Newland House School

Prize

Awarded to ~

Guy Dick

For Effort in U6L.

date July 1977.

THE HAUNTED SEA
Supernatural Stories

Other Books by Peter C. Smith

DESTROYER LEADER (*Kimber*)

TASK FORCE 57
> Foreword by Admiral of the Fleet Lord Fraser of North Cape, G.C.B., K.B.E. (*Kimber*)

PEDESTAL
> Foreword by Admiral Sir Richard Onslow, K.C.B., D.S.O. and Three Bars. (*Kimber*)

HARD LYING (*Kimber*)

WAR IN THE AEGEAN (With Edwin Walker) (*Kimber*)

DESTROYER ACTION
> (An anthology — as Editor) Foreword by Admiral Sir Gresham Nicholson, K.B.E., C.B., D.S.O., D.S.C. (*Kimber*)

HERITAGE OF THE SEA (*Balfour*)

ROYAL NAVY SHIPS' BADGES (*Balfour*)

R.A.F. SQUADRON BADGES (*Balfour*)

PER MARE PER TERRAM
> Foreword by Admiral of the Fleet Earl Mountbatten of Burma, K.G., P.C., G.C.B., O.M., G.C.S.I., G.C.I.E., G.C.V.O., D.S.O. (*Balfour*)

STUKA AT WAR
> Foreword by Oberstleutenant Hans Ulrich Rudel, holder of the Golden Oak Leaves with Swords and Diamonds to the Knights Cross of the Iron Cross (*Ian Allan*)

BATTLES OF THE MALTA STRIKING FORCES (With Edwin Walker). (*Ian Allan*)

BRITISH BATTLE CRUISERS (*Almark*)

THE STORY OF THE TORPEDO BOMBER (*Almark*)

THE
HAUNTED SEA

Supernatural Stories

Edited by

Peter C. Smith

WILLIAM KIMBER · LONDON

This collection first published in 1975 by
WILLIAM KIMBER & CO. LIMITED
Godolphin House, 22a Queen Anne's Gate
London SW1H 9AE

ISBN 0 7183 0483 7

Typeset by
Specialised Offset Services Ltd., Liverpool
Printed and bound in Great Britain by
REDWOOD BURN LIMITED
Trowbridge & Esher

Contents

I	Six Bells *by* 'Sea-Wrack'	9
II	The Haunted Ship *by* Wilhelm Hauff	20
III	The Ghost Ship *by* Richard Middleton	30
IV	The Call of Cthulhu *by* H.P. Lovecraft	41
V	Phantas *by* Oliver Onions	74
VI	The Sea Fit *by* Algernon Blackwood	90
VII	The Phantom Warships of Matapan *by* Admiral Aldo Cocchia	104
VIII	The Black Ferry *by* John Galt	108
IX	MS Found in a Bottle *by* Edgar Allan Poe	120
X	The Lagoon *by* Joseph Conrad	131
XI	In the Abyss *by* H.G. Wells	145
XII	Mrs Scarr *by* Elinor Mordaunt	162
XIII	The Voice in the Night *by* William Hope Hodgson	177
XIV	The Screaming Skull *by* F. Marion Crawford	190
XV	The Tale of Philo *by* Sir H. Rider Haggard	220
XVI	Confidences *by* 'Sea-Wrack'	231

Acknowledgements

The Editor would like to thank all those who have granted permission for stories within their copyright to be reprinted: to the Estate of E.H. Crebbin for permission to include *Six Bells* and *Confidences* by Sea-Wrack; to Hill, Quale & Hartmann, Wisconsin, and Arkham House for permission to include *The Call of Cthulhu* by H.P. Lovecraft; to the Estate of Oliver Onions and Chatto & Windus Ltd. for permission to include *Phantas* from *Widdershins* by Oliver Onions; to the Public Trustee and Paul Hamlyn Ltd. for permission to include *The Sea Fit* by Algernon Blackwood; to the Estate of H.G. Wells for permission to include *In the Abyss* from *The Short Stories* by H.G. Wells; to William Heinemann Ltd. for permission to include *Mrs Scarr* from *The Island* by Elinor Mordaunt; to The Estate of the late Sir H. Rider Haggard and Hutchinson & Co. Ltd. for permission to include *The Tale of Philo* from *Wisdom's Daughter* by Sir H. Rider Haggard; to William Kimber & Co. Ltd. for permission to include *The Phantom Warships of Matapan* by Admiral Aldo Cocchia; also to A.P. Watt & Son for their help in obtaining permission for the inclusion of some of these stories.

For
BRIAN J. SCOTT
remembering Ruby's, the Kismet
and Johnny Ticonderoga.

I

Six Bells

'Sea-Wrack'

It is one of the great delights of being asked to compile and edit an anthology of this type that one can garner all the tales one loves and has treasured over the years. Every anthology is only the anthology of the compiler and although one hopes that the reader will share the pleasures of all the tales it is inevitable that some will disagree with any choice. That being so, my inclusion of two of 'Sea-Wrack's' tales is a piece of total self-indulgence on my part. 'Sea-Wrack' was the pen-name of Lieutenant-Commander E.H. Crebbin.

The inn stood on a lonely headland on the east coast — a desolate, flat spit of land that echoed at night to the plaintive call of the curlew and to the snore of the surf that snarled monotonously round the protecting sea-wall. It was an old inn with, appropriately enough, an old sailor as its landlord; and as I trudged back to it, tired and cold at the end of a day after duck in the marshes, I thought with a pleasant sense of anticipation of its primitive, homely comfort. The doctor's words recurred to me as I watched a yellow square of light appear in the parlour window: 'A change — and rest is indicated,' he had said briskly. 'It's no good telling you to rest, but something might be done about the change. Go and stalk duck in the fens — with a walking-stick if you like, or a sketching-block: it'll answer the purpose just as well as a gun, and make travelling easier."

'A fat lot you know about duck-shooting,' I had retorted. 'D'you expect mallard to come and browse round my feet while I sketch them nimbly with a pencil and make notes of their colouring in the dusk?'

The doctor had grinned. 'Well, that's the idea, old man,' he had insisted, 'and if you let me know where you fetch up, I might be able to run up that way for a week-end and we can eat cheese and drink beer and listen to the local rustics telling us what's wrong with the country.'

I had taken the doctor's advice, and here I was at the end of my first day, feeling better already and looking forward to a hot bath, food, and then bed.

About an hour after I had got back, I was pottering round the inn-parlour examining the various sea-treasures and sailors' relics it contained when my attention was caught by a ship's bell that stood mounted on an oak tripod in a corner of the room. I was about to put out a hand to touch the bell when Captain Swan, the landlord, came into the parlour. 'Don't strike that bell — or touch it, sir, if you please,' he said, in an odd kind of voice which seemed to carry a note of fear in its intense tones.

I turned round in some amazement and saw that Swan's face was pale. Round his clenched lips little beads of sweat glistened. 'Why, Captain Swan,' I protested, 'what on earth's wrong with the bell. Are you afraid of it breaking loose from its moorings? The tripod looks solid enough to stand a much heavier weight?'

The old man shambled to a settee and with gnarled unsteady fingers began filling his pipe. As I waited for him to reply to my question, I heard from far away the honk of flighting geese, the sound merging and blending with the monotone bass of the rasping surf as if from time immemorial constant association had scored them into the same musical piece.

The old gnarled fingers had lost their deftness, and still Captain Swan did not reply. Somewhere an old clock ticked away with an occasional rumbling from the depths of its worn case. And as I watched that gaunt figure seated there on the settee, the odd idea came to me that Captain Swan, ashore in his snug anchorage, was probably more lonely than he had ever been at sea — even in the rolling wastes of the South Atlantic. Across the marshes there came a squall of wind that, booming and reverberating round the solid walls of the inn, drowned with its vehemence the sound of the ticking clock and screeched away into the distance as if frustrated in its design to gain admittance, it soared away to find flimsier victims.

Then at last Captain Swan spoke, and the sound of a human voice after that elemental chorus seemed somehow but to increase, to underline, the desolation, the solitude of the inn-parlour, so that we might have been alone in a dim-light cave on a desert island. Yet when I had approached the inn that evening from the marshes and seen the square of yellow light, I had received an impression of comfort, of rough good cheer. And it was suddenly borne in on me that it was Captain Swan who seemed to neutralize the glow of the good fire and the thickness of the hearthrug — as if he exuded an atmosphere of solitude and close-knit concentration, like a man wrapt up hopelessly in years of futile meditation and brooding.

'You've been a seaman yourself,' said Captain Swan suddenly. 'I might tell you, for I've never yet spoken the truth of it and that's a fact.' Back to his face came that curious shut-in expression, as if he were listening for some voice far away: a voice he expected, yet one that filled him with apprehension.

'I would like to tell someone,' said Swan. 'Maybe ordinary people would think it was only the ramblings of an old sailor whose reason has been clouded by the loneliness of marsh-life coming on top of years at sea. . . .'

The old man broke off abruptly and stared moodily at the floor, taking all the while huge puffs of his clay-pipe until he was sitting in the midst of a smoke-screen of sweet-smelling tobacco-smoke. Through the smoke I could just see flashing across his features hesitation, doubt, then a kind of resigned desperation. He muttered under his breath and I thought he said: 'Townley wouldn't care, no, he wouldn't care. It's all so long ago. . . .'

I said: 'Tell me, Captain Swan — I'm interested.' And putting my tobacco-pouch on the table in front of him, I added: 'Try some of that if you finish your pipe before the end of the story.'

'Aye,' he said gloomily, 'but is there any end to the story? You'll see, though. I'll tell you. . . .'

'We were running down our easting round the Horn in the old *Lilian Gay* — full-rigged ship,' said Captain Swan. 'It was the usual Cape. Stiff weather, blowing mor'n a capful of wind from the nor-west, but we were well loaded down with a cargo of nitrate out of Iquique, bound for Liverpool, and the wind was favourable — just abaft the port beam.

'The *Lilian Gay* was lying over to it with her starboard rails awash, and every now and again a big Cape Stiff greybeard roared along past the bulwarks, mainyard-high. But homeward-bound is homeward-bound, and as night fell, you could ha' heard young Townley playing his accordion in the fo'c'sle.

'We'd taken in t'gallant sails, and were running under fore, main, and mizzen tops'ls and foresail — snugged down for the night. I remember the storm canvas was billowing out and straining fit to tear the bolt-ropes out of her.

'We spoke two outward-bounders, lying-to, and they gave us a cheer as we passed, surging alone and logging our eleven knots.

'Well, the first watch came and passed, and then the middle started. All hands had been called but twice so far, but now the wind backed to west and blew in great squalls. It was the Mate's watch, and he thought it was time to lighten her, so we took in foresail, and a rare tussle we had doing it. After that, though, she seemed to ride the big following sea much easier.

'At ten minutes before three in the middle watch one of the fore t'gallant back stays parted with a noise like a cannon shot and the whole foremast shook in its housing. We were standing by, though, and in five minutes we'd got her shipshape again with a preventer and jury-stay.'

Captain Swan paused and a troubled expression crept into his eyes. 'A few minutes before six bells,' he went on, 'Townley — the young able-seaman who played the accordion — walked for'ard to the break of the fo'c'sle to strike six bells.'

Captain Swan's knuckles showed white as he gripped his bony old knees. 'Townley was always joking,' he went on, and his voice quavered. 'He had a jest on his lips then as he went for'ard. And he had a sort of swagger in his way of walking.' Captain Swan shook his old body in a grotesque movement, which yet conveyed some sort of idea of what he meant. 'I can see him now, swaggering his way forward, the cold moonlight gleaming on his wet oilskins, then standing with his hand up near the bell-lanyard. He struck the first two — you know of course how a ship's bell is struck, you who are a seaman yourself, one-two, one-two. . . . Before he could strike any more, the stern of the ship rose with the suddenness of an express lift: the bow dipped, and a huge following sea threw the ship sideways and down into the trough. Above the swirl and sluice of the water pouring through the waist and the bellowing of the canvas, we heard a loud crack, like the discharge of a gun. It was the back-stay — the jury-rigged one this time. At the time, we were standing just below at the foot of the foresail.

'"She's gone" — a man standing next to me yelled out. "Look-out, mates! The fore-topgallant mast's falling!"

'The bos'un had rushed to the halliards and let go at the run the fore and main — thereby saving the main t'gallant mast from being mixed up in the ruin. He acted just in time.

'As the heavy spar crashed, bringing with it the royal mast and all the yards above the lower fore t'gallant yard, the air became full of flying blocks and parted rigging.

'And there was Townley standing right under it — at the break of the fo'c'sle, with two bells struck and four still to come. I can see his face now — showing white under the moonlight, as he looked up suddenly — too late.

'Before a man of us could stir, the t'gallant mast had thundered down bringing with it a mass of wreckage that blotted Townley out. But the curious thing — and we never noticed it until afterwards — the curious thing was that though the bell had been struck with a force that scored it deep, not one of us, when we spoke of it later, could say as how he heard it give out a sound. . . .'

'And Townley?' I asked the old sailor.

The old man nodded his head gloomily. 'Aye,' he said, 'Townley was killed — but not outright.

'I was the first to reach him, though all hands rushed to the wreckage and tore it away as best they could. We found him still alive, with a great jagged wound in the forehead and half the broken t'gallant mast pinning his body to the deck.

'He spoke once, and his words have been ringing in my ears

ever since. He said: "I'll be back again. Strike two bells, mate, and I'll come back later and strike the other four." At the time' — Captain Swan's voice faltered and his voice rose into a quaver again, so that suddenly I realized he was a very old man — 'at the time, I didn't think much of his meaning, but later. . . .' Captain Swan put a clenched bony hand on the table. 'Why, now I come to think of it, I've heard nothing else all these years but those words — especially o' nights when the wind howls round this old place and I can hear the distant beat of the surf. It's then' — the old man spoke with a sort of suppressed intensity that startled me — 'It's then I see again poor Townley's twisted smile, half-hidden by the stream of blood pouring the last supreme jest that he uttered — for he spoke those words . . . and died.'

A shaft of moonlight, that same moonlight that had lighted up the well-deck of the *Lilian Gay* those many years ago, crept through the parlour window and turned to feathery silver the white hair of the speaker while rendering deeper the harsh craggy lines of his troubled old face.

'We buried him there off Van Diemen's Land,' Captain Swan continued jerkily, 'in the wild seas of the Horn, with great flakes of snow falling like a shroud over his body before he slipped quietly away off the grating into the shoulder of a great wave. And for many a day after that men went forward in the night-watches and hurried past the spot, looking over their shoulders, for he had said: "I'll be back again." . . .' The old sailor made a gesture as if excusing his old-time mates: 'You know what seamen were — and are — how superstitious they get: it's the loneliness and the desolation of those solitary miles of great waves all around you, and the nights with the strange calls of sea-birds echoing through the shrouds. Your thoughts seem to get unhitched and wander like an evening star.

'But if the thoughts are long, a sailor's memory is short, and by the time we had bent on our old canvas for the tropics and had passed through the rains and lightning of the doldrums, Townley and the bell were nigh forgotten. In the course of time, we made Liverpool and paid off, and although, as was usual towards the end of long voyages, men talked of what they were going to do when they went ashore, how they would save their money this time, and how they must meet their mates when they were snug ashore in some soft billet, the most of them were at sea again within a few days with all their money gone, and, for the most part, with only a hazy idea of how they had arrived in a ship's fo'c'sle once more.' The old man sighed, as he brooded over the past. 'Oh, those sailors' resolutions,' he muttered sombrely. 'I recollect sitting out in the night, maybe waiting for the call of "All Hands!" in driving rain, in bright moonlight with a clear sky and the fleecy white clouds of the trade-wind, or in a snoring westerly gale off Ushant — voyages without number, they seem now, and some I've clean forgot; but on all of 'em I remember sitting round in the lee of the windward bulwarks and talking, talking of this and that: of long-forgotten families, sisters, brothers who took on a strangely splendid aspect, and who seemed bigger, finer than anyone else's brothers and sisters simply because they were half-lost in the fogs of memories which themselves were growing dim. And always we talked of how we should stay ashore — this time, and not be reckless with our money. . . .' Captain Swan sighed again.

'Well, the years rolled by, and the war of 1914, and with it, I found myself aboard a man-of-war. I was getting old but they took me as a carpenter in the R.N.R. and one fine day when my ship was in the South Atlantic, I was lowered in a whaler to board a sailing-ship which was slowly foundering. She had been attacked by a U-boat and abandoned, so there was not a soul aboard. I had almost forgotten by then my time in sail, but as we approached this old sailing-ship, looking somehow strangely forlorn and neglected in her shabby white paint and with her untended sails and running rigging, something in her lines stirred my memory. I looked at her more closely, then suddenly slapped my knee. "Why, it's the *Lilian Gay*," I shouted. The others in the whaler, pulling at the oars, grinned. "Heave ho, Chips; an old ship?" they said. "You'll be able to show us the cuddy and maybe find us a tot from the locker."

'By the time we boarded her I had begun to feel strangely excited. You see, she was like a ghost from the buried past; and as I set foot on her sharply-listing deck, my mind was beset with memories, for every fitting — almost every fathom of running-tackle — spoke to me of some incident, storm and wind and the bellow of the Mate and the drumming of heavy seaboots, and the call of my shipmates working alongside me in the swirl of water sluicing round the deck-houses. . . .

'But I was recalled to the present work, for the *Lilian Gay* was sinking fast. Already, clear over her t'gallant fo'c'sle the long Atlantic swell was rolling. The Captain had said: "Get her bell if you can — and her papers, if they haven't gone already."

'I directed the others aft to the saloon, then I took one look at the *Lilian Gay*'s fast-disappearing bows and raced forward. The main bell was slung under the break of the poop, aft: I could get that last. But for'ard . . . was Townley's bell. Somehow, I felt as if I had never wanted anything so much in my life, for Jack Townley had been a "raggie" of mine — that's Navy language, as you know, for great friend.

'I saw that it was going to be a close thing. The water was up to my waist, and the green smooth swell was cascading off the t'gallant fo'c'sle all round and over me as I wrenched and prised out the clamps and screws holding the bell. But I got it, and half-swam, half-stumbled aft. I had secured Townley's bell. As I made my way aft, a hand roared at me from the poop. "She's going!" he yelled; "any moment now! Shake a leg, Chips, or you'll go with her."

'There was still the bell aft, but I found when I reached the poop that someone else had taken it already.

'We jumped for the whaler, just as a big swell rolled up the waist and submerged the whole forepart of the ship. We shoved off quickly, and before we were fifty fathoms away from her side, the *Lilian Gay* gave a kind of shudder, and with a terrible sort of groaning noise, threw up her stern and plunged suddenly head foremost straight down. . . .'

The old man broke off and stared in front of him with a faint smile that somehow seemed sadder than tears. 'The Captain let me keep Townley's bell,' he said, at last, and his voice quavered. 'You see, I told him — about it. Well, that is the bell, over there. It's never been struck since. . . . Townley struck the first two strokes of six bells, that wild night off Van Diemen's Land. . . . Sometimes' — the gnarled bony hands were clenched on the table in front of him, and the old sailor spoke jerkily, hoarsely, as if the words were wrenched from his lips — 'sometimes, it calls, that bell, calls and calls again, so that wherever I am I just have to go and stand near it and stare at those scored grooves in its bright surface. And then I hear Townley's voice again, and the parlour's gone: all I can see is wild seas ranging up over the bulwarks and the bell glinting in the moonlight, and . . . and a figure walking with a swagger, walking forward to strike the bell. And all the time, even before I see him, I hear Townley's voice' — the old man's speech died to a whisper that froze my blood as I listened — 'Townley's voice saying: "Strike two bells, mate, and I'll be back again and strike the other four."

'You see,' Captain Swan said, averting his face, 'you see, it is so real: it *is* real. You must understand I don't try to see Townley: to hear him: he comes' — the whisper died almost away — 'for years and years I have been thinking what I can do, but still Townley's voice comes back. And I'm an old man now. Shall I never know what I should do? Is the spirit of my old raggie uneasy? Should I strike two bells? Can you tell me, sir. You don't know what a relief it is to me to have been able at last after all these years to tell someone about the bell — and Townley.'

I looked across at the old sailor and what I saw in his face — though I'm no doctor — made my thoughts grave. Telling the story, he had re-lived that episode which, it was clear, had haunted his life ever afterwards. His face now appeared ghastly in its gaunt, immobile impassivity — as if all the vitality of the aged body had travelled to the burning eyes. It was as if Captain Swan's soul looked out from behind a mask, a mask roughly hewed to resemble human features. For years, it seemed, that troubled, simple soul had wrestled and brooded, gradually relinquishing the ordinary human thoughts until the mind became the battleground of one overpowering obsession, encouraged and facilitated by the solitude and desolation of its surroundings.

And yet, it occurred to me, as I stared back gravely into those burning eyes and revolved in my own mind the simple alternatives, and it really mattered little what I advised. Captain Swan was far beyond taking, or even weighing up, advice. But even as I spoke I knew my own night's rest was going to be forfeit. The story of Townley's bell had got hold of me, too. I should spend most of the night-watches recalling those words: 'Strike two bells and I'll be back again to strike the other four.' The actual phraseology, I noted, varied a little in the old sailor's narrative, but those were the words I remembered, and would remember for some considerable time. My eyes strayed to the bell, as it hung in its mount. The dying firelight cast glints of dull gold from the polished surface.

'I shouldn't strike two bells, Captain Swan,' I said at last, averting my eyes from the glitter and gleam of the brass. Shortly after that we went to bed.

The troubled sleep I fell into could not have visited me before two o'clock, and my dreams were shot with gripping, spasmodic pictures, like little vignettes, of huge seas roaring past low bulwarks, while in the distance I heard the tolling of a bell. I awoke from a troubled sleep with the sonorous vibrations of a deep bell reverberating all round my mind and seemingly spreading outwards from it to the room and then to the whole house. In a flash, I was wide awake and sitting up in bed, shivering. Round the room squalls of wind screeched and howled. Then, in an instant, I was out of bed, for memory had stretched back infallibly out of the limbo of sleep the significant points of the story Captain Swan had told me only a few hours before. It seemed almost as if my mind, in sleep, had been the vehicle for a shaft of predestination, for clear to my ears, then, as I stood trembling at my bedside, there came suddenly the rich, resonant boom of a bell being struck twice.

I stood like a figure of stone while the sonorous vibrations echoed through the house, to be followed almost immediately by a hoarse cry. It was the sound I had dreaded — but, as soon as it came, the sound I knew I had expected, intuitively — as though this was some inexorable end to a story I had already read. The cry stung me to quick action. In a moment I had, somehow, a lighted candle in my hand, and even as I was thrusting open the door by its dim light I heard the dull crash from under my feet, and then the sound of four more rapid strokes on the bell, each getting louder than the preceding one, so that the last seemed to sound a veritable tocsin of triumph, of victory.

As I made my way fearfully downstairs a terrible feeling of fatality preceded me, so that I seemed to be catching it up all the way down. When I arrived at the parlour-door, I knew as certainly as I was standing there, that tragedy was in the very atmosphere: all around me: as solid as the walls, yet as difficult to analyse as the reasons of my intuition. I opened the door at last with a shaky hand and went in.

Just inside the room I stood still and my leart leapt. Opposite me, Captain Swan lay face-downwards on the parlour-floor and across his head and shoulders lay the bell and the oak-stand. I walked across and, taking the bell firmly by its lanyard, I lifted it carefully so that the tongue could not strike, and I put the bell down on the floor as far away as I could. One glance into the old sailor's face, as I turned him gently over, was enough to tell me that he had died suddenly and mercifully — probably from a heart-attack. The bell had not harmed him, and all the worry and perplexity had left his features. He looked like a man enjoying a rest after a hard-run race. Fine featured in life, the arrival of death had but added an indestructible impression of dignity to his face which was somehow symbolic of that great, hidden cyclic rhythm which is the Immutable Law.

I found a cushion with which to pillow the silvery hair, and as I turned to summon assistance, the old clock in the parlour struck softly. It was three o'clock — six bells.

II

The Haunted Ship

Wilhelm Hauff

The title story of this collection is one set to a classic theme. The mysterious abandoned ship found drifting through the oceans by her own volition, has been repeated often and the true episode of the Mary Celeste *has added its own attraction over the years. Edgar Allan Poe used a similar theme for his* MS found in a Bottle *also reprinted in this book, and it was further developed in his strange,* Arthur Gordon Pym.*

The Haunted Ship, although in the classic mould, is refreshingly written by this German author, who died at an early age in 1827, as a fairy tale and as such the story takes on an added attraction in its very simplicity.

My father kept a small shop at Balsora. He was neither poor nor rich, and one of these people who are afraid of venturing anything lest they should lose the little they possess. He brought me up plainly and virtuously, and soon I was enabled to assist him in his trade. Scarcely had I reached my eighteenth year, and hardly had he made his first large speculation, when he died, probably from grief at having confided a thousand pieces of gold to the sea.

I could not help thinking him lucky afterwards on account of his death, for a few weeks later the news arrived that the ship to which my father had entrusted his goods had sunk. This mishap, however, did not curb my youthful courage. I converted everything that my father had left into money, and set forth to try my fortune abroad, accompanied only by my father's old servant, who from long attachment would not separate himself from me and my fate.

We took ship at Balsora and left the haven with a favourable wind. The ship in which we embarked was bound for India. When we had sailed some fifteen days over the ordinary track, the Captain predicted a storm. He looked very serious, for it appeared that he was not sufficiently acquainted with the course in these parts to await a storm with composure. He had all sail furled, and we drifted along quite gently. The night had fallen. It was cold and clear, and the Captain began to think he had been deceived by false indications of the storm. All at once a ship which we had not observed before drove past at a little distance from our own. Wild shouts and cheers resounded from her deck; at which, in such an anxious hour before a tempest, I wondered not a little. The Captain, who stood by my side, turned as pale as death. 'My ship is doomed!' he cried; 'yonder sails death.' Before I could question him as to the meaning of this strange exclamation, the sailors came running towards us, howling and crying. 'Have you seen it?' they cried. 'It is all over with us.'

But the Captain caused some consolatory verses to be read out of the Koran, and placed himself at the helm. All in vain! Visibly the storm increased in fury, and before an hour had passed the ship crashed and stuck fast. The boats were lowered, and scarcely had the last sailors saved themselves, when the ship sank before our eyes, and I was launched on the sea, a beggar. Further miseries yet awaited us. The storm raged more furiously, our boat became unmanageable. I had clasped my old servant tightly, and we vowed never to part from one another. At length day broke. But at the first dawn of morning a squall caught the boat in which we were seated and capsized it. I never saw my shipmates again. I was stunned by the shock; and when I awoke, I found myself in the arms of my old and faithful servant, who had saved himself on the overturned boat and dragged me after him. The tempest had subsided. Nothing more was seen of our ship. We discovered, however, not far from us another ship, towards which the waves were drifting us. As we drew near I recognized it as the same ship that had dashed past us on the preceding night, and which had terrified our Captain so much. I was inspired with a singular horror at the sight of this vessel. The expression of the Captain which had been so terribly fulfilled, the desolate aspect of the ship, on which, near as we were and loudly as we shouted, no one appeared, frightened me. However, this was our only means of safety, therefore we praised the Prophet who had so wonderfully preserved us.

Over the ship's bow hung a long cable. We paddled with

hands and feet towards it in order to grasp it. At length we succeeded. Loudly I raised my voice, but all was silent on board. We then climbed up by the rope, I as the youngest going first. Oh, horror! What a spectacle met my gaze as I stepped upon the deck! The planks were reddened with blood; twenty or thirty corpses in Turkish dresses lay on the deck. Close to the mainmast stood a man, richly attired, a sabre in his hand, but with features pale and distorted; a great nail driven through his forehead pinned him to the mainmast. He also was dead.

Terror shackled my steps. I scarcely ventured to breathe. At last my companion had also come up. He too was struck at the sight of the deck, on which nothing living was to be seen, only so many frightful corpses. After a time we ventured, after having invoked the aid of the Prophet in anguish of heart, to go forward. At each step we glanced around expecting to discover something new and yet more terrible. But all was the same. Far and wide nothing was living but ourselves and the ocean. We dared not even speak aloud, lest the dead Captain spitted to the mast should turn his ghastly eyes upon us, or one of the corpses move its head. At last we reached a hatchway which led to the ship's hold. There we both stopped, involuntarily, and looked at each other, for neither dared to speak his thoughts.

'O Master,' said my faithful servant, 'something awful has happened here! Yet, though the hold below be full of murderers, I would rather give myself up to their mercy than remain here any longer among these corpses.' I thought the same. We grew bold and, full of expectation, descended. But here likewise all was still as death, and only our steps sounded on the ladder. We stood at the door of the cabin. I placed my ear against it and listened. Nothing could be heard. I opened it, and the cabin presented a disorderly appearance. Dresses, weapons, and other things lay in confusion. Everything was out of its place. The crew, or at least the Captain must have been carousing not long since, for all was still lying about.

We went from place to place and from cabin to cabin, and everywhere found splendid stores of silk, pearls, sugar, and the like. I was beside myself with joy at this sight, for since no one was on board, I thought I had a right to appropriate all to myself; but Ibrahim reminded me that we were doubtless far from land, which we could never reach without the help of man.

We refreshed ourselves with the meats and drinks, of which we found an ample supply, and finally ascended again to the deck. But here we shuddered at the sight of the ghastly corpses. We resolved upon freeing ourselves from them by throwing them overboard. But how awful was the dread which we felt when we found that not one could be moved from his position! So firmly fixed were they to the flooring, that we should have had to take up the planks of the deck in order to remove them, and for this purpose we had no tools. Neither could we loose the Captain from the mainmast, nor wrest his sabre from his rigid grasp.

We passed the day in sad contemplation of our position, and when night began to fall I allowed old Ibrahim to lie down to sleep, while I kept watch on deck spying for some means of deliverance. But when the moon had come out, and I reckoned by the stars that it was about eleven o'clock, such an irresistible sleep took possession of me that I involuntarily fell behind a cask that stood on the deck. However, this was more stupefaction than sleep, for I distinctly heard the sea beating against the side of the ship, and the sails creaking and whistling in the wind. All of a sudden I thought I heard voices and men's footsteps on the deck. I endeavoured to get up to see what it was, but an invisible power held my limbs fettered; I could not even open my eyes. The voices, however, grew more distinct, and it appeared to me as if a merry crew was rushing about on the deck. Now and then I thought I heard the sonorous voice of a commander, and also distinctly the hoisting and lowering of cordage and sails. But by degrees my senses left me, I sank into a deeper sleep, in which I only thought I could hear a clatter of arms, and only awoke when the sun was far above the horizon and scorching my face.

I stared about in astonishment. Storm, ship, the dead, and what I had heard during the night, appeared to me like a dream, but when I glanced around I found everything as on the previous day. Immovable lay the dead, immovable stood the Captain spitted to the mast. I laughed over my dream, and rose up to seek the old man.

He was seated, absorbed in reflection in the cabin. 'Oh, Master,' he exclaimed, as I entered, 'I would rather lie at the bottom of the sea than pass another night in this bewitched ship.' I inquired the cause of his trouble, and he thus answered me: 'After I had slept some hours, I awoke and heard people running about above my head, rushing to and fro, aloft, and I also heard calling and shouting. At last heavy steps came down the cabin. Upon this I became insensible, and only now and then my consciousness returned for a few moments, and then I saw the same man who is nailed to the mast overhead, sitting there at that table, singing and drinking, while the man in the scarlet dress, who is close to him on the floor, sat beside him and drank with him.' Such was my old servant's narrative.

Believe me, my friends, I did not feel at all at ease, for it was no illusion. I had also heard the dead men quite plainly. To sail in such company was gruesome to me. My Ibrahim, however, relapsed into profound meditation. 'I have just hit it!' he exclaimed at last. He recalled a little formula, which his grandfather, a man of experience and a great traveller, had taught him, which was a charm against ghosts and sorcery. He likewise affirmed that we might ward off the unnatural sleep during the coming night, by diligently saying verses from the Koran.

The proposal of the old man pleased me. In anxious expectation we saw the night approach. Adjoining the cabin was a narrow berth, into which we resolved to retire. We bored several holes through the door, large enough to overlook the whole cabin: we then locked the door as well as we could inside, and Ibrahim wrote the name of the Prophet in all four corners. Thus we awaited the terrors of the night. It might be about eleven o'clock when I began to feel very drowsy. My companion therefore advised me to say some verses from the Koran, which indeed helped me. All at once everything grew animated above, the cordage creaked, feet paced the deck, and several voices became clearly heard. We had thus sat for some time in intense expectation, when we heard something descending the steps of the cabin stairs. The old man on hearing this commenced to recite the formula which his grandfather had taught him against ghosts and sorcery:—

> If you are spirits from the air,
> Or come from depths of sea,
> Have in dark sepulchres your lair,
> Or if from fire you be.
> Allah is your God and Lord,
> All spirits must obey His word.

I must confess I did not quite believe in this charm, and my hair stood on end as the door opened. In stepped that tall majestic man whom I had seen nailed to the mainmast. The nail still passed through his skull, but his sword was sheathed. Behind him followed another person less richly dressed; him also I had seen stretched on deck. The Captain, for there was no doubt it was he, had a pale face, a large black beard and fiery eyes, with which he looked around the whole cabin. I could see him quite distinctly as he passed our door; but he did not seem to notice the door at all, which hid us. Both seated themselves at the table which stood in the middle of the cabin, speaking loudly and almost shouting to one another in an unknown tongue. They grew more and more hot and excited, until at last the Captain brought his fist down upon the table, so that the cabin shook. The other jumped up with a wild laugh and beckoned the Captain to follow him. The latter rose, tore his sabre out of its sheath, and both left the cabin.

After they had gone we breathed more freely, but our alarm was not to terminate yet. Louder and louder grew the noise on deck. We heard rushing backwards and forwards, shouting, laughing and howling. At last a most fiendish noise was heard, so we thought the deck together with all its sails was coming down on us, clashing of arms and shrieks — and suddenly a dead silence followed. When, after many hours, we ventured to ascend, we found everything as before; not one had shifted his place; all lay as stiff as wood.

Thus we passed many days on board this ship, and constantly steered on an eastern course, where according to my calculation land should be found; but although we seemed to cover many miles by day, yet at night it seemed to go back, for we were always in the same place at the rising of the sun. We could not understand this, except that the dead crew each night navigated the ship in a directly opposite course with full sails. In order to prevent this, we furled all the sails before night fell, and employed the same means as we had used on the cabin door. We wrote the name of the prophet, and the formula prescribed by Ibrahim's grandfather, upon a scroll of parchment, and wound it round the furled sails. Anxiously we awaited the result in our berths. The noise now seemed to increase more violently than ever; but behold, on the following morning, the sails were still furled, as we had left them. By day we only hoisted as many sails as were needed to carry the ship gently along, and thus in five days we covered a considerable tract.

At last on the sixth morning we discovered land at a short distance, and thanked Allah and his Prophet for our miraculous deliverance. This day and on the following night we sailed along a coast, and on the seventh morning we thought at a short distance we saw a town. With much difficulty we dropped our anchor, which at once struck ground, lowered a little boat, which was on deck, and rowed with all our strength towards the town. After the lapse of half-an-hour we entered a river which ran into the sea, and landed. On entering the gate of the town we asked the name of it, and learnt that it was an Indian town, not far from where I had intended to land at first. We went towards a caravanserai and refreshed ourselves after our adventurous journey. I also inquired there after some wise and intelligent man, intimating to the landlord that I wished to consult one on matters relating to sorcery. He led me to some remote street to a mean-looking house and knocked. I was allowed to enter, and simply told to ask for Muley.

In the house I met a little old man, with a grey beard and a long nose, who asked me what I wanted. I told him I desired to see the wise Muley, and he answered me that he was Muley. I now asked his advice what I should do with the corpses, and how I was to set about to remove them from he ship. He answered me that very likely the ship's crew were spell-bound on the ocean on account of some crime; and he believed the charm might be broken by bringing them on land, which, however, could only be done by taking up the planks on which they lay. The ship, together with all its goods, by divine and human law belonged to me, because I had as it were found it. I was, however, to keep all very secret, and make him a little present of my abundance, in return for which he and his slaves would assist me in removing the dead. I promised to reward him richly, and we set forth followed by five slaves provided with saws and hatchets. On the road the magician Muley could not sufficiently laud the happy thought of tacking the Koran verses upon the sails. He said that this had been the only means of our deliverance.

It was yet early morning when we reached the vessel. We all set to work immediately, and in an hour four lay already in the boat. Some of the slaves had to row them to land to bury them there. They related on their return that the corpses had saved them the trouble of burial, for hardly had they been put on the ground when they crumbled into dust. We continued sawing off the corpses, and before evening all had been removed to land except one, namely he who was nailed to the mast. In vain we endeavoured to draw the nail out of the wood. Every effort could not displace it a hair's-breadth. I did not know what to do, for it was impossible to cut down the mast to bring him to land. Muley, however, devised an expedient. He ordered a slave quickly to row to land, in order to bring him a pot filled with earth. When it was brought, the magician pronounced some mystic words over it, and emptied the earth upon the head of the corpse. Immediately he opened his eyes, heaved a deep sigh, and the wound of the nail in his forehead began to bleed. We now extracted the nail easily, and the wounded man fell into the arms of one of the slaves.

'Who has brought me hither?' he said, after having slightly recovered. Muley pointed to me, and I approached him. 'Thanks be to thee, unknown stranger, for thou hast rescued me from a long martyrdom. For fifty years has my corpse been floating upon these waves, and my spirit was condemned to reanimate it each night; but now earth having touched my head, I can return to my fathers reconciled.'

I begged him to tell us how he had fallen into this awful condition, and he answered: 'Fifty years ago I was a man of power and rank, and lived in Algiers. The longing after gain induced me to fit out a vessel in order to engage in piracy. I had already carried on this business for some time, when one day I took on board at Zante a Dervish, who asked for a free passage. My companions and myself were wild fellows, and paid no respect for the sanctity of the man, but rather mocked him. But one day, when he had reproached me in his holy zeal with my sinful mode of living, I became furious at night, after having drunk a great deal with my steersman in my cabin. Enraged at what a Dervish had told me, and what I would not even allow a Sultan to tell me, I rushed upon deck, and plunged my dagger in his breast. As he died, he cursed me and my crew, that we might neither live nor die till our heads should touch the earth. The Dervish died, and we threw him into the sea, laughing at his menaces; but in the same night his words were fulfilled.

'Some of my crew mutinied against me. We fought with insane fury until my adherents were defeated, and I was nailed to the mainmast. But the mutineers also expired of their wounds, and my ship soon became but an immense tomb. My eyes also grew dim, my breathing ceased, I thought I was dying. But it was only a kind of numbness that seized me. The very next night, and at the precise hour that we had thrown the Dervish into the sea, I and all my companions awoke, we were alive, but we could only do and say what we had said and done on that night. Thus we have been sailing these fifty years unable to live or die: for how could we reach land? It was with a savage joy that we sailed many times with full sail in the storm, hoping that at length we might strike some rock, and rest our wearied heads at the bottom of the sea. We did not succeed. But now I shall die. Thanks once more, my unknown deliverer, and if treasures can reward thee, accept my ship as a mark of my gratitude.'

After having said this, the Captain's head fell upon his breast, and he expired. Immediately his body also, like the crew's, crumbled to dust. We collected it in a little urn and buried him on shore. I engaged, however, workmen from the town, who repaired my ship thoroughly. After having bartered the goods which I had on board for others at a great profit, I collected a crew, rewarded my friend Muley handsomely, and set sail towards my native place. I made, however, a detour, and landed on many islands and countries where I sold my goods. The Prophet blessed my enterprise.

After a lapse of nine months, twice as wealthy as the dying Captain had made me, I reached Balsora. My fellow-citizens were astonished at my riches and my fortune, and did not believe anything else but that I must have found the diamond valley of the celebrated traveller Sinbad. I left their belief undisturbed, but henceforth the young people of Balsora, when they were scarcely eighteen years old, were obliged to go out into the world in order like myself to seek their fortune. But I lived quietly and peacefully, and every five years undertook a journey to Mecca, in order to thank the Lord for His blessing at this sacred shrine, and pray for the Captain and his crew that He might receive them into His Paradise.

III

The Ghost Ship

Richard Middleton

Richard Barham Middleton (1882-1911) was born at Staines, Middlesex. A descendant of Richard Harris Barham, author of the Ingoldsby Legends, he was fated to be relegated to the horrors of a job as an insurance clerk through lack of finance to send him to university. After six years of such hell his artistic nature rebelled and he found a limited freedom with a Bohemian group, writing a few stories one of which won him five guineas in the New Leader. *By 1911 he had run the gamut of his bad luck and ill fortune, and, his talent and skill ignored, he went to Brussels in 1911 where he committed suicide at the age of twenty-nine.*

In tragic contrast to his poor, miserable life, the story we reproduce here in tribute to his memory, The Ghost Ship, *is a delightful and gay spoof on the traditional sea tale of terror.*

Fairfield is a little village lying near the Portsmouth Road about half-way between London and the sea. Strangers who find it by accident now and then, call it a pretty, old-fashioned place; we who live in it and call it home don't find anything very pretty about it, but we should be sorry to live anywhere else. Our minds have taken the shape of the inn and the church and the green, I suppose. At all events, we never feel comfortable out of Fairfield.

Of course the Cockneys, with their vasty houses and noise-ridden streets, can call us rustics if they choose, but for all that Fairfield is a better place to live in than London. Doctor says that when he goes to London his mind is bruised with the weight of the houses, and he was a Cockney born. He had to live there himself when he was a little chap, but he knows better now. You gentlemen may laugh — perhaps some of you come from London way — but it seems to me that a witness like that is worth a gallon of arguments.

Dull? Well, you might find it dull, but I assure you that I've listened to all the London yarns you have spun tonight, and they're absolutely nothing to the things that happen at Fairfield. It's because of our way of thinking and minding our own business. If one of your Londoners were set down on the green of a Saturday night when the ghosts of the lads who died in the war keep tryst with the lasses who lie in the churchyard, he couldn't help being curious and interfering and then the ghosts would go somewhere where it was quieter. But we just let them come and go and don't make any fuss, and in consequence Fairfield is the ghostliest place in all England. Why, I've seen a headless man sitting on the edge of the well in broad daylight, and the children playing about his feet as if he were their father. Take my word for it, spirits know when they are well off as much as human beings.

Still, I must admit that the thing I'm going to tell you about was queer even for our part of the world, where three packs of ghost-hounds hunt regularly during the season, and blacksmith's great-grandfather is busy all night shoeing the dead gentlemen's horses. Now that's a thing that wouldn't happen in London, because of their interfering ways, but blacksmith he lies up aloft and sleeps as quiet as a lamb. Once when he had a bad head he shouted down to them not to make so much noise, and in the morning he found an old guinea left on the anvil as an apology. He wears it on his watch chain now. But I must get on with my story; if I start telling you about the queer happenings at Fairfield I'll never stop.

It all came of the great storm in the spring of '97, the year that we had two great storms. This was the first one, and I remember it very well, because I found in the morning that it had lifted the thatch of my pigsty into the widow's garden as clean as a boy's kite. When I looked over the hedge, widow — Tom Lamport's widow that was — was prodding for her nasturtiums with a daisy-grubber. After I had watched her for a little I went down to the Fox and Grapes to tell landlord what she had said to me. Landlord he laughed, being a married man and at ease with the sex. 'Come to that,' he said, 'the tempest has blowed something into my field. A kind of a ship I think it would be.'

I was surprised at that until he explained that it was only a ghost ship and would do no hurt to the turnips. We argued that it had been blown up from the sea at Portsmouth, and then we talked of something else. There were two slates down at the parsonage and a big tree in Lumley's meadow. It was a rare storm.

I reckon the wind had blown our ghosts all over England. They were coming back for days afterwards with foundered horses and as footsore, as possible, and they were so glad to get back to Fairfield that some of them walked up the street crying like little children. Squire said that his great-grandfather's great-grandfather hadn't looked so dead-beat since the Battle of Naseby, and he's an educated man.

What with one thing and another, I should think it was a week before we got straight again, and then one afternoon I met the landlord on the green and he had a worried face. 'I wish you'd come and have a look at that ship in my field,' he said to me: 'it seems to me it's leaning real hard on the turnips. I can't bear thinking what the missus will say when she sees it.'

I walked down the lane with him, and sure enough there was a ship in the middle of his field, but such a ship as no man had seen on the water for three hundred years, let alone in the middle of a turnip field. It was all painted black and covered with carvings, and there were a great bay window in the stern for all the world like the Squire's drawing-room. There was a crowd of little black cannon on deck and looking out of her portholes, and she was anchored at each end to the hard ground. I have seen the wonders of the world on picture-postcards, but I have never seen anything to equal that.

'She seems very solid for a ghost ship,' I said, seeing the landlord was bothered.

'I should say it's a betwixt and between,' he answered, puzzling it over, 'but it's going to spoil a matter of fifty turnips, and missus she'll want it moved.' We went up to her and touched the side, and it was as hard as a real ship. 'Now there's folks in England would call that very curious,' he said.

Now I don't know much about ships, but I should think that that ghost ship weighed a solid two hundred tons, and it seemed to me that she had come to stay, so that I felt sorry for the landlord, who was a married man. 'All the horses in Fairfield won't move her out of my turnips,' he said, frowning at her.

Just then we heard a noise on her deck, and we looked up and saw that a man had come out of her front cabin and was looking down at us very peaceably. He was dressed in a black uniform set out with rusty gold lace, and he had a great cutlass by his side in a brass sheath. 'I'm Captain Bartholomew Roberts,' he said, in a gentleman's voice, 'put in for recruits. I seem to have brought her rather far up the harbour.'

'Harbour!' cried landlord; 'why, you're fifty miles from the sea.'

Captain Roberts didn't turn a hair. 'So much as that, is it?' he said coolly. 'Well, it's of no consequence.'

Landlord was a bit upset at this. 'I don't want to be unneighbourly,' he said, 'but I wish you hadn't brought your ship into my field. You see, my wife sets great store on these turnips.'

The captain took a pinch of snuff out of a fine gold box that he pulled out of his pocket, and dusted his fingers with a silk handkerchief in a very genteel fashion. 'I'm only here for a few months,' he said; 'but if a testimony of my esteem would pacify your good lady I should be content,' and with the words he loosed a great gold brooch from the neck of his coat and tossed it down to landlord.

Landlord blushed as red as a strawberry. 'I'm not denying she's fond of jewellery,' he said, 'but it's too much for half a sackful of turnips.' And indeed it was a handsome brooch.

The captain laughed. 'Tut, man,' he said, 'it's a forced sale, and you deserve a good price. Say no more about it.' And nodding good-day to us, he turned on his heel and went into the cabin. Landlord walked back up the lane like a man with a weight off his mind. 'That tempest has blowed me a bit of luck,' he said; 'the missus will be main pleased with that brooch. It's better than blacksmith's guinea, any day.'

Ninety-seven was Jubilee year, the year of the second Jubilee, you remember, and we had great doings at Fairfield, so that we hadn't much time to bother about the ghost ship, though anyhow it isn't our way to meddle in things that don't concern us. Landlord, he saw his tenant once or twice when he was hoeing his turnips and passed the time of day, and landlord's wife wore her new brooch to church every Sunday. But we didn't mix much with the ghosts at any time, all except an idiot lad there was in the village, and he didn't know the difference between a man and a ghost, poor innocent! On Jubilee Day, however, somebody told Captain Roberts why the church bells were ringing, and he hoisted a flag and fired off his guns like a loyal Englishman. 'Tis true the guns were shotted, and one of the round shot knocked a hole in Farmer Johnstone's barn, but nobody thought much of that in such a season of rejoicing.

It wasn't till our celebrations were over that we noticed that anything was wrong in Fairfield. 'Twas shoemaker who told me first about it one morning at the Fox and Grapes. 'You know my great great-uncle?' he said to me.

'You mean Joshua, the quiet lad,' I answered, knowing him well.

'Quiet!' said shoemaker indignantly. 'Quiet you call him, coming home at three o'clock every morning as drunk as a magistrate and waking up the whole house with his noise.'

'Why, it can't be Joshua!' I said, for I knew him for one of the most respectable young ghosts in the village.

'Joshua it is,' said shoemaker; 'and one of these nights he'll find himself out in the street if he isn't careful.'

This kind of talk shocked me, I can tell you, for I don't like to hear a man abusing his own family, and I could hardly believe that a steady youngster like Joshua had taken to drink. But just then in came butcher Aylwin in such a temper that he could hardly drink his beer. 'The young puppy! the young puppy!' he kept on saying; and it was some time before shoemaker and I found out that he was talking about his ancestor that fell at Senlac.

'Drink?' said shoemaker hopefully, for we all like company in our misfortunes, and butcher nodded grimly.

'The young noodle,' he said, emptying his tankard.

Well, after that I kept my ears open, and it was the same story all over the village. There was hardly a young man among all the ghosts of Fairfield who didn't roll home in the small hours of the morning the worse for liquor. I used to wake up in the night and hear them stumble past my house, singing outrageous songs. The worst of it was we couldn't keep the scandal to ourselves, and the folk at Greenhill began to talk of 'sodden Fairfield', and taught their children to sing a song about us:

Sodden Fairfield, sodden Fairfield, has no use for bread-and-butter;
Rum for breakfast, rum for dinner, rum for tea, and rum for supper!

We are easy-going in our village, but we didn't like that.

Of course we soon found out where the young fellows went to get the drink, and landlord was terribly cut up that his tenant should have turned out so badly, but his wife wouldn't hear of parting with the brooch, so that he couldn't give the Captain notice to quit. But as time went on, things grew from bad to worse, and at all hours of the day you would see those young reprobates sleeping it off on the village green. Nearly every afternoon a ghost wagon used to jolt down to the ship with a lading of rum, and though the older ghosts seemed inclined to give the Captain's hospitality the go-by, the youngsters were neither to hold nor to bind.

So one afternoon when I was taking my nap I heard a knock at the door, and there was parson looking very serious, like a man with a job before him that he didn't altogether relish. 'I'm going down to talk to the Captain about all this drunkenness in the village, and I want you to come with me,' he said straight out.

I can't say that I fancied the visit much myself, and I tried to hint to parson that as, after all, they were only a lot of ghosts, it didn't very much matter.

'Dead or alive, I'm responsible for their good conduct,' he said, 'and I'm going to do my duty and put a stop to this continued disorder. And you are coming with me, John Simmons.' So I went, parson being a persuasive kind of man.

We went down to the ship, and as we approached her I could see the Captain tasting the air on deck. When he saw parson he took off his hat very politely, and I can tell you that I was relieved to find that he had a proper respect for the cloth. Parson acknowledged his salute and spoke out stoutly enough. 'Sir, I should be glad to have a word with you.'

'Come on board, sir; come on board,' said the Captain, and I could tell by his voice that he knew why we were there. Parson and I climbed up an uneasy kind of ladder, and the Captain took us into the great cabin at the back of the ship, where the bay window was. It was the most wonderful place you ever saw in your life, all full of gold and silver plate, swords and jewelled scabbards, carved oak chairs, and great chests that looked as though they were bursting with guineas. Even parson was surprised, and he did not shake his head very hard when the Captain took down some silver cups and poured us out a drink of rum. I tasted mine, and I don't mind saying that it changed my view of things entirely. There was nothing betwixt and between about that rum, and I felt that it was ridiculous to blame the lads for drinking too much of stuff like that. It seemed to fill my veins with honey and fire.

Parson put the case squarely to the Captain, but I didn't listen much to what he said; I was busy sipping my drink and looking through the window at the fishes swimming to and fro over landlord's turnips. Just then it seemed the most natural thing in the world that they should be there, though afterwards, of course, I could see that that proved it was a ghost ship.

But even then I thought it was queer when I saw a drowned sailor float by in the thin air with his hair and beard all full of bubbles. It was the first time I had seen anything quite like that at Fairfield.

All the time I was regarding the wonders of the deep, parson was telling Captain Roberts how there was no peace or rest in the village owing to the curse of drunkenness, and what a bad example the youngsters were setting to the older ghosts. The Captain listened very attentively, and only put in a word now and then about boys being boys and young men sowing their wild oats. But when parson had finished his speech he filled up our silver cups and said to parson, with a flourish, 'I should be sorry to cause trouble anywhere where I have been made welcome, and you will be glad to hear that I put to sea tomorrow night. And now you must drink me a prosperous voyage.' So we all stood up and drank the toast with honour, and that noble rum was like hot oil in my veins.

After that Captain showed us some of the curiosities he had brought back from foreign parts, and we were greatly amazed, though afterwards I couldn't clearly remember what they were. And then I found myself walking across the turnips with parson, and I was telling him of the glories of the deep that I had seen through the window of the ship. He turned on me severely. 'If I were you, John Simmons,' he said, 'I should go straight home to bed.' He has a way of putting things that wouldn't occur to an ordinary man, has parson, and I did as he told me.

Well, next day it came on to blow, and it blew harder and harder, till about eight o'clock at night I heard a noise and looked out into the garden. I dare say you won't believe me, it seems a bit tall even to me, but the wind had lifted the thatch of my pigsty into the widow's garden a second time. I thought I wouldn't wait to hear what widow had to say about it, so I went across the green to the Fox and Grapes, and the wind was so strong that I danced along on tiptoe like a girl at the fair. When I got to the inn landlord had to help me shut the door; it seemed as though a dozen goats were pushing against it to come in out of the storm.

'It's a powerful tempest,' he said, drawing the beer. 'I hear there's a chimney down at Dickory End.'

'It's a funny thing how these sailors know about the weather,' I answered. 'When Captain said he was going tonight, I was thinking it would take a capful of wind to carry the ship back to sea, but now here's more than a capful.'

'Ah, yes,' said landlord, 'it's tonight he goes true enough, and, mind you, though he treated me handsome over the rent, I'm not sure it's a loss to the village. I don't hold with gentrice who fetch their drink from London instead of helping local traders to get their living.'

'But you haven't got any rum like his,' I said, to draw him out.

His neck grew red above the collar, and I was afraid I'd gone too far; but after a while he got his breath with a grunt.

'John Simmons,' he said, 'if you've come down here this windy night to talk a lot of fool's talk, you've wasted a journey.'

Well, of course, then I had to smooth him down with praising his rum, and Heaven forgive me for swearing it was better than Captain's. For the like of that rum no living lips have tasted save mine and parson's. But somehow or other I brought landlord round, and presently we must have a glass of his best to prove its quality.

'Beat that if you can!' he cried, and we both raised our glasses to our mouths, only to stop half-way and look at each other in amaze. For the wind that had been howling outside like an outrageous dog had all of a sudden turned as melodious as the carol-boys of a Christmas Eve.

'Surely that's not my Martha,' whispered landlord; Martha being his great-aunt that lived in the loft overhead.

We went to the door, and the wind burst it open so that the handle was driven clean into the plaster of the wall. But we didn't think about that at the time; for over our heads, sailing very comfortably through the windy stars, was the ship that had passed the summer in landlord's field. Her portholes and her bay window were blazing with lights, and there was a noise of singing and fiddling on her decks. 'He's gone,' shouted landlord above the storm, 'and he's taken half the village with him!' I could only nod in answer, not having lungs like bellows of leather.

In the morning we were able to measure the strength of the storm, and over and above my pigsty there was damage enough wrought in the village to keep us busy. True it is that the children had to break down no branches for the firing that autumn, since the wind had strewn the woods with more than they could carry away. Many of our ghosts were scattered abroad, but this time very few came back, all the young men having sailed with Captain; and not only ghosts, for a poor half-witted lad was missing, and we reckoned that he had stowed himself away or perhaps shipped as cabin-boy, not knowing any better.

What with the lamentations of the ghost-girls and the grumblings of families who had lost an ancestor, the village was upset for a while, and the funny thing was that it was the folk who had complained most of the carryings-on of the youngsters, who made most noise now that they were gone. I hadn't any sympathy with shoemaker or butcher, who ran about saying how much they missed their lads, but it made me grieve to hear the poor bereaved girls calling their lovers by name on the village green at nightfall. It didn't seem fair to me that they should have lost their men a second time, after giving up life in order to join them, as like as not. Still, not even a spirit can be sorry for ever, and after a few months we made up our mind that the folk who had sailed in the ship were never coming back, and we didn't talk about it any more.

And then one day, I dare say it would be a couple of years after, when the whole business was quite forgotten, who should come trapesing along the road from Portsmouth but the daft lad who had gone away with the ship, without waiting till he was dead to become a ghost. You never saw such a boy as that in all your life. He had a great rusty cutlass hanging to a string at his waist, and he was tatooed all over in fine colours, so that even his face looked like a girl's sampler. He had a handkerchief in his hand full of foreign shells and old-fashioned pieces of small money, very curious, and he walked up to the well outside his mother's house and drew himself a drink as if he had been nowhere in particular.

The worst of it was that he had come back as soft-headed as he went, and try as we might we couldn't get anything reasonable out of him. He talked a lot of gibberish about keel-hauling and walking the plank and crimson murders — things which a decent sailor should know nothing about, so that it seemed to me that for all his manners Captain had been more of a pirate than a gentleman mariner. But to draw sense out of that boy was as hard as picking cherries off a crab-tree. One silly tale he had that he kept on drifting back to, and to hear him you would have thought that it was the only thing that happened to him in his life.

'We was at anchor,' he would say, 'off an island called the Basket of Flowers, and the sailors had caught a lot of parrots and we were teaching them to swear. Up and down the decks, up and down the decks, and the language they used was dreadful. Then we looked up and saw the masts of the

Spanish ship outside the harbour. Outside the harbour they were, so we threw the parrots in the sea and sailed out to fight. And all the parrots were drownded in the sea and the language they used was dreadful.' That's the sort of boy he was, nothing but silly talk of parrots when we asked him about the fighting. And we never had a chance of teaching him better, for two days after he ran away again, and hasn't been seen since.

That's my story, and I assure you that things like that are happening at Fairfield all the time. The ship has never come back, but somehow as people grow older they seem to think that one of these windy nights she'll come sailing in over the hedges with all the lost ghosts on board. Well, when she comes, she'll be welcome. That's one ghost-lass that has never grown tired of waiting for her lad to return. Every night you'll see her out on the green, straining her poor eyes with looking for the mast-lights among the stars. A faithful lass you'd call her, and I'm thinking you'd be right.

Landlord's field wasn't a penny the worse for the visit, but they do say that since then the turnips that have been grown in it have tasted of rum.

IV

The Call of Cthulhu

H.P. Lovecraft

H.P. Lovecraft, that lonely recluse who died in 1937, was ignored in his own time as are so many talented people. This mystic dreamer inherited the qualities of Dunsey, Hodgson and Poe which he utilised to create a whole myth pattern of remarkable depth and quality. Our tale is the basis of the Cthulhu mythos which was founded on the theory that the earth was inhabited by other races eons before man evolved and that survivors of these ancient races still exist in the earth's dark places, 'dreaming but not dead as we know the word', awaiting a call to renew their old domination.

This myth pattern has today been seized on by scores of 'original thinkers' but Lovecraft was its major prophet. It was fashionable for critics to sneer at his work when he was alive and today it is still thought desirable for the 'experts' to look down upon the Lovecraft stories. However anyone who has bothered to study these tales will be amazed by their breathtaking range and vision. He foresaw the effects of nuclear radiation in his Colour out of Space *while* Shadow over Innsmouth *and* Shadow out of Time *both build to a peak of culminating horror in a masterly fashion. Perhaps his greatest work is* At the Mountains of Madness *but* The Call of the Cthulhu *gives a perfect illustration of his style and power.*

> *Of such great powers or beings there may be conceivably a survival ... a survival of a hugely remote period when ... consciousness was manifested, perhaps, in shapes and forms long since withdrawn before the tide of advancing humanity ... forms of which poetry and legend alone have caught a flying memory and called them gods, monsters, mythical beings of all sorts and kinds ...*
> --ALGERNON BLACKWOOD

The Horror in Clay

The most merciful thing in the world, I think, is the inability of the human mind to correlate all its contents. We live on a placid island of ignorance in the midst of black seas of infinity, and it was not meant that we should voyage far. The sciences, each straining in its own direction, have hitherto harmed us little; but some day the piecing together of dissociated knowledge will open up such terrifying vistas of reality, and of our frightful position therein, that we shall either go mad from the revelation or flee from the deadly light into the peace and safety of a new dark age.

Theosophists have guessed at the awesome grandeur of the cosmic cycle wherein our world and human race form transient incidents. They have hinted at strange survivals in terms which would freeze the blood if not masked by a bland optimism. But it is not from them that there came the single glimpse of forbidden eons which chills me when I think of it and maddens me when I dream of it. That glimpse, like all dread glimpses of truth, flashed out from an accidental piecing together of separated things — in this case an old newspaper item and the notes of a dead professor. I hope that no one else will accomplish this piecing out; certainly, if I live, I shall never knowingly supply a link in so hideous a chain. I think that the professor, too, intended to keep silent regarding the part he knew, and that he would have destroyed his notes had not sudden death seized him.

My knowledge of the thing began in the winter of 1926-27 with the death of my grand uncle, George Gammell Angell, Professor Emeritus of Semitic Languages in Brown University, Providence, Rhode Island. Professor Angell was widely known as an authority on ancient inscriptions, and had frequently been resorted to by the heads of prominent museums; so that his passing at the age of ninety-two may be recalled by many. Locally, interest was intensified by the obscurity of the cause of death. The professor had been stricken whilst returning from the Newport boat; falling suddenly, as witnesses said, after having been jostled by a nautical-looking negro who had come from one of the queer dark courts on the precipitous hillside which formed a short cut from the waterfront to the deceased's home in Williams Street. Physicians were unable to find any visible disorder, but concluded after perplexed debate that some obscure lesion of the heart, induced by the brisk ascent of so steep a hill by so elderly a man, was responsible for the end. At the time I saw no reason to dissent from this dictum, but latterly I am inclined to wonder — and more than wonder.

As my granduncle's heir and executor, for he died a childless widower, I was expected to go over his papers with some thoroughness; and for that purpose moved his entire set of files and boxes to my quarters in Boston. Much of the material which I correlated will be later published by the American Archaeological Society, but there was one box which I found exceedingly puzzling, and which I felt much averse from showing to other eyes. It had been locked, and I did not find the key till it occurred to me to examine the personal ring which the professor carried always in his pocket. Then, indeed, I succeeded in opening it, but when I did so seemed only to be confronted by a greater and more closely locked barrier. For what could be the meaning of the queer clay bas-relief and the disjointed jottings, ramblings, and cuttings which I found? Had my uncle, in his latter years, become credulous of the most superficial impostures? I resolved to search out the eccentric sculptor responsible for this apparent disturbance of an old man's peace of mind.

The bas-relief was a rough rectangle less than an inch thick and about five by six inches in area; obviously of modern origin. Its designs, however, were far from modern in atmosphere and suggestion; for, although the vagaries of cubism and futurism are many and wild, they do not often reproduce that cryptic regularity which lurks in prehistoric writing. And writing of some kind the bulk of these designs seemed certainly to be; though my memory, despite much familiarity with the papers and collections of my uncle, failed in any way to identify this particular species, or even hint at its remotest affiliations.

Above these apparent hieroglyphics was a figure of evidently pictorial intent, though its impressionistic execution forbad a very clear idea of its nature. It seemed to be a sort of monster, or symbol representing a monster, of a form which only a diseased fancy could conceive. If I say that my somewhat extravagant imagination yielded simultaneous pictures of an octopus, a dragon, and a human caricature, I shall not be unfaithful to the spirit of the thing.

A pulpy, tentacled head surmounted a grotesque and scaly body with rudimentary wings; but it was the *general outline* of the whole which made it most shockingly frightful. Behind the figure was a vague suggestion of a Cyclopean architectural background.

The writing accompanying this oddity was, aside from a stack of press cuttings, in Professor Angell's most recent hand; and made no pretense to literary style. What seemed to be the main document was headed 'CTHULHU CULT' in characters painstakingly printed to avoid the erroneous reading of a word so unheard-of. This manuscript was divided into two sections, the first of which was headed '1925 — Dream and Dream Work of H.A. Wilcox, 7 Thomas St., Providence, R.I.,' and the second, 'Narrative of Inspector John R. Legrasse, 121 Bienville St., New Orleans, La., at 1908 A. A. S. Mtg. — Notes on Same, & Prof. Webb's Acct.' The other manuscript papers were all brief notes, some of them accounts of the queer dreams of different persons, some of them citations from theosophical books and magazines (notably W. Scott-Elliott's *Atlantis and the Lost Lemuria*), and the rest comments on long-surviving secret societies and hidden cults, with references to passages in such mythological and anthropological source-books as Frazer's *Golden Bough* and Miss Murray's *Witch-Cult in Western Europe*. The cuttings largely alluded to outré mental illness and outbreaks of group folly or mania in the spring of 1925.

The first half of the principal manuscript told a very peculiar tale. It appears that on March 1st, 1925, a thin, dark young man of neurotic and excited aspect had called upon Professor Angell bearing the singular clay bas-relief, which was then exceedingly damp and fresh. His card bore the name of Henry Anthony Wilcox, and my uncle had recognized him as the youngest son of an excellent family slightly known to him, who had latterly been studying sculpture at the Rhode Island School of Design and living alone at the Fleur-de-Lys Building near that institution. Wilcox was a precocious youth of known genius but great eccentricity, and had from childhood excited attention through the strange stories and odd dreams he was in the habit of relating. He called himself 'psychically hypersensitive', but the staid folk of the ancient commercial city dismissed him as merely 'queer'. Never mingling much with his kind, he had dropped gradually from social visibility, and was now known only to a small group of aesthetes from other towns. Even the Providence Art Club, anxious to preserve its conservatism, had found him quite hopeless.

On the occasion of the visit, ran the professor's manuscript, the sculptor abruptly asked for the benefit of his host's archeological knowledge in identifying the hieroglyphics on the bas-relief. He spoke in a dreamy, stilted manner which suggested pose and alienated sympathy; and my uncle showed some sharpness in replying, for the conspicuous freshness of the tablet implied kinship with anything but archeology. Young Wilcox's rejoinder, which impressed my uncle enough to make him recall and record it verbatim, was of a fantastically poetic cast which must have typified his whole conversation, and which I have since found highly characteristic of him. He said, 'It is new, indeed, for I made it last night in a dream of strange cities; and dreams are older than brooding Tyre, or the contemplative Sphinx, or garden-girdled Babylon.'

It was then that he began that rambling tale which suddenly played upon a sleeping memory and won the fevered interest of my uncle. There had been a slight earthquake tremor the night before, the most considerable felt in New England for some years; and Wilcox's imagination had been keenly affected. Upon retiring, he had had an unprecedented dream of great Cyclopean cities of Titan blocks and sky-flung monoliths, all dripping with green ooze and sinister with latent horror. Hieroglyphics had covered the walls and pillars, and from some undetermined point below had come a voice that was not a voice; a chaotic sensation which only fancy could transmute into sound, but which he attempted to render by the almost unpronounceable jumble of letters, '*Cthulhu fhtagn*'.

This verbal jumble was the key to the recollection which excited and disturbed Professor Angell. He questioned the sculptor with scientific minuteness; and studied with almost frantic intensity the bas-relief on which the youth had found himself working, chilled and clad only in his nightclothes, when waking had stolen bewilderingly over him. My uncle blamed his old age, Wilcox afterward said, for his slowness in recognizing both hieroglyphics and pictorial design. Many of his questions seemed highly out of place to his visitor, especially those which tried to connect the latter with strange cults or societies; and Wilcox could not understand the repeated promises of silence which he was offered in exchange for an admission of membership in some wide-spread mystical or paganly religious body.

When Professor Angell became convinced that the sculptor was indeed ignorant of any cult or system of cryptic lore, he besieged his visitor with demands for future reports of dreams. This bore regular fruit, for after the first interview the manuscript records daily calls of the young man, during which he related startling fragments of nocturnal imagery whose burden was always some terrible Cyclopean vista of dark and dripping stone, with a subterrene voice or intelligence shouting monotonously in enigmatical sense-impacts uninscribable save as gibberish. The two sounds most frequently repeated are those rendered by the letters 'Cthulhu' and 'R'lyeh'.

On March 23, the manuscript continued, Wilcox failed to appear; and inquiries at his quarters revealed that he had been stricken with an obscure sort of fever and taken to the home of his family in Waterman Street. He had cried out in the night, arousing several other artists in the building, and had manifested since then only alternations of unconsciousness and delirium. My uncle at once telephoned the family, and from that time forward kept close watch of the case; calling often at the Thayer Street office of Dr. Tobey, whom he learned to be in charge. The youth's febrile mind, apparently, was dwelling on strange things; and the doctor shuddered now and then as he spoke of them. They included not only a repetition of what he had formerly dreamed, but touched wildly on a gigantic thing 'miles high' which walked or lumbered about. He at no time fully described this object but occasional frantic words, as repeated by Dr. Tobey, convinced the professor that it must be identical with the nameless monstrosity he had sought to depict in his dream-sculpture. Reference to this object, the doctor added, was invariably a prelude to the young man's subsidence into lethargy. His temperature, oddly enough, was not greatly above normal; but the whole condition was otherwise such as to suggest true fever rather than mental disorder.

On April 2 at about 3 p.m. every trace of Wilcox's malady suddenly ceased. He sat upright in bed, astonished to find himself at home and completely ignorant of what had happened in dream or reality since the night of March 22. Pronounced well by his physician, he returned to his quarters in three days; but to Professor Angell he was of no further assistance. All traces of strange dreaming had vanished with his recovery, and my uncle kept no record of his night-thoughts after a week of pointless and irrelevant accounts of thoroughly usual visions.

Here the first part of the manuscript ended, but references to certain of the scattered notes gave me much material for thought — so much, in fact, that only the ingrained scepticism then forming my philosophy can account for my continued distrust of the artist. The notes in question were those descriptive of the dreams of various persons covering the same period as that in which young Wilcox had had his strange visitations. My uncle, it seems, had quickly instituted a prodigiously far-flung body of inquiries amongst nearly all the friends whom he could question without impertinence, asking for nightly reports of their dreams, and the dates of any notable visions for some time past.

The reception of his request seems to have been varied; but he must, at the very least, have received more responses than any ordinary man could have handled without a secretary. This original correspondence was not preserved, but his notes formed a thorough and really significant digest. Average people in society and business — New England's traditional 'salt of the earth' — gave an almost completely negative result, though scattered cases of uneasy but formless nocturnal impressions appear here and there, always between March 23 and April 2 — the period of young Wilcox's delirium. Scientific men were little more affected, though four cases of vague description suggest fugitive glimpses of strange landscapes, and in one case there is mentioned a dread of something abnormal.

It was from the artists and poets that the pertinent answers came, and I know that panic would have broken loose had they been able to compare notes. As it was, lacking their original letters, I half suspected the compiler of having asked leading questions, or of having edited the correspondence in corroboration of what he had latently resolved to see. That is why I continued to feel that Wilcox, somehow cognizant of the old data which my uncle had possessed, had been imposing on the veteran scientist. These responses from aesthetes told a disturbing tale. From February 28 to April 2 a large proportion of them had dreamed very bizarre things, the intensity of the dreams being immeasurably the stronger during the period of the sculptor's delirium. Over a fourth of those who reported anything, reported scenes and half-sounds not unlike those which Wilcox had described; and some of the dreamers confessed acute fear of the gigantic nameless thing visible toward the last.

One case, which the note describes with emphasis, was very sad. The subject, a widely known architect with leanings toward theosophy and occultism, went violently insane on the date of young Wilcox's seizure, and expired several months later after incessant screamings to be saved from some escaped denizen of hell. Had my uncle referred to these cases by name instead of merely by number, I should have attempted some corroboration and personal investigation; but as it was, I succeeded in tracing down only a few. All of these, however, bore out the notes in full. I have often wondered if all the objects of the professor's questioning felt as puzzled as did this fraction. It is well that no explanation shall ever reach them.

The press cuttings, as I have intimated, touched on cases of panic, mania, and eccentricity during the given period. Professor Angell must have employed a cutting bureau, for the number of extracts was tremendous, and the sources scattered throughout the globe. Here was a nocturnal suicide in London, where a lone sleeper had leaped from a window after a shocking cry. Here likewise a rambling letter to the editor of a paper in South America, where a fanatic deduces a dire future from visions he has seen. A dispatch from California describes a theosophic colony as donning white robes en masse for some 'glorious fulfilment' which never arrives, whilst items from India speak guardedly of serious native unrest toward the end of March. Voodoo orgies multiply in Haiti, and African outposts report ominous mutterings. American officers in the Philippines find certain tribes bothersome about this time, and New York policemen are mobbed by hysterical Levantines on the night of March 22-23. The west of Ireland, too, is full of wild rumour and legendry, and a fantastic painter named Ardois-Bonnot hangs a blasphemous *Dream Landscape* in the Paris spring salon of 1926. And so numerous are the recorded troubles in insane asylums that only a miracle can have stopped the medical fraternity from noting strange parallelisms and drawing mystified conclusions.

A weird bunch of cuttings, all told; and I can at this date scarcely envisage the callous rationalism with which I set them aside. But I was then convinced that young Wilcox had known of the older matters mentioned by the professor.

The Tale of Inspector Legrasse

The old matters which had made the sculptor's dream and bas-relief so significant to my uncle formed the subject of the second half of his long manuscript. Once before, it appears, Professor Angell had seen the hellish outlines of the nameless monstrosity, puzzled over the unknown hieroglyphics, and heard the ominous syllables which can be rendered only as '*Cthulhu*'; and all this in so stirring and horrible a connection that it is small wonder he pursued young Wilcox with queries and demands for data.

This earlier experience had come in 1908, seventeen years before, when the American Archaeological Society held its annual meeting in St. Louis. Professor Angell, as befitted one of his authority and attainments, had had a prominent part in all the deliberations; and was one of the first to be approached by the several outsiders who took advantage of the convocation to offer questions for correct answering and problems for expert solution.

The chief of these outsiders, and in a short time the focus of interest for the entire meeting, was a commonplace-looking middle-aged man who had travelled all the way from New Orleans for certain special information unobtainable from any local source. His name was John Raymond Legrasse, and he was by profession an inspector of police. With him he bore the subject of his visit, a grotesque, repulsive, and apparently very ancient stone statuette whose origin he was at a loss to determine.

It must not be fancied that Inspector Legrasse had the least interest in archaeology. On the contrary, his wish for enlightenment was prompted by purely professional considerations. The statuette, idol, fetish, or whatever it was, had been captured some months before in the wooded swamps south of New Orleans during a raid on a supposed voodoo meeting; and so singular and hideous were the rites connected with it, that the police could not but realize that they had stumbled on a dark cult totally unknown to them, and infinitely more diabolic than even the blackest of the African voodoo circles. Of its origin, apart from the erratic and unbelievable tales extorted from the captured members, absolutely nothing was to be discovered; hence the anxiety of the police for any antiquarian lore which might help them to place the frightful symbol, and through it track down the cult to its fountain-head.

Inspector Legrasse was scarcely prepared for the sensation which his offering created. One sight of the thing had been enough to throw the assembled men of science into a state of tense excitement, and they lost no time in crowding around him to gaze at the diminutive figure whose utter strangeness and air of genuinely abysmal antiquity hinted so potently at unopened and archaic vistas. No recognized school of sculpture had animated this terrible object, yet centuries and even thousands of years seemed recorded in its dim and greenish surface of unplaceable stone.

The figure, which was finally passed slowly from man to man for close and careful study, was between seven and eight inches in height, and of exquisitely artistic workmanship. It represented a monster of vaguely anthropoid outline, but with an octopuslike head whose face was a mass of feelers, a scaly, rubbery-looking body, prodigious claws on hind and fore feet, and long, narrow wings behind. This thing, which seemed instinct with a fearsome and unnatural malignancy, was of a somewhat bloated corpulence, and squatted evilly on a rectangular block or pedestal covered with undecipherable characters. The tips of the wings touched the back edge of the block, the seat occupied the centre, whilst the long, curved claws of the doubled-up, crouching hind legs gripped the front edge and extended a quarter of the way down toward the bottom of the pedestal. The cephalopod head was bent forward, so that the ends of the facial feelers brushed the backs of huge fore-paws which clasped the croucher's elevated knees. The aspect of the whole was abnormally lifelike, and the more subtly fearful because its source was so totally unknown. Its vast, awesome, and incalculable age was unmistakable; yet not one link did it show with any known type of art belonging to civilization's youth — or indeed to any other time.

Totally separate and apart, its very material was a mystery; for the soapy, greenish-black stone with its golden or iridescent flecks and striations resembled nothing familiar to geology or mineralogy. The characters along the base were equally baffling; and no member present, despite a representation of half the world's expert learning in this field, could form the least notion of even their remotest linguistic kinship. They, like the subject and material, belonged to something horribly remote and distinct from mankind as we know it; something frightfully suggestive of old and unhallowed cycles of life in which our world and our conceptions have no part.

And yet, as the members severally shook their heads and confessed defeat at the inspector's problem, there was one man in that gathering who suspected a touch of bizarre familiarity in the monstrous shape and writing, and who presently told with some diffidence of the odd trifle he knew. This person was the late William Channing Webb, professor of anthropology in Princeton University, and an explorer of no slight note.

Professor Webb had been engaged, forty-eight years before, in a tour of Greenland and Iceland in search of some Runic inscriptions which he failed to unearth; and whilst high up on the West Greenland coast had encountered a singular tribe or cult of degenerate Eskimos whose religion, a curious form of devil-worship, chilled him with its deliberate bloodthirstiness and repulsiveness. It was a faith of which other Eskimos knew little, and which they mentioned only with shudders, saying that it had come down from horribly ancient eons before ever the world was made. Besides nameless rites and human sacrifices there were certain queer hereditary rituals addressed to a supreme elder devil or *tornasuk*; and of this Professor Webb had taken a careful phonetic copy from an aged *angekok* or wizard-priest, expressing the sounds in Roman letters as best he knew how. But just now of prime significance was the fetish which this cult had cherished, and around which they danced when the aurora leaped high over the ice cliffs. It was, the professor stated, a very crude bas-relief of stone, comprising a hideous picture and some cryptic writing. And as far as he could tell it was a rough parallel in all essential features of the bestial thing now lying before the meeting.

These data, received with suspense and astonishment by the assembled members, proved doubly exciting to Inspector Legrasse; and he began at once to ply his informant with questions. Having noted and copied an oral ritual among the swamp cult-worshipers his men had arrested, he besought the professor to remember as best he might the syllables taken down amongst the diabolist Eskimos. There then followed an exhaustive comparison of details, and a moment of really awed silence when both detective and scientist agreed on the virtual identity of the phrase common to two hellish rituals so many worlds of distance apart. What, in substance, both the Eskimo wizards and the Louisiana swamp-priests had chanted to their kindred idols was something very like this — the word-divisions being guessed at from traditional breaks in the phrase as chanted aloud:

'*Ph'nglui mglw'nafh Cthulhu R'lyeh wgah'nagl fhtagn.*'

Legrasse had one point in advance of Professor Webb, for several among his mongrel prisoners had repeated to him what older celebrants had told them the words meant. This text, as given, ran something like this:

'In his house at R'lyeh dead Cthulhu waits dreaming.'

And now, in response to a general urgent demand, Inspector Legrasse related as fully as possible his experience with the swamp worshippers; telling a story to which I could see my uncle attached profound significance. It savoured of the wildest dreams of myth-maker and theosophist, and disclosed an astonishing degree of cosmic imagination among such half-castes and pariahs as might be least expected to possess it.

On November 1, 1907, there had come to New Orleans police a frantic summons from the swamp and lagoon country to the south. The squatters there, mostly primitive but good-natured descendants of Lafitte's men, were in the grip of stark terror from an unknown thing which had stolen upon them in the night. It was voodoo, apparently, but voodoo of a more terrible sort than they had ever known; and some of their women and children had disappeared since the malevolent tom-tom had begun its incessant beating far within the black haunted woods where no dweller ventured. There were insane shouts and harrowing screams, soul-chilling chants and dancing devil-flames; and, the frightened messenger added, the people could stand it no more.

So a body of twenty police, filling two carriages and an automobile, had set out in the late afternoon with the shivering squatter as a guide. At the end of the passable road they alighted, and for miles splashed on in silence through the terrible cypress woods where day never came. Ugly roots and malignant hanging nooses of Spanish moss beset them, and now and then a pile of dank stones or fragments of a rotting wall intensified by its hint of morbid habitation a depression which every malformed tree and every fungus islet combined to create. At length the squatter settlement, a miserable huddle of huts, hove in sight; and hysterical dwellers ran out to cluster around the group of bobbing lanterns. The muffled beat of tom-toms was now faintly audible far, far ahead; and a curdling shriek came at infrequent intervals when the wind shifted. A reddish glare, too, seemed to filter through the pale undergrowth beyond endless avenues of forest night. Reluctant even to be left alone again, each one of the cowed squatters refused point-blank to advance another inch toward the scene of

unholy worship, so Inspector Legrasse and his nineteen
colleagues plunged on unguided into black arcades of horror
that none of them had ever trod before.

The region now entered by the police was one of
traditionally evil repute, substantially unknown and un-
traversed by white men. There were legends of a hidden lake
unglimpsed by mortal sight, in which dwelt a huge, formless
white polypous thing with luminous eyes; and squatters
whispered that bat-winged devils flew up out of caverns in
inner earth to worship it at midnight. They said it had been
there before D'Iberville, before La Salle, before the Indians,
and before even the wholesome beasts and birds of the
woods. It was nightmare itself, and to see it was to die. But it
made men dream, and so they knew enough to keep away.
The present voodoo orgy was, indeed, on the merest fringe of
this abhorred area, but that location was bad enough; hence
perhaps the very place of the worship had terrified the
squatters more than the shocking sounds and incidents.

Only poetry or madness could do justice to the noises
heard by Legrasse's men as they ploughed on through the
black morass toward the red glare and the muffled tom-toms.
There are vocal qualities peculiar to men, and vocal qualities
peculiar to beasts; and it is terrible to hear the one when the
source should yield the other. Animal fury and orgiastic
licence here whipped themselves to demoniac heights by
howls and squawking ecstasies that tore and reverberated
through those nighted woods like pestilential tempests from
the gulfs of hell. Now and then the less organized ululations
would cease, and from what seemed a well-drilled chorus of
hoarse voices would rise in singsong chant that hideous
phrase or ritual:

'Ph'nglui mglw'nafh Cthulhu R'lyeh wgah'nagl fhtagn.'

Then the men, having reached a spot where the trees were
thinner, came suddenly in sight of the spectacle itself. Four
of them reeled, one fainted, and two were shaken into a
frantic cry which the mad cacophony of the orgy fortunately
deadened. Legrasse dashed swamp water on the face of the
fainting man, and all stood trembling and nearly hypnotized
with horror.

In a natural glade of the swamp stood a grassy island of

perhaps an acre's extent, clear of trees and tolerably dry. On this now leaped and twisted a more indescribable horde of human abnormality than any but a Sime or an Angarola could paint. Void of clothing, this hybrid spawn were braying, bellowing and writhing about a monstrous ring-shaped bonfire; in the centre of which, revealed by occasional rifts in the curtain of flame, stood a great granite monolith some eight feet in height; on top of which, incongruous in its diminutiveness, rested the noxious carven statuette. From a wide circle of ten scaffolds set up at regular intervals with the flame-girt monolith as a centre hung, head downward, the oddly marred bodies of the helpless squatters who had disappeared. It was inside this circle that the ring of worshippers jumped and roared, the general direction of the mass motion being from left to right in endless bacchanale between the ring of bodies and the ring of fire.

It may have been only imagination and it may have been only echoes which induced one of the men, an excitable Spaniard, to fancy he heard antiphonal responses to the ritual from some far and unillumined spot deeper within the wood of ancient legendry and horror. This man, Joseph D. Galvez, I later met and questioned; and he proved distractingly imaginative. He indeed went so far as to hint of the faint beating of great wings, and of a glimpse of shining eyes and mountainous white bulk beyond the remotest trees — but I suppose he had been hearing too much native superstition.

Actually, the horrified pause of the men was of comparatively brief duration. Duty came first; and although there must have been nearly a hundred mongrel celebrants in the throng, the police relied on their firearms and plunged determinedly into the nauseous rout. For five minutes the resultant din and chaos were beyond description. Wild blows were struck, shots were fired, and escapes were made; but in the end Legrasse was able to count some forty-seven sullen prisoners, whom he forced to dress in haste and fall into line between two rows of policemen. Five of the worshippers lay dead, and two severely wounded ones were carried away on improvised stretchers by their fellow-prisoners. The image on the monolith, of course, was carefully removed and carried back by Legrasse.

Examined at headquarters after a trip of intense strain and

weariness, the prisoners all proved to be men of a very low, mixed-blooded, and mentally aberrant type. Most were seamen, and a sprinkling of negroes and mulattoes, largely West Indians or Brava Portuguese from the Cape Verde Islands, gave a colouring of voodooism to the heterogeneous cult. But before many questions were asked, it became manifest that something far deeper and older than negro fetishism was involved. Degraded and ignorant as they were, the creatures held with surprising consistency to the central idea of their loathsome faith.

They worshipped, so they said, the Great Old Ones who lived ages before there were any men, and who came to the young world out of the sky. These Old Ones were gone now, inside the earth and under the sea; but their dead bodies had told their secrets in dreams to the first man, who formed a cult which had never died. This was the cult, and the prisoners said it had always existed and always would exist, hidden in distant wastes and dark places all over the world until the time when the great priest Cthulhu, from his dark house in the mighty city of R'lyeh under the waters, should rise and bring the earth again beneath his sway. Some day he would call, when the stars were ready, and the secret cult would always be waiting to liberate him.

Meanwhile no more must be told. There was a secret which even torture could not extract. Mankind was not absolutely alone among the conscious things of earth, for shapes came out of the dark to visit the faithful few. But these were not the Great Old Ones. No man had ever seen the Old Ones. The carven idol was great Cthulhu, but none might say whether or not the others were precisely like him. No one could read the old writing now, but things were told by word of mouth. The chanted ritual was not the secret — that was never spoken aloud, only whispered. The chant meant only this: 'In his house at R'lyeh dead Cthulhu waits dreaming.'

Only two of the prisoners were found sane enough to be hanged, and the rest were committed to various institutions. All denied a part in the ritual murders, and averred that the killing had been done by Black-winged Ones which had come to them from their immemorial meeting-place in the haunted wood. But of those mysterious allies no coherent account could ever be gained. What the police did extract came mainly from an immensely aged mestizo named Castro, who claimed to have sailed to strange ports and talked with undying leaders of the cult in the mountains of China.

Old Castro remembered bits of hideous legend that paled the speculations of theosophists and made man and the world seem recent and transient indeed. There had been eons when other Things ruled on the earth, and They had had great cities. Remains of Them, he said the deathless Chinamen had told him, were still to be found as Cyclopean stones on islands in the Pacific. They all died vast epochs of time before man came, but there were arts which could revive Them when the stars had come round again to the right positions in the cycle of eternity. They had, indeed, come themselves from the stars, and brought Their images with Them.

These Great Old Ones, Castro continued, were not composed altogether of flesh and blood. They had shape — for did not this star-fashioned image prove it? — but that shape was not made of matter. When the stars were right, They could plunge from world to world through the sky; but when the stars were wrong, They could not live. But although They no longer lived, They would never really die. They all lay in stone houses in Their great city of R'lyeh, preserved by the spells of mighty Cthulhu for a glorious resurrection when the stars and the earth might once more be ready for Them. But at that time some force from outside must serve to liberate Their bodies. The spells that preserved Them intact likewise prevented Them from making an initial move, and They could only lie awake in the dark and think whilst uncounted millions of years rolled by. They knew all that was occurring in the universe, for Their mode of speech was transmitted thought. Even now They talked in Their tombs. When, after infinities of chaos, the first men came, the Great Old Ones spoke to the sensitive among them by molding their dreams; for only thus could Their language reach the fleshy minds of mammals.

Then, whispered Castro, those first men formed the cult around small idols which the Great Ones showed them; idols brought in dim eras from dark stars. That cult would never die till the stars came right again, and the secret priests would take great Cthulhu from His tomb to revive His subjects and resume His rule of earth. The time would be easy to know, for then mankind would have become as the Great Old Ones; free and wild and beyond good and evil, with laws and morals thrown aside and all men shouting and killing and reveling in joy. Then the liberated Old Ones would teach them new ways to shout and kill and revel and enjoy themselves, and all the earth would flame with a holocaust of ecstasy and freedom. Meanwhile the cult, by appropriate rites, must keep alive the memory of those ancient ways and shadow forth the prophecy of their return.

In the elder time chosen men had talked with the entombed Old Ones in dreams, but then something had happened. The great stone city R'lyeh, with its monoliths and sepulchers, had sunk beneath the waves; and the deep waters, full of the one primal mystery through which not even thought can pass, had cut off the spectral intercourse. But the memory never died, and high priests said that the city would rise again when the stars were right. Then came out of the earth the black spirits of earth, mouldy and shadowy, and full of dim rumours picked up in caverns beneath forgotten sea-bottoms. But of them old Castro dared not speak much. He cut himself off hurriedly, and no amount of persuasion or subtlety could elicit more in this direction. The *size* of the Old Ones, too, he curiously declined to mention. Of the cult, he said that he thought the centre lay amid the pathless deserts of Arabia, where Irem, the City of Pillars, dreams hidden and untouched. It was not allied to the European witch-cult, and was virtually unknown beyond its members. No book had ever really hinted of it, though the deathless Chinamen said that there were double meanings in the *Necronomicon* of the mad Arab Abdul Alhazred which the initiated might read as they chose, especially the much discussed couplet:

> That is not dead which can eternal lie,
> And with strange eons even death may die.

Legrasse, deeply impressed and not a little bewildered, had inquired in vain concerning the historic affiliations of the cult. Castro, apparently, had told the truth when he said that it was wholly secret. The authorities at Tulane University could shed no light upon either cult or image, and now the detective had come to the highest authorities in the country and met with no more than the Greenland tale of Professor Webb.

The feverish interest aroused at the meeting by Legrasse's tale, corroborated as it was by the statuette, is echoed in the subsequent correspondence of those who attended; although scant mention occurs in the formal publication of the society. Caution is the first care of those accustomed to face occasional charlatanry and imposture. Legrasse for some time lent the image to Professor Webb, but at the latter's death it was returned to him and remains in his possession, where I viewed it not long ago. It is truly a terrible thing, and unmistakably akin to the dream-sculpture of young Wilcox.

That my uncle was excited by the tale of the sculptor I did not wonder, for what thoughts must arise upon hearing, after a knowledge of what Legrasse had learned of the cult, of a sensitive young man who had *dreamed* not only the figure and exact hieroglyphics of the swamp-found image and the Greenland devil tablet, but had come *in his dreams* upon at least three of the precise words of the formula uttered alike by Eskimo diabolists and mongrel Louisianans? Professor Angell's instant start on an investigation of the utmost thoroughness was eminently natural; though privately I suspected young Wilcox of having heard of the cult in some indirect way, and of having invented a series of dreams to heighten and continue the mystery at my uncle's expense. The dream-narratives and cuttings collected by the professor were, of course, strong corroboration; but the rationalism of my mind and the extravagance of the whole subject led me to adopt what I thought the most sensible conclusions. So, after thoroughly studying the manuscript again and correlating the theosophical and anthropological notes with the cult narrative of Legrasse, I made a trip to Providence to see the sculptor and give him the rebuke I thought proper for so boldly imposing upon a learned and aged man.

Wilcox still lived alone in the Fleur-de-Lys Building in Thomas Street, a hideous Victorian imitation of Seventeenth Century Breton architecture which flaunts its stuccoed front amidst the lovely Colonial houses on the ancient hill, and under the very shadow of the finest Georgian steeple in America. I found him at work in his rooms, and at once conceded from the specimens scattered about that his genius is indeed profound and authentic. He will, I believe, be heard of sometime as one of the great decadents; for he has crystallized in clay and will one day mirror in marble those nightmares and fantasies which Arthur Machen evokes in prose, and Clark Ashton Smith makes visible in verse and in painting.

Dark, frail, and somewhat unkempt in aspect, he turned languidly at my knock and asked me my business without rising. When I told him who I was, he displayed some interest; for my uncle had excited his curiosity in probing his strange dreams, yet had never explained the reason for the study. I did not enlarge his knowledge in this regard, but sought with some subtlety to draw him out.

In a short time I became convinced of his absolute sincerity for he spoke of the dreams in a manner none could mistake. They and their subconscious residuum had influenced his art profoundly, and he showed me a morbid statue whose contours almost made me shake with the potency of its black suggestion. He could not recall having seen the original of this thing except in his own dream bas-relief, but the outlines had formed themselves insensibly under his hands. It was, no doubt, the giant shape he had raved of in delirium. That he really knew nothing of the hidden cult, save from what my uncle's relentless catechism had let fall, he soon made clear; and again I strove to think of some way in which he could possibly have received the weird impressions.

He talked of his dreams in a strangely poetic fashion; making me see with terrible vividness the damp Cyclopean city of slimy green stone — whose *geometry*, he oddly said, was *all wrong* — and hear with frightened expectancy the ceaseless, half-mental calling from underground: '*Cthulhu fhtagn*,' '*Cthulhu fhtagn*.'

These words had formed part of that dread ritual which told of dead Cthulhu's dream-vigil in his stone vault at R'lyeh, and I felt deeply moved despite my rational beliefs.

Wilcox, I was sure, had heard of the cult in some casual way, and had soon forgotten it amidst the mass of his equally weird reading and imagining. Later, by virtue of its sheer impressiveness, it had found subconscious expression in dreams, in the bas-relief, and in the terrible statue I now beheld; so that his imposture upon my uncle had been a very innocent one. The youth was of a type, at once slightly affected and slightly ill-mannered, which I could never like; but I was willing enough now to admit both his genius and his honesty. I took leave of him amicably, and wish him all the success his talent promises.

The matter of the cult still remained to fascinate me, and at times I had visions of personal fame from researches into its origin and connections. I visited New Orleans, talked with Legrasse and others of that old-time raiding-party, saw the frightful image, and even questioned such of the mongrel prisoners as still survived. Old Castro, unfortunately, had been dead for some years. What I now heard so graphically at first hand, though it was really no more than a detailed confirmation of what my uncle had written, excited me afresh; for I felt sure that I was on the track of a very real, very secret, and very ancient religion whose discovery would make me an anthropologist of note. My attitude was still one of absolute materialism *as I wish it still were*, and I discounted with a most inexplicable perversity the coincidence of the dream notes and odd cuttings collected by Professor Angell.

One thing which I began to suspect, and which I now fear I *know*, is that my uncle's death was far from natural. He fell on a narrow hill street leading up from an ancient waterfront swarming with foreign mongrels, after a careless push from a negro sailor. I did not forget the mixed blood and marine pursuits of the cult-members in Louisiana, and would not be surprised to learn of secret methods and poison needles as ruthless and as anciently known as the cryptic rites and beliefs. Legrasse and his men, it is true, have been let alone; but in Norway a certain seaman who saw things is dead. Might not the deeper inquiries of my uncle after encountering the sculptor's data have come to sinister ears? I think Professor Angell died because he knew too much, or because he was likely to learn too much. Whether I shall go as he did remains to be seen, for I have learned much now.

The Madness from the Sea

If heaven ever wishes to grant me a boon, it will be a total effacing of the results of a mere chance which fixed my eye on a certain stray piece of shelf-paper. It was nothing on which I would naturally have stumbled in the course of my daily round, for it was an old number of an Australian journal, *Sydney Bulletin* for April 18, 1925. It had escaped even the cutting bureau which had at the time of its issuance been avidly collecting material for my uncle's research.

I had largely given over my inquiries into what Professor Angell called the 'Cthulhu Cult', and was visiting a learned friend of Paterson, New Jersey; the curator of a local museum and a mineralogist of note. Examining one day the reserve specimens roughly set on the storage shelves in a rear room of the museum, my eye was caught by an odd picture in one of the old papers spread beneath the stones. It was the *Sydney Bulletin* I have mentioned, for my friend has wide affiliations in all conceivable foreign parts; and the picture was a half-tone cut of a hideous stone image almost identical with that which Legrasse had found in the swamp.

Eagerly clearing the sheet of its precious contents, I scanned the item in detail; and was disappointed to find it of only moderate length. What it suggested, however, was of portentous significance to my flagging quest; and I carefully tore it out for immediate action. It read as follows:

MYSTERY DERELICT FOUND AT SEA

Vigilant Arrives with Helpless Armed New Zealand Yacht in Tow. One Survivor and Dead Man Found Aboard. Tale of Desperate Battle and Deaths at Sea. Rescued Seaman Refuses Particulars of Strange Experience. Odd Idol Found in His Possession. Inquiry to Follow.

The Morrison Co.'s freighter *Vigilant*, bound from Valparaiso, arrived this morning at its wharf in Darling Harbour, having in tow the battled and disabled but heavily armed steam yacht *Alert* of Dunedin, N.Z., which was sighted April 12th in S. Latitude 34° 21', W. Longitude 152° 17', with one living and one dead man aboard.

The *Vigilant* left Valparaiso March 25th, and on April 2nd was driven considerably south of her course by exceptionally heavy storms and monster waves. On April 12th the derelict was sighted; and though apparently deserted, was found upon boarding to contain one survivor in a half-delirious condition and one man who had evidently been dead for more than a week.

The living man was clutching a horrible stone idol of unknown origin, about a foot in height, regarding whose nature authorities at Sydney University, the Royal Society, and the Museum in College Street all profess complete bafflement, and which the survivor says he found in the cabin of the yacht, in a small carved shrine of common pattern.

This man, after recovering his senses, told an exceedingly strange story of piracy and slaughter. He is Gustaf Johansen, a Norwegian of some intelligence, and had been second mate of the two-masted schooner *Emma* of Auckland, which sailed for Callao February 20th, with a complement of eleven men.

The *Emma*, he says, was delayed and thrown widely south of her course by the great storm of March 1st, and on March 22nd, in S. Latitude 49° 51', W. Longitude 128° 34', encountered the *Alert*, manned by a queer and evil-looking crew of Kanakas and half-castes. Being ordered peremptorily to turn back, Capt. Collins refused; whereupon the strange crew began to fire savagely and without warning upon the schooner with a peculiarly heavy battery of brass cannon forming part of the yacht's equipment.

The *Emma*'s men showed fight, says the survivor, and though the schooner began to sink from shots beneath the waterline they managed to heave alongside their enemy and board her, grappling with the savage crew on the yacht's deck, and being forced to kill them all, the number being slightly superior, because of their particularly abhorrent and desperate though rather clumsy mode of fighting.

Three of the *Emma*'s men, including Capt. Collins and First Mate Green, were killed; and the remaining eight under Second Mate Johansen proceeded to navigate the captured yacht, going ahead in their original direction to see if any reason for their ordering back had existed.

The next day, it appears, they raised and landed on a small island, although none is known to exist in that part of the ocean; and six of the men somehow died ashore, though Johansen is queerly reticent about this part of his story and speaks only of their falling into a rock chasm.

Later, it seems, he and one companion boarded the yacht and tried to manage her, but were beaten about by the storm of April 2nd.

From that time till his rescue on the 12th, the man remembers little, and he does not even recall when William Briden, his companion, died. Briden's death reveals no apparent cause, and was probably due to excitement or exposure.

Cable advices from Dunedin report that the *Alert* was well known there as an island trader, and bore an evil reputation along the waterfront. It was owned by a curious group of half-castes whose frequent meetings and night trips to the woods attracted no little curiosity; and it had set sail in great haste just after the storm and earth tremors of March 1st.

Our Auckland correspondent gives the *Emma* and her crew an excellent reputation, and Johansen is described as a sober and worthy man.

The admiralty will institute an inquiry on the whole matter beginning tomorrow, at which every effort will be made to induce Johansen to speak more freely than he has done hitherto.

This was all, together with the picture of the hellish image; but what a train of ideas it started in my mind! Here were new treasuries of data on the Cthulhu Cult, and evidence that it had strange interests at sea as well as on land. What motive prompted the hybrid crew to order back the *Emma* as they sailed about with their hideous idol? What was the unknown island on which six of the *Emma*'s crew had died, and about which the mate Johansen was so secretive? What had the vice-admiralty's investigation brought out, and what was known of the noxious cult in Dunedin? And most marvellous of all, what deep and more than natural linkage of dates was this which gave a malign and now undeniable significance to the various turns of event so carefully noted by my uncle?

March 1st — our February 28th according to the International Date Line — the earthquake and storm had come. From Dunedin the *Alert* and her noisome crew had darted eagerly forth as if imperiously summoned, and on the other side of the earth poets and artists had begun to dream of a strange, dank Cyclopean city whilst a young sculptor had molded in his sleep the form of the dreaded Cthulhu. March 23rd the crew of the *Emma* landed on an unknown island and left six men dead; and on that date the dreams of sensitive men assumed a heightened vividness and darkened with dread of a giant monster's malign pursuit, whilst an architect had gone mad and a sculptor had lapsed suddenly into delirium! And what of this storm of April 2nd — the date on which all dreams of the dank city ceased, and Wilcox emerged unharmed from the bondage of strange fever? What of all this — and of those hints of old Castro about the sunken, star-born Old Ones and their coming reign; their faithful cult *and their mastery of dreams*? Was I tottering on the brink of cosmic horrors beyond man's power to bear? If so, they must be horrors of the mind alone, for in some way the second of April had put a stop to whatever monstrous menace had begun its siege of mankind's soul.

That evening, after a day of hurried cabling and arranging, I bade my host adieu and took a train for San Francisco. In less than a month I was in Dunedin: where, however, I found that little was known of the strange cult-members who had lingered in the old sea taverns. Waterfront scum was far too common for special mention; though there was vague talk about one island trip these mongrels had made, during which faint drumming and red flame were noted on the distant hills.

In Auckland I learned that Johansen had returned *with yellow hair turned white* after a perfunctory and inconclusive questioning at Sydney, and had thereafter sold his cottage in West Street and sailed with his wife to his old home in Oslo. Of his stirring experience he would tell his friends no more than he had told the admiralty officials, and all they could do was to give me his Oslo address.

After that I went to Sydney and talked profitlessly with seamen and members of the vice-admiralty court. I saw the *Alert*, now sold and in commercial use, at Circular Quay in Sydney Cove, but gained nothing from its noncommittal bulk. The crouching image with its cuttlefish head, dragon body, scaly wings, and hieroglyphed pedestal, was preserved in the Museum at Hyde Park; and I studied it long and well, finding it a thing of balefully exquisite workmanship, and with the same utter mystery, terrible antiquity, and unearthly strangeness of material which I had noted in Legrasse's smaller specimen. Geologists, the curator told me, had found it a monstrous puzzle; for they vowed that the world held no rock like it. Then I thought with a shudder of what old Castro had told Legrasse about the primal Great Ones: 'They had come from the stars, and had brought Their images with Them.'

Shaken with such a mental revolution as I had never before known, I now resolved to visit Mate Johansen in Oslo. Sailing for London, I re-embarked at once for the Norwegian capital; and one autumn day landed at the trim wharves in the shadow of the Egeberg.

Johansen's address, I discovered, lay in the Old Town of King Harold Haardrada, which kept alive the name of Oslo during all the centuries that the greater city masqueraded as 'Christiania'. I made the brief trip by taxicab, and knocked with palpitant heart at the door of a neat and ancient building with plastered front. A sad-faced woman in black answered my summons, and I was stung with disappointment when she told me in halting English that Gustaf Johansen was no more.

He had not long survived his return, said his wife, for the doings at sea in 1925 had broken him. He had told her no more than he had told the public, but had left a long manuscript — of 'technical matters' as he said — written in English, evidently in order to safeguard her from the peril of casual perusal. During a walk through a narrow lane near the Gothenburg dock, a bundle of papers falling from an attic window had knocked him down. Two Lascar sailors at once helped him to his feet, but before the ambulance could reach him he was dead. Physicians found no adequate cause for the end, and laid it to heart trouble and a weakened constitution.

I now felt gnawing at my vitals that dark terror which will never leave me till I, too, am at rest; 'accidentally' or otherwise. Persuading the window that my connection with her husband's 'technical matters' was sufficient to entitle me to his manuscript, I bore the document away and began to read it on the London boat.

It was a simple, rambling thing — a naïve sailor's effort at a post-facto diary — and strove to recall day by day that last awful voyage. I can not attempt to transcribe it verbatim in all its cloudiness and redundance, but I will tell its gist enough to show why the sound of the water against the vessel's sides became so unendurable to me that I stopped my ears with cotton.

Johansen, thank God, did not know quite all, even though he saw the city and the Thing, but I shall never sleep calmly again when I think of the horrors that lurk ceaselessly behind life in time and in space, and of those unhallowed blasphemies from elder stars which dream beneath the sea, known and favoured by a nightmare cult ready and eager to loose them on the world whenever another earthquake shall heave their monstrous stone city again to the sun and air.

Johansen's voyage had begun just as he told it to the vice-admiralty. The *Emma*, in ballast, had cleared Auckland on February 20th, and had felt the full force of that earthquake-born tempest which must have heaved up from the sea-bottom the horrors that filled men's dreams. Once more under control, the ship was making good progress when held up by the *Alert* on March 22nd, and I could feel the mate's regret as he wrote of her bombardment and sinking. Of the swarthy cult-fiends on the *Alert* he speaks with significant horror. There was some peculiarly abominable quality about them which made their destruction seem almost a duty, and Johansen shows ingenuous wonder at the charge of ruthlessness brought against his party during the proceedings of the court of inquiry. Then, driven ahead by curiosity in their captured yacht under Johansen's command, the men sight a great stone pillar sticking out of the sea, and in S. Latitude 47° 9', W. Longitude 126° 43', come upon a coastline of mingled mud, ooze, and weedy Cyclopean masonry which can be nothing less than the tangible substance of earth's supreme terror — the nightmare corpse-city of R'lyeh, that was built in measureless eons behind history by the vast, loathsome shapes that seeped down from the dark stars. There lay great Cthulhu and his hordes, hidden in green slimy vaults and sending out at last, after cycles incalculable, the thoughts that spread fear to the dreams of the sensitive and called imperiously to the faithful to come on a pilgrimage of liberation and restoration. All this Johansen did not suspect, but God knows he soon saw enough!

I suppose that only a single mountain-top, the hideous monolith-crowned citadel whereon great Cthulhu was buried, actually emerged from the waters. When I think of the *extent* of all that may be brooding down there I almost wish to kill myself forthwith. Johansen and his men were awed by the cosmic majesty of this dripping Babylon of elder demons, and must have guessed without guidance that it was nothing of this or of any sane planet. Awe at the unbelievable size of the greenish stone blocks, at the dizzying height of the great carven monolith, and at the stupefying identity of the colossal statues and bas-reliefs with the queer image found in the shrine on the *Alert*, is poignantly visible in every line of the mate's frightened description.

Without knowing what futurism is like, Johansen achieved something very close to it when he spoke of the city; for instead of describing any definite structure or building, he dwells only on the broad impressions of vast angles and stone surfaces — surfaces too great to belong to any thing right or proper for this earth, and impious with horrible images and hieroglyphs. I mention his talk about *angles* because it suggests something Wilcox had told me of his awful dreams.

He had said that the *geometry* of the dream-place he saw was abnormal, non-Euclidean, and loathsomely redolent of spheres and dimensions apart from ours. Now an unlettered seaman felt the same thing whilst gazing at the terrible reality.

Johansen and his men landed at a sloping mud-bank on this monstrous acropolis, and clambered slipperily over titan oozy blocks which could have been no mortal staircase. The very sun of heaven seemed distorted when viewed through the polarizing miasma welling out from this sea-soaked perversion, and twisted menace and suspense lurked leeringly in those crazily elusive angles of carven rock where a second glance showed concavity after the first showed convexity.

Something very like fright had come over all the explorers before anything more definite than rock and ooze and weed was seen. Each would have fled had he not feared the scorn of the others, and it was only half-heartedly that they searched — vainly, as it proved — for some portable souvenir to bear away.

It was Rodriguez the Portuguese who climbed up the foot of the monolith and shouted of what he had found. The rest followed him, and looked curiously at the immense carved door with the now familiar squid-dragon bas-relief. It was, Johansen said, like a great barn-door; and they all felt that it was a door because of the ornate lintel, threshold, and jambs around it, though they could not decide whether it lay flat like a trap door or slantwise like an outside cellar-door. As Wilcox would have said, the geometry of the place was all wrong. One could not be sure that the sea and the ground were horizontal, hence the relative position of everything else seemed fantasmally variable.

Briden pushed at the stone in several places without result. Then Donovan felt over it delicately around the edge, pressing each point separately as he went. He climbed interminably along the grotesque stone molding — that is, one would call it climbing if the thing was not after all horizontal — and the men wondered how any door in the universe could be so vast. Then, very softly and slowly, the acre-great panel began to give inward at the top; and they saw that it was balanced.

Donovan slid or somehow propelled himself down or along the jamb and rejoined his fellows, and everyone watched the queer recession of the monstrously carven portal. In this fantasy of prismatic distortion it moved anomalously in a diagonal way, so that all the rules of matter and perspective seemed upset.

The aperture was black with a darkness almost material. That tenebrousness was indeed a *positive quality*; for it obscured such parts of the inner walls as ought to have been revealed, and actually burst forth like smoke from its eon-long imprisonment, visibly darkening the sun as it slunk away into the shrunken and gibbous sky on flapping membranous wings. The odour arising from the newly opened depths was intolerable, and at length the quick-eared Hawkins thought he heard a nasty, slopping sound down there. Everyone listened, and everyone was listening still when It lumbered slobberingly into sight and gropingly squeezed Its gelatinous green immensity through the black doorway into the tainted outside air of that poison city of madness.

Poor Johansen's handwriting almost gave out when he wrote of this. Of the six men who never reached the ship, he thinks two perished of pure fright in that accursed instant. The Thing can not be described — there is no language for such abysms of shrieking and immemorial lunacy, such eldritch contradictions of all matter, force, and cosmic order. A mountain walked or stumbled. God! What wonder that across the earth a great architect went mad, and poor Wilcox raved with fever in that telepathic instant? The Thing of the idols, the green, sticky spawn of the stars, had awaked to claim his own. The stars were right again, and what an age-old cult had failed to do by design, a band of innocent sailors had done by accident. After vigintillions of years great Cthulhu was loose again, and ravening for delight.

Three men were swept up by the flabby claws before anybody turned. God rest them, if there be any rest in the universe. They were Donovan, Guerrera and Angstrom. Parker slipped as the other three were plunging frenziedly over endless vistas of green-crusted rock to the boat, and Johansen swears he was swallowed up by an angle of masonry which shouldn't have been there; an angle which was acute, but behaved as if it were obtuse. So only Briden and Johansen reached the boat, and pulled desperately for the *Alert* as the mountainous monstrosity flopped down the slimy stones and hesitated, floundering at the edge of the water. Steam had not been suffered to go down entirely, despite the departure of all hands for the shore; and it was the work of only a few moments of feverish rushing up and down between wheels and engines to get the *Alert* under way. Slowly, amidst the distorted horrors of that indescribable scene, she began to churn the lethal waters; whilst on the masonry of that charnel shore that was not of earth the titan Thing from the stars slavered and gibbered like Polypheme cursing the fleeing ship of Odysseus. Then, bolder than the stored Cyclops, great Cthulhu slid greasily into the water and began to pursue with vast wave-raising strokes of cosmic potency. Briden looked back and went mad, laughing at intervals till death found him one night in the cabin whilst Johansen was wandering deliriously.

But Johansen had not given out yet. Knowing that the Thing could surely overtake the *Alert* until steam was fully up, he resolved on a desperate chance; and, setting the engine for full speed, ran lightning-like on deck and reversed the wheel. There was a mighty eddying and foaming in the noisome brine, and as the steam mounted higher and higher the brave Norwegian drove his vessel head on against the pursuing jelly which rose above the unclean froth like the stern of a demon galleon. The awful squid-head with writhing feelers came nearly up to the bowsprit of the sturdy yacht, but Johansen drove on relentlessly.

There was a bursting as of an exploding bladder, a slushy nastiness as of a cloven sunfish, a stench as of a thousand opened graves, and a sound that the chronicler would not put on paper. For an instant the ship was befouled by an acrid and blinding green cloud, and then there was only a venomous seething astern; where – God in heaven! – the scattered plasticity of that nameless sky-spawn was nebulously *recombining* in its hateful original form, whilst its distance widened every second as the *Alert* gained impetus from its mounting steam. That was all. After that Johansen only brooded over the idol in the cabin and attended to a few matters of food for himself and the laughing maniac by his side. He did not try to navigate after the first bold flight; for the reaction had taken something out of his soul. Then came the storm of April 2nd, and a gathering of the clouds about his consciousness. There is a sense of spectral whirling through liquid gulfs of infinity, of dizzying rides through reeling universes on a comet's tail, and of hysterical plunges from the pit to the moon and from the moon back again to the pit, all livened by a cachinnating chorus of the distorted, hilarious elder gods and the green, bat-winged mocking imps of Tartarus.

Out of that dream came rescue — the *Vigilant*, the vice-admiralty court, the streets of Dunedin, and the long voyage back home to the old house by the Egeberg. He could not tell — they would think him mad. He would write of what he knew before death came, but his wife must not guess. Death would be a boon if only it could blot out the memories.

That was the document I read, and now I have placed it in the tin box beside the bas-relief and the papers of Professor Angell. With it shall go this record of mine — this test of my own sanity, wherein is pieced together that which I hope may never be pieced together again. I have looked upon all that the universe has to hold of horror, and even the skies of spring and the flowers of summer must eve afterwards be poison to me. But I do not think my life will be long. As my uncle went, as poor Johansen went, so I shall go. I know too much, and the cult still lives.

Cthulhu still lives, too, I suppose, again in that chasm of stone which has shielded him since the sun was young. His accursed city is sunken once more, for the *Vigilant* sailed over the spot after the April storm; but his ministers on earth still bellow and prance and slay around idol-capped monoliths in lonely places. He must have been trapped by the sinking whilst within his black abyss, or else the world would by now be screaming with fright and frenzy. Who knows the end? What has risen may sink, and what has sunk may rise. Loathsomeness waits and dreams in the deep, and decay spreads over the tottering cities of men. A time will come — but I must not and can not think! Let me pray that, if I do not survive this manuscript, my executors may put caution before audacity and see that it meets no other eye.

V

Phantas

Oliver Onions

The spirit of the sea is handed on from generation to generation and it burns especially bright in the history of Great Britain. From the time of the Armada up to within a few decades ago Britain was firmly established as the Maritime Nation. Until this long dominance was cast aside unheedingly by politicians the existence of such a continuity was accepted without question. How this great heritage and knowledge was preserved in succeeding generations down the long centuries is brought out by Oliver Onions in Phantas, *written at a time when that continuing theme seemed inviolate. It is also a first-class ghost story, and one that also strays over into the popular world of science fiction if its implications are taken to their logical conclusion.*

For, barring all pother,
With this, or the other,
Still Britons are Lords of the Main.
THE CHAPTER OF ADMIRALS

As Abel Keeling lay on the galleon's deck, held from rolling down it only by his own weight and the sun-blackened hand that lay outstretched upon the planks, his gaze wandered, but ever returned to the bell that hung, jammed with the dangerous heel-over of the vessel, in the small ornamental belfry immediately abaft the mainmast. The bell was of cast bronze, with half-obliterated bosses upon it that had been the heads of cherubs; but wind and salt spray had given it a thick incrustation of bright, beautiful, lichenous green. It was this colour that Abel Keeling's eyes liked.

For wherever else on the galleon his eyes rested they found only whiteness — the whiteness of extreme eld. There were slightly varying degrees of her whiteness; here she was of a white that glistened like salt-granules, there of a greyish chalky white, and again her whiteness had the yellowish cast of decay; but everywhere it was the mild, disquieting whiteness of materials out of which the life had departed. Her cordage was bleached as old straw is bleached, and half her ropes kept their shape little more firmly than the ash of a string keeps its shape after the fire has passed; her pallid timbers were white and clean as bones found in sand; and even the wild frankincense with which (for lack of tar, at her last touching of land) she had been pitched, had dried to a pale hard gum that sparkled like quartz in her open seams. The sun was yet so pale a buckler of silver through the still white mists that not a cord or timber cast shadow; and only Abel Keeling's face and hands were black, carked and cinder-black from exposure to his pitiless rays.

The galleon was the *Mary of the Tower*, and she had a frightful list to starboard. So canted was she that her mainyard dipped one of its steel sickles into the glassy water, and, had her foremast remained, or more than the broken stump of her bonaventure mizzen, she must have turned over completely. Many days ago they had stripped the mainyard of its course, and had passed the sail under the *Mary*'s bottom, in the hope that it would stop the leak. This it had partly done as long as the galleon had continued to glide one way; then, without coming about, she had begun to glide the other, the ropes had parted, and she had dragged the sail after her, leaving a broad tarnish on the silver sea.

For it was broadside that the galleon glided, almost imperceptibly, ever sucking down. She glided as if a loadstone drew her, and, at first, Abel Keeling had thought it was a loadstone, pulling at her iron, drawing her through the pearly mists that lay like face-cloths to the water and hid at a short distance the tarnish left by the sail. But later he had known that it was no loadstone drawing at her iron. The motion was due — must be due — to the absolute deadness of the calm in that silent, sinister, three-miles-broad waterway. With the eye of his mind he saw that loadstone now as he lay against a gun-truck, all but toppling down the deck. Soon that would happen again which had happened for five days past. He would hear again the chattering of monkeys and screaming of parrots, the mat of green and yellow weeds would creep in towards the *Mary* over the quicksilver sea, once more the sheer wall of rock would rise, and the men would run. . . .

But no; the men would not run this time to drop the fenders. There were no men left to do so, unless Bligh was still alive. Perhaps Bligh was still alive. He had walked half way down the quarter-deck steps a little before the sudden nightfall of the day before, had then fallen and lain for a minute (dead, Abel Keeling had supposed, watching him from his place by the gun-truck), and had then got up again and tottered forward to the forecastle, his tall figure swaying and his long arms waving. Abel Keeling had not seen him since. Most likely, he had died in the forecastle during the night. If he had not been dead he would have come aft again for water. . . .

At the remembrance of the water Abel Keeling lifted his head. The strands of lean muscle about his emaciated mouth worked, and he made a little pressure of his sun-blackened hand on the deck, as if to verify its steepness and his own balance. The mainmast was some seven or eight yards away. . . . He put one stiff leg under him and began, seated as he was, to make shuffling movements down the slope.

To the mainmast, near the belfry, was affixed his contrivance for catching water. It consisted of a collar of rope set lower at one side than at the other (but that had been before the mast had steeved so many degrees away from the zenith), and tallowed beneath. The mists lingered later in that gully of a strait than they did on the open ocean, and the collar of rope served as a collector of the dews that condensed on the mast. The drops fell into a small earthen pipkin placed on the deck beneath it.

Abel Keeling reached the pipkin and looked into it. It was nearly a third full of fresh water. Good. If Bligh, the mate, was dead, so much the more water for Abel Keeling, master of the *Mary of the Tower*. He dipped two fingers into the pipkin and put them into his mouth. This he did several times. He did not dare to raise the pipkin to his black and broken lips for dread of a remembered agony, he could not have told how many days ago, when a devil had whispered to him and he had gulped down the contents of the pipkin in the morning, and for the rest of the day had gone waterless. . . . Again he moistened his fingers and sucked them; then he lay sprawling against the mast, idly watching the drops of water as they fell.

It was odd how the drops formed. Slowly they collected at the edge of the tallowed collar, trembled in their fullness for an instant, and fell, another beginning the process instantly. It amused Abel Keeling to watch them. Why (he wondered) were all the drops the same size? What cause and compulsion did they obey that they never varied, and what frail tenuity held the little globules intact? It must be due to some Cause. . . . He remembered that the aromatic gum of the wild frankincense with which they had parcelled the seams had hung on the buckets in great sluggish gouts, obedient to a different compulsion; oil was different again, and so were juices and balsams. Only quicksilver (perhaps the heavy and motionless sea put him in mind of quicksilver) seemed obedient to no law. . . . Why was it so?

Bligh, of course, would have had his explanation: it was the Hand of God. That sufficed for Bligh, who had gone forward the evening before, and whom Abel Keeling now seemed vaguely and as at a distance to remember as the deep-voiced fanatic who had sung his hymns, as, man by man, he had committed /the bodies of the ship's company to the deep. Bligh was that sort of man; accepted things without question; was content to take things as they were and be ready with the fenders when the wall of rock rose out of the opalescent mists. Bligh, too, like the waterdrops, had his Law, that was his and nobody else's. . . .

There floated down from some rotten rope up aloft a flake of scurf, that settled in the pipkin. Abel Keeling watched it dully as it settled towards the pipkin's rim. When presently he again dipped his fingers into the vessel the water ran into a little vortex, drawing the flake with it. The water settled again; and again the minute flake determined towards the rim and adhered there, as if the rim had power to draw it. . . .

It was exactly so that the galleon was gliding towards the wall of rock, the yellow and green weeds, and the monkeys and parrots. Put out into mid-water again (while there had

been men to put her out) she had glided to the other wall.
One force drew the chip in the pipkin and the ship over the
tranced sea. It was the Hand of God, said Bligh. . . .

Abel Keeling, his mind now noting minute things and now
clouded with torpor, did not at first hear a voice that was
quakingly lifted up over by the forecastle — a voice that drew
nearer, to an accompaniment of swirling water.

> O Thou, that Jonas in the fish
>   Three days didst keep from pain,
> Which was a figure of Thy death
>   And rising up again —

It was Bligh, singing one of his hymns:

> O Thou, that Noah keptst from flood
>   And Abram, day by day,
> As he along through Egypt passed
>   Didst guide him in the way —

The voice ceased, leaving the pious period uncompleted.
Bligh was alive, at any rate. . . . Abel Keeling resumed his
fitful musing.

Yes, that was the Law of Bligh's life, to call things the
Hand of God; but Abel Keeling's Law was different; no
better, no worse, only different. The Hand of God, that drew
chips and galleons, must work by some method; and Abel
Keeling's eyes were dully on the pipkin again as if he sought
the method there. . . .

Then conscious thought left him for a space, and when he
resumed it was without obvious connection.

Oars, of course, were the thing. With oars, men could laugh
at calms. Oars, that only pinnaces and galliasses now used,
had had their advantages. But oars (which was to say a
method, for you could say if you liked that the Hand of God
grasped the loar-loom, as the Breath of God filled the
sail) — oars were antiquated, belonged to the past, and meant
a throwing-over of all that was good and new and a return to
fine lines, a battle-formation abreast to give effect to the
shock of the ram, and a day or two at sea and then to port
again for provisions. Oars . . . no. Abel Keeling was one of the

new men, the men who swore by the line-ahead, the broadside fire of sakers and demi-cannon, and weeks and months without a landfall. Perhaps one day the wits of such men as he would devise a craft, not oar-driven (because oars would not penetrate into the remote seas of the world) — not sail-driven (because men who trusted to sails found themselves in an airless, three-mile strait, suspended motionless between cloud and water, ever gliding to a wall of rock — but a ship . . . a ship. . . .

> To Noah and his sons with him
> God spake, and this said He:
> A cov'nant set I up with you
> And your posterity —

It was Bligh again, wandering somewhere in the waist. Abel Keeling's mind was once more a blank. Then slowly, slowly, as the water drops collected on the collar of rope, his thoughts took shape again.

A galliasse? No, not a galliasse. The galliasse made shift to be two things, and was neither. This ship, that the hand of man should one day make for the Hand of God to manage, should be a ship that should take and conserve the force of the wind, take it and store it as she stored her victuals; at rest when she wished, going ahead when she wished; turning the forces both of calm and storm against themselves. For, of course, her force must be wind — stored wind — a bag of the winds, as the children's tale had it — wind probably directed upon the water astern, driving it away and urging forward the ship, acting by reaction. She would have a wind-chamber, into which wind would be pumped with pumps. . . .

Bligh would call that equally the Hand of God, this driving-force of the ship of the future that Abel Keeling dimly foreshadowed as he lay between the mainmast and the belfry, turning his eyes now and then from ashy white timbers to the vivid green bronze-rust of the bell above him. . . .

Bligh's face, liver-coloured with the sun and ravaged from inwards by the faith that consumed him, appeared at the head of the quarter-deck steps. His voice beat uncontrolledly out.

And in the earth here is no place,
Of refuge to be found,
Nor in the deep and water-course
That passeth underground —

Bligh's eyes were lidded, as if in contemplation of his inner ecstasy. His head was thrown back, and his brows worked up and down tormentedly. His wide mouth remained open as his hymn was suddenly interrupted on the long-drawn note. From somewhere in the shimmering mists the note was taken up, and there drummed and rang and reverberated through the strait a windy, hoarse, and dismal bellow, alarming and sustained. A tremor rang through Bligh. Moving like a sightless man, he stumbled forward from the head of the quarter-deck steps, and Abel Keeling was aware of his gaunt figure behind him, taller for the steepness of the deck. As that vast empty sound died away, Bligh laughed in his mania.

'Lord, hath the grave's wide mouth a tongue to praise Thee? Lo, again — '

Again the cavernous sound possessed the air, louder and nearer. Through it came another sound, a slow throb, throb — throb, throb — Again the sounds ceased.

'Even Leviathan lifteth up his voice in praise!' Bligh sobbed.

Abel Keeling did not raise his head. There had returned to him the memory of that day when, before the morning mists had lifted from the strait, he had emptied the pipkin of the water that was the allowance until night should fall again. During the agony of thirst he had seen shapes and heard sounds with other than his mortal eyes and ears, and even in the moments that had alternated with his lightness, when he had known these to be hallucinations, they had come again. He had heard the bells on a Sunday in his own Kentish home, the calling of children at play, the unconcerned singing of men at their daily labour, and the laughter and gossip of the women as they had spread the linen on the hedge or distributed bread upon the platters. These voices had rung in his brain, interrupted now and then by the groans of Bligh and of two other men who had been alive then. Some of the voices he had heard had been silent on earth this many a long year, but Abel Keeling, thirst-tortured, had heard them, even as he was now hearing that vacant moaning with the intermittent throbbing that filled the strait with alarm. . . .

'Praise Him, Praise Him, Praise Him!' Bligh was calling deliriously.

Then a bell seemed to sound in Abel Keeling's ears, and, as if something in the mechanism of his brain had slipped, another picture rose in his fancy — the scene when the *Mary of the Tower* had put out, to a bravery of swinging bells and shrill fifes and valiant trumpets. She had not been a leper-white galleon then. The scroll-work on her prow had twinkled with gilding; her belfry and stern-galleries and elaborate lanterns had flashed in the sun with gold; and her fighting-tops and the war-pavesse about her waist had been gay with painted coats and scutcheons. To her sails had been switched gaudy ramping lions of scarlet saye, and from her mainyard, now dipping in the water, had hung the broad two-tailed pennant with the Virgin and Child embroidered upon it. . . .

Then suddenly a voice about him seemed to be saying, 'And a half-seven — and a half-seven —' in a twink the picture in Abel Keeling's brain changed again. He was at home again, instructing his son, young Abel, in the casting of the lead from the skiff they had pulled out of the harbour.

'And a half-seven!' the boy seemed to be calling.

Abel Keeling's blackened lips muttered: 'Excellently well cast, Abel, excellently well cast!'

'And a half-seven — and a half-seven — seven — seven — '

'Ah,' Abel Keeling murmured, 'the last was not a clear cast, give me the line — thus it should go . . . ay, so . . . Soon you shall sail the seas with me in the *Mary of the Tower*. You are already perfect in the stars and the motions of the planets; tomorrow I will instruct you in the use of the backstaff. . . .'

For a minute or two he continued to mutter; then he dozed. When again he came to semi-consciousness it was once more to the sound of bells, at first faint, then louder, and finally becoming a noisy clamour immediately above his head. It was Bligh. Bligh, in a fresh attack of delirium, had seized the bell-lanyard and was ringing the bell insanely. The cord, broke in his fingers, but he thrust at the bell with his hand, and again called aloud.

'Upon an harp and an instrument of ten strings ... let Heaven and Earth praise Thy Name! ...'

He continued to call aloud, and to beat on the bronze-rusted bell.

'Ship ahoy! What ship's that?'

One would have said that a veritable hail had come out of the mists; but Abel Keeling knew those hails that came out of the mists. They came from ships which were not there. 'Ay, ay, keep a good lookout, and have a care to your lode-manage,' he muttered again to his son. . . .

But, as sometimes a sleeper sits up in his dream, or rises from his couch and walks, so all of a sudden Abel Keeling found himself on his hands and knees on the deck, looking back over his shoulder. In some deep-seated region of his consciousness he was dimly aware that the cant of the deck had become more perilous, but his brain received the intelligence and forgot it again. He was looking out into the bright and baffling mists. The buckler of the sun was of a more ardent silver; the sea below it was lost in brilliant evaporation; and between them, suspended in the haze, no more substantial than the vague darknesses that float before dazzled eyes, a pyramidal phantom-shape hung. Abel Keeling passed his hand over his eyes, but when he removed it the shape was still there, gliding slowly towards the *Mary*'s quarter. Its form changed as he watched it. The spirit-grey shape that had been a pyramid seemed to dissolve into four upright members, slightly graduated in tallness, the nearest the *Mary*'s stern the tallest and that to the left the lowest. It might have been the shadow of the gigantic set of reed-pipes on which that vacant mournful note had been sounded.

And as he looked, with fooled eyes, again his ears became fooled:

'Ahoy there! What ship's that? Are you a ship? ... Here, give me that trumpet — ' Then a metallic barking. 'Ahoy there! What the devil are you? Didn't you ring a bell? Ring it again, or blow a blast or something, and go dead slow!'

All this came, as it were, indistinctly, and through a sort of high singing in Abel Keeling's own ears. Then he fancied a

short bewildered laugh, followed by a colloquy from somewhere between sea and sky.

'Here, Ward, just pinch me, will you? Tell me what you see
there. I want to know if I'm awake.'

'See where?'

'There, on the starboard bow. (Stop that ventilating fan; I
can't hear myself think.) See anything? Don't tell me it's that
damned Dutchman — don't pitch me that old Vanderdecken
tale — give me an easy one first, something about a sea-
serpent. . . . You did hear that bell, didn't you?'

'Shut up a minute — listen — '

Again Bligh's voice was lifted up.

> 'This is the cov'nant that I make:
> From henceforth nevermore
> Will I again the world destroy
> With water, as before.'

Bligh's voice died away again in Abel Keeling's ears.

'Oh — my — fat — Aunt — Julia!' the voice that seemed to
come from between sea and sky sounded again. Then it spoke
more loudly. 'I say,' it began with careful politeness, 'if you
are a ship, do you mind telling us where the masquerade is to
be? Our wireless is out of order, and we hadn't heard of
it. . . . Oh, you do see it, Ward, don't you? . . . Please, please,
tell us what the hell you are!'

Again Abel Keeling had moved as a sleepwalker moves. He
had raised himself up by the belfry timbers, and Bligh had
sunk in a heap on the deck. Abel Keeling's movement
overturned the pipkin, which raced the little trickle of its
contents down the deck and lodged where the still and
brimming sea made, as it were, a chain with a carved
balustrade of the quarter-deck — one link a still gleaming
edge, then a dark baluster, and then another gleaming link.
For one moment only Abel Keeling found himself noticing
that that which had driven Bligh aft had been the rising of
the water in the waist as the galleon settled by the head — the
waist was now entirely submerged; then once more he was
absorbed in his dream, its voices, and its shape in the mist,
which had again taken the form of a pyramid before his
eyeballs.

'Of course,' a voice seemed to be complaining anew, and still through that confused dinning in Abel Keeling's ears, 'we can't turn a four-inch on it ... And, of course, Ward, I don't believe in 'em. D'you hear, Ward? I don't believe in 'em I say.... Shall we call down to old A.B.? This might interest His Scientific Skippership...."

'Oh, lower a boat and pull out to it — into it — over it — through it — '

'Look at our chaps crowded on the barbette yonder. They've seen it. Better not give an order you know won't be obeyed....'

Abel Keeling, cramped against the antique belfry, had begun to find his dream interesting. For, though he did not know her build, that mirage was the shape of a ship. No doubt it was projected from his brooding on ships of half an hour before; and that was odd.... But, perhaps, after all, it was not very odd. He knew that she did not really exist; only the appearance of her existed; but things had to exist like that before they really existed. Before the *Mary of the Tower* had existed she had been a shape in some man's imagination; before that, some dreamer had dreamed the form of a ship with oars; and before that, far away in the dawn and infancy of the world, some seer had seen in a vision the raft before man had ventured to push out over the water on his two planks. And since this shape that rode before Abel Keeling's eyes was a shape in his, Abel Keeling's dream, he, Abel Keeling, was the master of it. His own brooding brain had contrived her, and she was launched upon the illimitable ocean of his own mind....

> 'And I will not unmindful be
> Of this, My cov'nant, passed
> Twixt Me and you and every flesh
> Whiles that the world should last.'

sang Bligh, rapt....

But as a dreamer, even in his dream, will scratch upon the wall by his couch some key or word to put him in mind of his vision on the morrow when it has left him, so Abel Keeling found himself seeking some sign to be a proof to those to whom no vision is vouchsafed. Even Bligh sought that — could not be silent in his bliss, but lay on the deck there, uttering great passionate Amens and praising his Maker, as he said, upon a harp and an instrument of ten strings. So with Abel Keeling. It would be the Amen of his life to have praised God, not upon a harp, but upon a ship that should carry her own power, that should store wind or its equivalent as she stored her victuals, that should be something wrested from the chaos of uninvention and ordered and disciplined and subordinated to Abel Keeling's will. . . . And there she was, that ship-shaped thing of spirit-grey, with the four pipes that resembled a phantom organ now broadside and of equal length. And the ghost-crew of that ship were speaking again. . . .

The interrupted silver chain by the quarter-deck balustrade had now become continuous, and the balusters made a herring-bone over their own motionless reflections. The spilt water from the pipkin had dried, and the pipkin was not to be seen. Abel Keeling stood beside the mast, erect as God made man to go. With his leathery hand he smote upon the bell. He waited for the space of a minute, and then cried:

'Ahoy! . . . Ship ahoy! . . . What ship's that?'

We are not conscious in a dream that we are playing a game the beginning and end of which are in ourselves. In this dream of Abel Keeling's a voice replied:

'Hallo, it's found its tongue. . . . Ahoy there! What are you?'

Loudly and in a clear voice Abel Keeling called: 'Are you a ship?'

With a nervous giggle the answer came:

'We are a ship, aren't we, Ward? I hardly feel sure. . . . Yes, of course, we're a ship. No question about us. The question is what the dickens you are.'

Not all the words these voices used were intelligible to Abel Keeling, and he knew not what it was in the tone of these last words that reminded him of the honour due to the *Mary of the Tower*. Blister-white and at the end of her life as she was, Abel Keeling was still jealous of her dignity; the voice had a youngish ring; and it was not fitting that young chins should be wagged about his galleon. He spoke curtly.

'You that spoke — are you the master of that ship?'

'Officer of the watch,' the words floated back; 'the captain's below.'

'Then send for him. It is with masters that masters hold speech,' Abel Keeling replied.

He could see the two shapes, flat and without relief, standing on a high narrow structure with rails. One of them gave a low whistle, and seemed to be fanning his face; but the other rumbled something into a sort of funnel. Presently the two shapes became three. There was a murmuring, as to a consultation, and then suddenly a new voice spoke. At its thrill and tone a sudden tremor ran through Abel Keeling's frame. He wondered what response it was that that voice found in the forgotten recesses of his memory. . . .

'Ahoy!' seemed to call this new yet faintly remembered voice. 'What's all this about? Listen. We're His Majesty's destroyer *Seapink*, out of Devonport last October, and nothing particular the matter with us. Now who are you?'

'The *Mary of the Tower*, out of the Port of Rye on the day of Saint Anne, and only two men — '

A gasp interrupted him.

'Out of *where*?' that voice that so strangely moved Abel Keeling said unsteadily, while Bligh broke into groans of renewed rapture.

'Out of the Port of Rye, in the County of Sussex. . . . nay, give ear, else I cannot make you hear me while this man's spirit and flesh wrestle so together! . . . Ahoy! Are you gone?' For the voices had become a low murmur, and the ship-shape had faded before Abel Keeling's eyes. Again and again he called. He wished to be informed of the disposition and economy of the wind chamber. . . .

'The wind-chamber!' he called, in an agony lest the knowledge almost within his grasp should be lost. 'I would know about the wind-chamber. . . .'

Like an echo, there came back the words, uncomprehendingly uttered, 'The wind-chamber? . . .'

' . . . that driveth the vessel — perchance 'tis not wind — a steel bow that is bent also conserveth force — the force you store, to move at will through calm and storm. . . .'

'Can you make out what it's driving at?'

'Oh, we shall all wake up in a minute. . . .'

'Quiet, I have it; the engines; it wants to know about our engines. It'll be wanting to see our papers presently. Rye Port! . . . Well, no harm in humouring it; let's see what it can make of this. Ahoy there!' came the voice to Abel Keeling, a little more strongly, as if a shifting wind carried it, and speaking faster and faster as it went on. 'Not wind, but steam; d'you hear? Steam, steam. Steam, in eight Yarrow water-tube boilers. S-t-e-a-m, steam. Got it? And we've twin-screw triple expansion engines, indicated horse-power, four thousand, and we can do 430 revolutions per minute; savvy? Is there anything your phantomhood would like to know about our armament? . . .'

Abel Keeling was muttering fretfully to himself. It annoyed him that words in his own vision should have no meaning for him. How did words come to him in a dream that he had no knowledge of when wide awake? The *Seapink* — that was the name of this ship; but a pink was long and narrow, low-carged and square-built aft. . . .

'And as for our armament,' the voice with the tones that so profoundly troubled Abel Keeling's memory continued, 'we've two revolving Whithead torpedo-tubes, three six-pounders on the upper deck, and that's a twelve-pounder forward there by the conning-tower. I forgot to mention that we're nickel steel, with a coal capacity of sixty tons in most damnably placed bunkers, and that thirty and a quarter knots is about our top. Care to come aboard?'

But the voice was speaking still more rapidly and fever-ishly, as if to fill a silence with no matter what, and the shape that was uttering it was straining forward anxiously over the rail.

'Ugh! But I'm glad this happened in the daylight,' another voice was muttering.

'I wish I was sure it was happening at all . . . Poor old spook!'

'I suppose it would keep its feet if her deck was quite vertical. Think she'll go down or just melt?'

'Kind of go down . . . without wash. . . .'

'Listen — here's the other one now — '

For Bligh was singing again:

> For, Lord, Thou knows't our nature such
> If we great things obtain,
> And in the getting of the same
> Do feel no grief or pain,
> We little do esteem thereof;
> But, Hardly brought to pass,
> A thousand times we do esteem
> More than the other was.

'But oh, look — look — look at the other! . . . Oh, I say, wasn't he a grand old boy! Look!'

For, transfiguring Abel Keeling's form as a prophet's form is transfigured in the instant of his rapture, flooding his brain with the white eureka light of perfect knowledge, that for which he and his dream had been at a standstill had come. He knew her, this ship of the future, as if God's Finger had bitten her lines into his brain. He knew her as those already sinking into the grave know things, miraculously, completely, accepting Life's impossibilities with a nodded 'Of course.' From the ardent mouth of her eight furnaces to the last drip from her lubricators, from her bed-plates to the breeches of her quick-firers, he knew her — read her gauges, thumbed her bearings, gave the ranges from her range-finders, and lived the life he lived who was in command of her. And he would not forget on the morrow, as he had forgotten on many morrows, for at last he had seen the water about his feet, and knew that there would be no morrow for him in this world. . . .

And even in that moment, with but a sand or two to run in his glass, indomitable, insatiable, dreaming dream on dream, he could not die until he knew more. He had two questions to ask, and a master-question; and but a moment remained. Sharply his voice rang out.

'Ho, there! . . . This ancient ship, the *Mary of the Tower*, cannot steam thirty and a quarter knots, but yet she can sail the waters. What more does your ship? Can she soar above them, as the fowls of the air soar?'

'Lord, he thinks we're an aeroplane! . . . No, she can't . . .'

'And can you dive, even as the fishes of the deep?'

'No — those are submarines, we aren't a submarine . . . .

But Abel Keeling waited for no more. He gave an exulting chuckle.

'Oho, oho — thirty knots, and but on the face of the waters — no more than that? Oho! . . . Now my ship, the ship I see as a mother sees full-grown the child she has but conceived — my ship, I say — oho! — my ship shall. . . . Below there — trip that gun!'

The cry came suddenly and alertly, as a muffled sound came from below and an ominous tremor shook the galleon.

'By Jove, her guns are breaking loose below — that's her finish — '

'Trip that gun, and double-breech the others!'

Abel Keeling's voice rang out, as if there had been any to obey him. He had braced himself within the belfry frame; and then in the middle of the next order his voice suddenly failed him. His ship-shape, that for the moment he had forgotten, rode once more before his eyes. This was the end, and his master-question, apprehension for the answer to which was now torturing his face and well-nigh bursting his heart, was still unasked.

'Ho — he that spoke with me — the master,' he cried in a voice that ran high, 'is he there?'

'Yes, yes!' came the other voice across the water, sick with suspense. 'Oh, be quick!'

There was a moment in which hoarse cries from many voices, a heavy thud and rumble on wood, and a crash of timbers and a gurgle and a splash were indescribably mingled; the gun under which Abel Keeling had lain had snapped her rotten breechings and plunged down the deck, carrying Bligh's unconscious form with it. The deck came up vertical, and for one instant longer Abel Keeling clung to the belfry.

'I cannot see your face,' he screamed, 'but meseems your voice is a voice I know. What is your name?'

In a torn sob the answer came across the water.

'Keeling — Abel Keeling. . . . Oh, my God!'

And Abel Keeling's cry of triumph, that mounted to a victorious 'Huzza!' was lost in the downward plunge of the *Mary of the Tower*, that left the strait empty save for the sun's fiery blaze and the last smoke-like evaporation of the mists.

VI

The Sea Fit

Algernon Blackwood

A classic tale in the same mould as the Cthulhu mythos, The Sea Fit is from the masterly pen of that British doyen of the ghost story, Algernon Blackwood. A writer of prolific output, his stories none the less maintained a constantly high standard, and the two big collections assembled by Spring Books some years ago are a feast of delights. Blackwood, who died in 1951, has been described as the master of the spine-chilling situation set in an atmosphere of mystery and horror. He indeed possessed the special gift of building up an uncanny atmosphere out of an ordinary situation and I remember with delight and gratitude my first reading of his Ancient Sorceries *in an old anthology.*

The sea that night sang rather than chanted; all along the far-running shore a rising tide dropped thick foam, and the waves, white-crested, came steadily in with the swing of a deliberate purpose. Overhead, in a cloudless sky, that ancient Enchantress, the full moon, watched their dance across the sheeted sands, guiding them carefully while she drew them up. For through that moonlight, through that roar of surf, there penetrated a singular note of earnestness and meaning — almost as though these common processes of Nature were instinct with the flush of an unusual activity that sought audaciously to cross the borderland into some subtle degree of conscious life. A gauze of light vapour clung upon the surface of the sea, far out — a transparent carpet through which the rollers drove shorewards in a moving pattern.

In the low-roofed bungalow among the sand-dunes the three men sat. Foregathered for Easter, they spent the day fishing and sailing, and at night told yarns of the days when life was younger. It was fortunate that there were three —

and later four — because in the mouths of several witnesses an extraordinary thing shall be established — when they agree. And although whisky stood upon the rough table made of planks nailed to barrels, it is childish to pretend that a few drinks invalidate evidence, for alcohol, up to a certain point, intensifies the consciousness, focuses the intellectual powers, sharpens observation; and two healthy men, certainly three, must have imbibed an absurd amount before they all see, or omit to see, the same things.

The other bungalows still awaited their summer occupants. Only the lonely tufted sand-dunes watched the sea, shaking their hair of coarse white grass to the winds. The men had the whole spit to themselves — with the wind, the spray, the flying gusts of sand, and that great Easter full moon. There was Major Reese of the Gunners and his half-brother, Dr. Malcolm Reese, and Captain Erricson, their host, all men whom the kaleidoscope of life had jostled together a decade ago in many adventures, then flung for years apart about the globe. There was also Erricson's body-servant, 'Sinbad', sailor of big seas, and a man who had shared on many a ship all the lust of strange adventure that distinguished his great blonde-haired owner — an ideal servant and dog-faithful, divining his master's moods almost before they were born. On the present occasion, besides crew of the fishing-smack, he was cook, valet, and steward of the bungalow smoking-room as well.

'Big Erricson', Norwegian by extraction, student by adoption, wanderer by blood, a Viking reincarnated if ever there was one, belonged to that type of primitive man in whom burns an inborn love and passion for the sea that amounts to positive worship — devouring tide, a lust and fever in the soul. 'All genuine votaries of the old sea-gods have it', he used to say, by way of explaining his carelessness of worldly ambitions. 'We're never at our best away from salt water — never quite right. I've got it bang in the heart myself. I'd do a bit before the mast sooner than make a million on shore. Simply can't help it, you see, and never could! It's our gods calling us to worship.' And he had never tried to 'help it', which explains why he owned nothing in the world on land except this tumble-down, one-storey bungalow — more like a ship's cabin than anything else, to which he sometimes asked his bravest and most faithful friends — and a store of curious reading gathered in long, becalmed days at the ends of the world. Heart and mind, that is, carried a queer cargo. 'I'm sorry if you poor devils are uncomfortable in her. You must ask Sinbad for anything you want and don't see, remember.' As though Sinbad could have supplied comforts that were miles away, or converted a draughty wreck into a snug, taut, brand-new vessel.

Neither of the Reeses had cause for grumbling on the score of comfort, however, for they knew the keen joys of roughing it, and both weather and sport besides had been glorious. It was on another score this particular evening that they found cause for uneasiness, if not for actual grumbling. Erricson had one of his queer sea fits on — the Doctor was responsible for the term — and was in the thick of it, plunging like a straining boat at anchor, talking in a way that made them both feel vaguely uncomfortable and distressed. Neither of them knew exactly perhaps why he should have felt this growing *malaise*, and each was secretly vexed with the other for confirming his own unholy instinct that something uncommon was astir. The loneliness of the sandspit and that melancholy singing of the sea before their very door may have had something to do with it, seeing that both were landsmen; for Imagination is ever Lord of the Lonely Places, and adventurous men remain children to the last. But, whatever it was that affected both men in different fashion, Malcolm Reese, the doctor, had not thought it necessary to mention to his brother that Sinbad had tugged his sleeve on entering and whispered in his ear significantly: 'Full moon, sir, please, and he's better without too much! These high spring tides get him all caught off his feet sometimes — clean sea-crazy'; and the man had contrived to let the doctor see the hilt of a small pistol he carried in his hip-pocket.

For Erricson had got upon his old subject: that the gods were not dead, but merely withdrawn, and that even a single true worshipper was enough to draw them down again into touch with the world, into the sphere of humanity, even into active and visible manifestation. He spoke of humanity, even into active and visible manifestation. He spoke of queer things he had seen in queerer places. He was serious, vehement, voluble; and the others had let it pour out unchecked, hoping thereby for its speedier exhaustion. They puffed their pipes in comparative silence, nodding from time to time, shrugging their shoulders, the soldier mystified and bewildered, the doctor alert and keenly watchful.

'And I like the old idea,' he had been saying, speaking of these departed pagan deities, 'that sacrifice and ritual feed their great beings, and that death is only the final sacrifice by which the worshipper becomes absorbed into them. The devout worshipper' – and there was a singular drive and power behind the words – 'should go to his death singing, as to a wedding – the wedding of his soul with the particular deity he has loved and served all his life.' He swept his tow-coloured beard with one hand, turning his shaggy head towards the window, where the moonlight lay upon the procession of shaking waves. 'It's playing the whole game, I always think, man-fashion. . . . I remember once, some years ago, down there off the coast by Yucatan – '

And then, before they could interfere, he told an extraordinary tale of something he had seen years ago, but told it with such a horrid earnestness of conviction – for it was dreadful, though fine, this adventure – that his listeners shifted in their wicker chairs, struck matches, unnecessarily, pulled at their long glasses, and exchanged glances that attempted a smile yet did not quite achieve it. For the tale had to do with sacrifice of human life and a rather haunting pagan ceremonial of the sea, and at its close the room had changed in some indefinable manner – was not exactly as it had been before perhaps – as though the savage earnestness of the language had introduced some new element that made it less cosy, less cheerful, even less warm. A secret lust in the man's heart, born of the sea, and of his intense admiration of the pagan gods called a light into his eye not altogether pleasant.

'They were great Powers, at any rate, those ancient fellows,' Erricson went on, refilling his huge pipe bowl; 'to great to disappear altogether, though today they may walk the earth in another manner. I swear they're still going it – especially the – ' (he hesitated for a mere second) 'the old water Powers — the Sea Gods. Terrific beggars, every one of 'em.'

'Still move the tides and raise the winds, eh?' from the Doctor.

Erricson spoke again after a moment's silence, with impressive dignity. 'And I like, too, the way they manage to keep their names before us,' he went on, with a curious eagerness that did not escape the Doctor's observation, while it clearly puzzled the soldier. 'There's old Hu, the Druid god of justice, still alive in "Hue and Cry"; there's Typhon hammering his way against us in the typhoon; there's the mighty Hurakar, serpent god of the winds, you know, shouting to us in hurricane and *ouragan*; and there's — '

'Venus still at it as hard as ever,' interrupted the Major, facetiously, though his brother did not laugh because of their host's almost sacred earnestness of manner and uncanny grimness of face. Exactly how he managed to introduce that element of gravity — of conviction — into such talk neither of his listeners quite understood, for in discussing the affair later they were unable to pitch upon any definite detail that betrayed it. Yet there it was, alive and haunting, even distressingly so. All day he had been silent and morose, but since dusk, with the turn of the tide, in fact, these queer sentences, half mystical, half unintelligible, had begun to pour from him, till now that cabin-like room among the sand-dunes fairly vibrated with the man's emotion. And at last Major Reese, with blundering good intention, tried to shift the key from this portentous subject of sacrifice to something that might eventually lead towards comedy and laughter, and so relieve this growing pressure of melancholy and incredible things. The Viking fellow had just spoken of the possibility of the old gods manifesting themselves visibly, audibly, physically, and so the Major caught him up and made light mention of spiritualism and the so-called 'materialisation séances', where physical bodies were alleged to be built up out of the emanations of the medium and the sitters. This crude aspect of the Supernatural was the only possible link the soldier's mind could manage. He caught his brother's eye too late, it seems, for Malcolm Reese realised by this time that something untoward was afoot, and no

longer needed the memory of Sinbad's warning to keep him
sharply on the look-out. It was not the first time he had seen
Erricson 'caught' by the sea; but he had never known him
quite so bad, nor seen his face so flushed and white
alternately, nor his eyes so oddly shining. So that Major
Reese's well-intentioned allusion only brought wind to fire.

The man of the sea, once Viking, roared with a rush of
boisterous laughter at the comic suggestion, then dropped his
voice to a sudden hard whisper, awfully earnest, awfully
intense. Any one must have started at the abrupt change and
the life-and-death manner of the big man. His listeners
undeniably both did.

'Bunkum!' he shouted, 'bunkum, and be damned to it all!
There's only one real materialisation of these immense Outer
Beings possible, and that's when the great embodied
emotions, which are their sphere of action' — his words
became wildly incoherent, painfully struggling to get out —
'derived, you see, from their honest worshippers the world
over — constituting their Bodies, in fact — come down into
matter and get condensed, crystallised into form — to claim
that final sacrifice I spoke about just now, and to which any
man might feel himself proud and honoured to be
summoned. . . . No dying in bed or fading out from old age,
but to plunge full-blooded and alive into the great Body of
the god who has deigned to descend and fetch you — '

The actual speech may have been even more rambling and
incoherent than that. It came out in a torrent at white heat.
Dr. Reese kicked his brother beneath the table, just in time.
The soldier looked thoroughly uncomfortable and amazed,
utterly at a loss to know how he had produced the storm. It
rather frightened him.

'I know it because I've seen it,' went on the sea man, his
mind and speech slightly more under control, 'seen the
ceremonies that brought these whopping old Nature gods
down into form — seen 'em carry off a worshipper into
themselves — seen that worshipper, too, go off singing and
happy to his death, proud and honoured to be chosen.'

'Have you really — by George!' the Major exclaimed. 'You
tell us a queer thing, Erricson'; and it was then for the fifth
time that Sinbad cautiously opened the door, peeped in and

silently withdrew after giving a swiftly comprehensive glance round the room.

The night outside was windless and serene, only the growing thunder of the tide near the full woke muffled echoes among the sand-dunes.

'Rites and ceremonies,' continued the other, his voice booming with a singular enthusiasm, but ignoring the interruption, 'are simply means of losing one's self by temporary ecstasy in the God of one's choice — the God one has worshipped all one's life — of being partially absorbed into his being. And sacrifice completes the process — '

'At death, you said?' asked Malcolm Reese, watching him keenly.

'Or voluntary,' was the reply that came flash-like. 'The devotee becomes wedded to his Diety — goes bang into him, you see, by fire or water or air — as by a drop from a height — according to the nature of the particular God; at-one-ment, of course. A man's death that! Fine, you know!'

The man's inner soul was on fire now. He was talking at a fearful pace, his eyes alight, his voice turned somehow into a kind of sing-song that chimed well, singularly well, with the booming of waves outside, and from time to time he turned to the window to stare at the sea and the moon-blanched sands. And then a look of triumph would come into his face — that giant face framed by slow-moving wreaths of pipe smoke.

Sinbad entered for the sixth time without any obvious purpose, busied himself unnecessarily with the glasses and went out again, lingeringly. In the room he kept his eye hard upon his master. This time he contrived to push a chair and a heap of netting between him and the window. No one but Dr. Reese observed the manoeuvre. And he took the hint.

'The port-holes fit badly, Erricson,' he laughed, but with a touch of authority. 'There's a five-knot breeze coming through the cracks worse than an old wreck!' And he moved up to secure the fastening better.

'The room *is* confoundedly cold,' Major Reese put in; 'has been for the last half-hour, too.' The soldier looked what he felt — cold — distressed — creepy. 'But there's no wind really, you know,' he added.

Captain Erricson turned his great bearded visage form one to the other before he answered; there was a gleam of sudden suspicion in his blue eyes. 'The beggar's got that back door open again. If he's sent for any one, as he did once before, I swear I'll drown him in fresh water for his impudence — or perhaps — can it be already that he expects — ?' He left the sentence incomplete and rang the bell, laughing with a boisterousness that was clearly feigned. 'Sinbad, what's this cold in the place? You've got the back door open. Not expecting any one, are you — ?'

'Everything's shut tight, Captain. There's a bit of a breeze coming up from the east. And the tide's drawing in at a raging pace — '

'We can all hear *that*. But are you expecting any one? I asked,' repeated his master, suspiciously, yet still laughing. One might have said he was trying to give the idea that the man had some land flirtation on hand. They looked one another square in the eye for a moment, these two. It was the straight stare of equals who understood each other well.

'Some one — might be — on the way, as it were, Captain. Couldn't say for certain.'

The voice almost trembled. By a sharp twist of the eye, Sinbad managed to shoot a lightning and significant look at the Doctor.

'But this cold — this freezing, damp cold in the place? Are you sure no one's come — by the back ways?' insisted the master. He whispered it. 'Across the dunes, for instance?' His voice conveyed awe and delight, both kept hard under.

'It's all over the house, Captain, already,' replied the man, and moved across to put more sea-logs on the blazing fire. Even the soldier noticed then that their language was tight with allusion of another kind. To relieve the growing tension and uneasiness in his own mind he took up the word 'house' and made fun of it.

'As though it were a mansion,' he observed, with a forced chuckle, 'instead of a mere sea-shell!' Then, looking about him, he added: 'But, all the same, you know, there *is* a kind of fog getting into the room — from the sea, I suppose; coming up with the tide, or something, eh?' The air had certainly in the last twenty minutes turned thickish; it was not all tobacco smoke, and there was a moisture that began to precipitate on the objects in tiny, fine globules. The cold, too, fairly bit.

'I'll take a look round,' said Sinbad, significantly, and went out. Only the Doctor perhaps noticed that the man shook, and was white down to the gills. He said nothing, but moved his chair nearer to the window and to his host. It was really a little bit beyond comprehension how the wild words of this old sea-dog in the full sway of his 'sea fit' had altered the very air of the room as well as the personal equations of its occupants, for an extraordinary atmosphere of enthusiasm that was almost splendour pulsed about him, yet vilely close to something that suggested terror! Through the armour of every-day common sense that normally clothed the minds of these other two, had crept the faint wedges of a mood that made them vaguely wonder whether the incredible could perhaps sometimes — by way of bewildering exceptions — actually come to pass. The moods of their deepest life, that is to say, were already affected. An inner, and thoroughly unwelcome, change was in progress. And such psychic disturbances once started are hard to arrest. In this case it was well on the way before either the Army or Medicine had been willing to recognise the fact. There was something coming — coming from the sand-dunes or the sea. And it was invited, welcomed at any rate, by Erricson. His deep, volcanic enthusiasm and belief provided the channel. In lesser degree they, too, were caught in it. Moreover, it was terrific, irresistible.

And it was at this point — as the comparing of notes afterwards established — that Father Norden came in, Norden, the big man's nephew, having bicycled over from some point beyond Corfe Castle and raced along the hard Studland sand in the moonlight, and then hullood till a boat had ferried him across the narrow channel of Poole Harbour. Sinbad simply brought him in without any preliminary question or announcement. He could not resist the splendid night and the spring air, explained Norden. He felt sure his uncle could 'find a hammock' for him somewhere aft, as he put it. He did not add that Sinbad had telegraphed for him just before sundown from the coast-guard hut. Dr. Reese already knew him, but he was introduced to the Major. Norden was a member of the Society of Jesus, an ardent, not clever, and unselfish soul.

Erricson greeted him with obviously mixed feelings, and with an extraordinary sentence: 'It doesn't really matter,' he exclaimed, after a few commonplaces of talk, 'for all religions are the same if you go deep enough. All teach sacrifice, and, with exception, all seek final union by absorption into their Deity.' And then, under his breath, turning sideways to peer out of the window, he added a swift rush of half-smothered words that only Dr. Reese caught: 'The Army, the Church, the Medical Profession, and Labour — if they would only all come! What a fine result, what a grand offering! Alone — I seem so unworthy — insignificant. . . !'

But meanwhile young Norden was speaking before any one could stop him, although the Major did make one or two blundering attempts. For once the Jesuit's tact was at fault. He evidently hoped to introduce a new mood — to shift the current already established by the single force of his own personality. And he was not quite man enough to carry it off.

It was an error of judgment on his part. For the forces he found established in the room were too heavy to lift and alter, their impetus being already acquired. He did his best, anyhow. He began moving with the current — it was not the first sea fit he had combated in this extraordinary personality — then found, too late, that he was carried along with it himself like the rest of them.

'Odd — but couldn't find the bungalow at first,' he laughed, somewhat hardly. 'It's got a bit of seafog all to itself that hides it. I thought perhaps my pagan uncle — '

The Doctor interrupted him hastily, with great energy. 'The fog *does* lie caught in these sand hollows — like steam in a cup, you know,' he put in. But the other, intent on his own procedure, missed the cue.

' — thought it was smoke at first, and that you were up to some heathen ceremony or other,' laughing in Erricson's face; 'sacrificing to the full moon or the sea, or the spirits of the desolate places that haunt sand-dunes, eh?'

No one spoke for a second, but Erricson's face turned quite radiant.

'My uncle's such a pagan, you know,' continued the priest, 'that as I flew along those deserted sands from Studland I almost expected to hear old Triton blow his wreathed horn . . . or see fair Thetis's tinsel-slippered feet. . . .'

Erricson, suppressing violent gestures, highly excited, face happy as a boy's, was combing his great yellow beard with both hands, and the other two men had begun to speak at once, intent on stopping the flow of unwise allusion. Norden, swallowing a mouthful of cold soda-water, had put the glass down, spluttering over its bubbles, when the sound was first heard at the window. And in the back room the manservant ran, calling something aloud that sounded like 'It's coming, God save us, it's coming in . . .!' Though the Major swears some name was mentioned that he afterwards forgot — Glaucus — Proteus — Pontus — or some such word. The sound itself, however, was plain enough — a kind of imperious tapping on the window-panes as of a multitude of objects. Blown sand it might have been or heavy spray or, as Norden suggested later, a great water-soaked branch of giant seaweed. Every one started up, but Erricson was first upon his feet, and had the window wide open in a twinkling. His voice roared forth over those moonlit sand-dunes and out towards the line of heavy surf ten yards below.

'All along the shore of the Aegean,' he bellowed, with a kind of hoarse triumph that shook the heart, 'that ancient cry once rang. But it was a lie, a thumping and audacious lie. And He is not the only one. Another still lives — and, by Poseidon, He comes! He knows His own and His own know Him — and His own shall go to meet Him . . .!'

That reference to the Aegean 'cry'! It was so wonderful. Every one, of course, except the soldier, seized the allusion. It was a comprehensive, yet subtle, way of suggesting the idea. And meanwhile all spoke at once, shouted rather, for the Invasion was somehow — monstrous.

'Damn it — that's a bit too much. Something's caught my throat!' The Major, like a man drowning, fought with the furniture in his amazement and dismay. Fighting was his first instinct, of course. 'Hurts so infernally — takes the breath,' he cried, by way of explaining the extraordinarily violent impetus that moved him, yet half ashamed of himself for seeing nothing he could strike. But Malcolm Reese struggled to get between his host and the open window, saying in tense voice something like 'Don't let him get out! Don't let him get out!' While the shouts of warning from Sinbad in the little cramped back offices added to the general confusion. Only Father Norden stood quiet — watching with a kind of admiring wonder the expression of magnificence that had flamed into the visage of Erricson.

'Hark, you fools! Hark!' boomed the Viking figure, standing erect and splendid.

And through that open window, along the far-drawn line of shore from Canford Cliffs to the chalk bluffs of Studland Bay, there certainly ran a sound that was no common roar of surf. It was articulate — a message from the sea — an announcement — a thunderous warning of approach. No mere surf breaking on sand could have compassed so deep and multitudinous a voice of dreadful roaring — far out over the entering tide, yet at the same time close in along the entire sweep of shore, shaking all the ocean, both depth and surface, with its deep vibrations. Into the bungalow chamber came — the SEA!

Out of the night, from the moonlit spaces where it had been steadily accumulating, into that little cabined room so full of humanity and tobacco smoke, came invisibly — the Power of the Sea. Invisible, yes, but mighty, pressed forward by the huge draw of the moon, soft-coated with brine and moisture — the great Sea. And with it, into the minds of those three other men, leaped instantaneously, not to be denied, overwhelming suggestions of water-power, the tear and strain of thousand-mile currents, the irresistible pull and rush of tides, the suction of giant whirlpools — more, the massed and awful impetus of whole driven oceans. The air turned salt and briny, and a welter of seaweed clamped their very skins.

'Glaucus! I come to Thee, great God of the deep Waterways. . . . Father and Master!' Erricson cried aloud in a voice that most marvellously conveyed supreme joy.

The little bungalow trembled as from a blow at the foundations, and the same second the big man was through the window and running down the moonlight sands towards the foam.

'God in Heaven! Did you all see *that*?' shouted Major Reese, for the manner in which the great body slipped through the tiny window-frame was incredible. And then, first tottering with a sudden weakness, he recovered himself and rushed round by the door, followed by his brother. Sinbad, invisible, but not inaudible, was calling aloud from the passage at the back. Father Norden, slimmer than the others — well controlled, too — was through the little window before either of them reached the fringe of beach beyond the sand-dunes. They joined forces halfway down to the water's edge. The figure of Erricson, towering in the moonlight, flew before them, coasting rapidly along the wave-line.

No one of them said a word; they tore along side by side, Norden a trifle in advance. In front of them, head turned seawards, bounded Erricson in great flying leaps, singing as he ran, impossible to overtake.

Then, what they witnessed all three witnessed; the weird grandeur of it in the moonshine was too splendid to allow the smaller emotions of personal alarm, it seems. At any rate, the divergence of opinion afterwards was unaccountably insignificant. For, on a sudden, that heavy roaring sound far out at sea came close in with a swift plunge of speed, followed simultaneously — accompanied, rather — by a dark line that was no mere wave moving: enormously, up and across between the sea and sky it swept close in to shore. The moonlight caught it for a second as it passed, in a cliff of her bright silver.

And Erricson slowed down, bowed his great head and shoulders, spread his arms out and. . . .

And what? For not one of those amazed witnesses could swear exactly what then came to pass. Upon this impossibility of telling it in language they all three agreed. Only those eyeless dunes of sand that watched, only the white and silent moon overhead, only that long, curved beach of empty and deserted shore retain the complete record, to be revealed some day perhaps when a later Science shall have learned to develop the photographs that Nature takes incessantly upon her secret plates. For Erricson's rough suit of tweed went out in ribbons across the air; his figure somehow turned dark like strips of tide-sucked seaweed; something enveloped and overcame him, half shrouding him from view. He stood for one instant upright, his hair wild in the moonshine, towering, with arms again outstretched; then bent forward, turned, drew out most curiously sideways, uttering the singing sound of tumbling waters. The next instant, curving over like a falling wave, he swept along the glistening surface of the sands — and was gone. In fluid form, wave-like, his being slipped away into the Being of the Sea. A violent tumult convulsed the surface of the tide near in, but at once, and with amazing speed, passed careering away into the deeper water — far out. To his singular death, as to a wedding, Erricson had gone, singing, and well content.

'May God, who holds the sea and all its powers in the hollow of His mighty hand, take them *both* into Himself!' Norden was on his knees, praying fervently.

The body was never recovered . . . and the most curious thing of all was that the interior of the cabin, where they found Sinbad shaking with terror when they at length returned, was splashed and sprayed, almost soaked, with salt water. Up into the bigger dunes beside the bungalow, and far beyond the reach of normal tides, lay, too, a great streak and furrow as of a large invading wave, caking the dry sand. A hundred tufts of the coarse grass tussocks had been torn away.

The high tide that night, drawn by the Easter full moon, of course, was known to have been exceptional, for it fairly flooded Poole Harbour, flushing all the coves and bays towards the mouth of the Frome. And the natives up at Arne Bay and Wych always declare that the noise of the sea was heard far inland even up to the nine Barrows of the Purbeck Hills — triumphantly singing.

VII

The Phantom Warships of Matapan

Admiral Aldo Cocchia

That the sailor remained a central character in superstition and the supernatural tale even to the present day is no accident. At sea strange happenings are less easily explained away and the seaman lives too close to nature to scoff at what he does not understand. The love of the sailor for his craft has always been typified by the naming of ships, and because of that they are always known as 'she', is it any less logical then that the ship should reciprocate that feeling?

Admiral Cocchia's strange tale, taken from his memoirs, Submarines Attacking, *is set in the midst of a brutal naval battlefield in 1941, and takes up both these themes. The facts are that three Italian heavy cruisers and two large destroyers were surprised and pulverised into wrecks during a night action against Admiral Cunningham's three mighty battleships. The events that Admiral Cocchia relates in this yarn have been repeated by Admiral Cunningham and others on the British side, and even the Official British publication on the battle and the chart, contained in* East of Malta, West of Suez *(H.M.S.O. 1942), report the Cruiser that was not there!*

Much has been written, both in England and Italy, about the Battle of Cape Matapan. We know every last detail of that unhappy affair. We know the circumstances which led to the disastrous night-action; the courses of all the ships engaged; the positions of the British battleships and cruisers; the speed of the enemy destroyers which chased the damaged *Vittorio Veneto*, but failed to catch her; the movements of Admiral Cattaneo's cruisers, *Zara* and *Fiume*, which were both lost; and how it was that *Pola* came to find herself torpedoed and stationary in mid-ocean. In short, we know everything, both from Admiral Iachino's account and from the detailed analysis of the battle in Admiral Bernotti's history of the war. There would be no point in saying anything more, were it not for certain well-authenticated phenomena which occurred during the battle and of which mere common-sense can provide no explanation.

Not long ago, for example, a bottle was washed ashore containing a dying message from one of the ratings killed in the action off Matapan. The bottle was found on a beach in Sardinia. Inside was a paper bearing the words: 'Signori, tell my Mother I am dying for my country. Thank-you, signori, thank-you.' The writer was Francesco Chirico, a seaman from Futani; and his message was scribbled as his ship, the *Fiume*, was sinking. At the last moment he thought of something else and added after his name the words, 'Italia, Italia.' They expressed all that he felt, but did not know how to say, as his ship went down. He committed his message to the sea, and the sea faithfully delivered it eleven years later.

I have no wish to comment on this message from eternity. You will say that it was pure chance that a jettisoned bottle, adrift in the Mediterranean for eleven years, should find its way at last to an Italian beach. So it was. But it was a chance which fits exactly into the pattern of strange events surrounding Matapan. Some people may be able to find a prosaic explanation; but I cannot.

A great many things about the battle can be explained. We know, for example, why the British did not open fire at once after spotting the *Pola* by radar, but turned away in search of other ships, which might not have been there at all. We can understand how the course of our two cruisers came to coincide with that of the British 15-inch battleships and why it was that the British, well served by the planes from their aircraft-carrier, knew exactly which Italian ships were at sea, whereas we had only a general idea that Cunningham's battle fleet was out. All this, as I say, can be explained. What remains entirely inexplicable is why seamen on both sides — the British without exception and many Italians as well — saw during the action a light cruiser of the *Colleoni* class, which was not in fact there at all.

There is no need to give an account of the whole engagement. It is enough to recall that on the night of 28th March, the cruiser *Pola*, badly hit by an air-torpedo, was stationary, and that the heavy cruisers *Zara* and *Fiume*, with four destroyers under Admiral Cattaneo, had been sent to her aid. The cruisers were steaming in line ahead, *Zara* leading, followed by the destroyers. They were the only Italian ships moving in the area, *Pola*, though not far off, being still stationary. Yet all the British accounts maintain that ahead of *Zara*, the flagship, was a light cruiser of the *Colleoni* class. It was so reported at the time; and Admiral Cunningham has told the same story in his recent memoirs. There is thus no room for doubt that the British officers and men concerned did actually see this non-existent ship.

The precise time at which she was first picked up is given: 2228 hours. She was a light cruiser of the *Colleoni* class and was sailing ahead of *Zara*, like an outrider to the Italian formation. It is also stated that she was fired on and that fires were started on board, which forced her to break off the action.

Zara and *Fiume*, as we know, not being equipped with radar, were taken by surprise and were both sunk before they could fire a shot. *Pola*, a silent and inactive spectator of the fight, was also sunk. But what of the light cruiser? No ship of that class took part in the engagement at any stage, either that night off Cape Matapan or earlier in the day off Gavdo Island. Her appearance was a myth or the result of mass-hallucination. But can any illusion of that sort be strong enough to persuade a captain and his crew to open fire on a ship which isn't there; or an admiral to report afterwards that the ship in question caught fire?

If it was an illusion, it was a strange one; and it is made all the stranger by the fact that, eight months before, the *Bartolomeo Colleoni* herself had been sunk in those very waters by the Australian cruiser *Sydney*. The *Colleoni* can scarcely have been present at Matapan in person; but her ghost was certainly there, drawing the enemy's fire. The enemy saw her, and she was also seen from the deck of the helpless *Pola*. But no one could do much for the Italian ships that night, not even a visible but non-existent light cruiser.

But the strangest story which that sad night-action produced, is another one. Admiral Iachino mentions it in his *Gaudo e Matapan* and so do other writers. I was told it by a seaman from Naples who was with me in the Red Sea and in the Atlantic in *Torelli* and was afterwards posted to *Fiume*. All that

I can remember about him is that his name was Antonio. When he came to see me on *Da Recco*, he told me, with tears in his eyes, the story of *Fiume*'s loss. The first salvo had taken her by surprise. Her Captain, Giorgio Giorgis, had tried in vain to bring the resulting fires under control, and had finally given the order to abandon ship. He himself had stayed on board; and they had seen him in the stern lighting a cigarette as he made his way forward to the bridge for the last time.

The survivors were adrift on rafts and in boats for five days. They suffered a good deal; but it was not that which left its mark on Antonio, so much as a sight which they all saw at dawn on the second day:

'There was nothing in sight, only flat, oily sea. So we all saw her plain enough when she began to come up, four or five miles away. First the crow's nest, then the mast and funnels. We couldn't help but know her. It was our own ship, *Fiume*, coming back for us. We could see her bridge and her gun-turrets. She heaved herself out of the water till her decks were almost awash, but so slowly that we thought she was dying. We thought she had come to fetch us, because some of us were pretty far gone by then. But she stayed where she was without ever seeming to shake quite free of the water. Then, very slowly, she began to sink again and that was that.'

That was the story that Antonio told me more than a year later. Perhaps I ought to have spoken to him about mirages and the power of suggestion. But who was I to destroy his belief that his ship had made a dying effort to rescue her crew? Besides, I am still convinced that *Fiume* did come back with a message for those who would listen, the same message that she sent last year by the hand of Francesco Chirico of Futani.

VIII

The Black Ferry

John Galt

John Galt who lived from 1779 to 1839, was a prolific writer of novels, travel book, poems and dramas, and notably, three books on country life in Scotland, The Annals of the Parish, The Ayrshire Legatees, and The Entail. He was a friend of Byron's, and published a life of him in 1830. The Black Ferry, which builds slowly but surely to a terrifying climax, is typical of the period in which it was written.

I was then returning from my first session at college. The weather had for some time been uncommonly wet, every brook and stream was swollen far beyond its banks, the meadows were flooded, and the river itself was increased to a raging Hellespont, insomuch that the ferry was only practicable for an hour before and after high tide.

The day was showery and stormy, by which I was detained at the inn until late in the afternoon, so that it was dark before I reached the ferry-house, and the tide did not serve for safe crossing until midnight. I was therefore obliged to sit by the fire and wait the time, a circumstance which gave me some uneasiness, for the ferryman was old and infirm, and Dick his son, who usually attended the boat during the night, happened to be then absent, the day having been such that it was not expected any travellers would seek to pass over that night.

The presence of Dick was not, however, absolutely necessary, for the boat swung from side to side by a rope anchored in he middle of the stream, and, on account of the strong current, another rope had been stretched across by which passengers could draw themselves over without assistance, an easy task to those who had the sleight of it, but it was not so to me, who still wore my arm in a sling.

While sitting at the fireside conversing with the ferryman and his wife, a smart, good-looking country lad, with a recruit's cockade in his hat, came in, accompanied by a young woman who was far advanced in pregnancy. They were told the state of the ferry, and that unless the recruit undertook to conduct the boat himself, they must wait the return of Dick.

They had been only that day married, and were on their way to join a detachment of the regiment in which Ralph Nocton, as the recruit was called, had that evening enlisted, the parish officers having obliged him to marry the girl. Whatever might have been their former love and intimacy, they were not many minutes in the house when he became sullen and morose towards her; nor was she more amiable towards him. He said little, but he often looked at her with an indignant eye, as she reproached him for having so rashly enlisted, to abandon her and his unborn baby, assuring him that she would never part from him while life and power lasted.

Though it could not be denied that she possessed both beauty and an attractive person, there was yet a silly vixen humour about her ill calculated to conciliate. I did not therefore wonder to hear that Nocton had married her with reluctance; I only regretted that the parish officers were so inaccessible to commiseration, and so void of conscience as to be guilty of rendering the poor fellow miserable for life to avert the hazard of the child becoming a burden on the parish.

The ferryman and his wife endeavoured to reconcile them to their lot; and the recruit, who appeared to be naturally reckless and generous, seemed willing to be appeased; but his weak companion was capricious and pettish. On one occasion, when a sudden shower beat hard against the window, she cried out, with little regard to decorum, that she would go no farther that night.

'You may do as you please, Mary Blake,' said Nocton, 'but go I must, for the detachment marches tomorrow morning. It was only to give you time to prepare to come with me that the Captain consented to let me remain so late in the town.'

She, however, only remonstrated bitterly at his cruelty in

forcing her to travel, in her condition, and in such weather. Nocton refused to listen to her, but told her somewhat doggedly, more so than was consistent with the habitual cheerful cast of his physiognomy, 'that although he had already been ruined by her, he trusted she had not yet the power to make him a deserter'.

He then went out, and remained some time alone. When he returned, his appearance was surprisingly changed; his face was of an ashy paleness; his eyes bright, febrile and eager, and his lip quivered as he said:

'Come, Mary, I can wait no longer; the boat is ready, the river is not so wild, and the rain is over.'

In vain she protested; he was firm; and she had no option but either to go or to be left behind. The old ferryman accompanied them to the boat, saw them embark, and gave the recruit some instruction how to manage the ropes, as it was still rather early in the tide. On returning into the house, he remarked facetiously to his wife:

'I can never see why young men should be always blamed, and all pity reserved for the damsels.'

At this moment a rattling shower of rain and hail burst like a platoon of small shot on the window, and a flash of vivid lightning was followed by one of the most tremendous peals of thunder I have ever heard.

'Hark!' cried the old woman, starting, 'was not that a shriek?' We listened, but the cry was not repeated; we rushed to the door, but no other sound was heard than the raging of the river, and the roar of the sea-waves breaking on the bar.

Dick soon after came home, and the boat having swung back to her station, I embarked with him, and reached the opposite inn, where I soon went to bed. Scarcely had I laid my head on the pillow when a sudden inexplicable terror fell upon me; I shook with an unknown horror; I was, as it were, conscious that some invisible being was hovering beside me, and could hardly muster fortitude enough to refrain from rousing the house. At last I fell asleep; it was perturbed and unsound; strange dreams and vague fears scared me awake, and in them were dreadful images of a soldier murdering a female, and open graves, and gibbet-irons swinging in the wind. My remembrance has no parallel to such another night.

In the morning the cloud on my spirit was gone, and I rose at my accustomed hour, and cheerily resumed my journey. It was a bright morning, all things were glittering and fresh in the rising sun, the recruit and his damsel were entirely forgotten, and I thought no more of them.

But when the night returned next year, I was seized with an unaccountable dejection; it weighed me down; I tried to shake it off, but was unable; the mind was diseased, and could no more by resolution shake off its discomfort, than the body by activity can expel a fever. I retired to my bed greatly depressed, but nevertheless I fell asleep. At midnight, however, I was summoned to awake by a hideous and undefinable terror; it was the same vague consciousness of some invisible visitor being near that I had once before experienced, as I have described, and I again recollected Nocton and Mary Blake in the same instant; I saw — for I cannot now believe that it was less than apparitional — the unhappy pair reproaching one another.

As I looked, questioning the integrity of my sight, the wretched bride turned round and looked at me. How shall I express my horror, when, for the ruddy beauty which she once possessed, I beheld the charnel visage of a skull; I started up and cried aloud with such alarming vehemence that the whole inmates of the house, with lights in their hands, were instantly in the room — shame would not let me tell what I had seen, and, endeavouring to laugh, I accused the nightmare of the disturbance.

This happened while I was at a watering-place on the west coast. I was living in a boarding-house with several strangers; among them was a tall pale German gentleman, of a grave impressive physiognomy. He was the most intelligent and shrewdest observer I have ever met with, and he had to a singular degree the gift of a discerning spirit. In the morning when we rose from the breakfast-table, he took me by the arm, and led me out upon the lawn in front of the house; and when we were at some distance from the rest of the company, said:

'Excuse me, sir, for I must ask an impertinent question. Was it indeed the dream of the nightmare that alarmed you last night?'

'I have no objection to answer you freely; but tell me first why you ask such a question?'

'It is but reasonable. I had a friend who was a painter; none ever possessed an imagination which discerned better how nature in her mysteries should appear. One of his pictures was the scene of Brutus when his evil genius summoned him to Philippi, and strange to tell, you bear some resemblance to the painted Brutus. When, with the others, I broke into your room last night, you looked so like the Brutus in his picture that I could have sworn you were amazed with the vision of a ghost.'

I related to him what I have done to you.

'It is wonderful,' said he, 'what inconceivable sympathy hath linked you to the fate of these unhappy persons. There is something more in this renewed visitation than the phantasma of a dream.'

The remark smote me with an uncomfortable sensation of dread, and for a short time my flesh crawled as it were upon my bones. But the impression soon wore off, and was again entirely forgotten.

When the anniversary again returned, I was seized with the same heaviness and objectless horror of mind; it hung upon me with bodings and auguries until I went to bed, and then after my first sleep I was a third time roused by another fit of the same inscrutable panic. On this occasion, however, the vision was different. I beheld only Nocton, pale and wounded, stretched on a bed, and on the coverlet lay a pair of new epaulettes, as if just unfolded from a paper.

For seven years I was thus annually afflicted. The vision in each was different, but I saw no more of Mary Blake. On the fourth occasion, I beheld Nocton sitting in the uniform of an aide-de-camp at a table, with the customary tokens of conviviality before him; it was only part of a scene, such as one beholds in a mirror.

On the fifth occasion, he appeared to be ascending, sword in hand, the rampart of a battery; the sun was setting behind him, and the shadows and forms of a strange land, with the domes and pagodas of an oriental country, lay in wide extent around: it was a picture, but far more vivid than painting can exhibit.

On the sixth time, he appeared again stretched upon a couch; his complexion was sullen, not from wounds, but disease, and there appeared at his bedside the figure of a general officer, with a star on his breast, with whose conversation he appeared pleased, though languid.

But on the seventh and last occasion on which the horrors of the visions were repeated, I saw him on horseback in a field of battle; and while I looked at him, he was struck on the face by a sabre, and the blood flowed down upon his regimentals.

Years passed after this, during which I had none of these dismal exhibitions. My mind and memory resumed their healthful tone. I recollected, without these intervening years of oblivion, Nocton and Mary Blake, occasionally, as one thinks of things past, and I told my friends of the curious periodical returns of the visitations to me as remarkable metaphysical phenomena. By an odd coincidence, it so happened that my German friend was always present when I related my dreams. He in the intervals sometimes spoke to me of them, but my answers were vague, for my reminiscences were imperfect. It was not so with him. All I told he distinctly recorded and preserved in a book wherein he wrote down the minutest thing that I had witnessed in my visions. I do not mention his name, because he is a modest and retiring man, in bad health, and who has long sequestered himself from company. His rank, however, is so distinguished that his name could not be stated without the hazard of exposing him to impertinent curiosity.

But to proceed.

Exactly fourteen years — twice seven it was — I remember well, because for the first seven I had been haunted as I have described, and for the other seven I had been placid in my living. At the end of that period of fourteen years, my German friend paid me a visit here. He came in the forenoon, and we spent an agreeable day together, for he was a man of much recondite knowledge. I have seen none so wonderfully possessed of all sorts of occult learning.

He was an astrologer of the true kind, for in him it was not a pretence but a science; he scorned horoscopes and fortune-tellers with the just derision of a philosopher, but he had a beautiful conception of the reciprocal dependencies of nature. He affected not to penetrate to causes, but he spoke of effects with a luminous and religious eloquence. He described to me how the tides followed the phases of the moon; but he denied the Newtonian notion that they were caused by the procession of the lunar changes. He explained to me that when the sun entered Aries, and the other signs of the zodiac, how his progression could be traced on this earth by the development of plants and flowers, and the passions, diseases, and affections of animals and man; but that the stars were more than the celestial signs of these terrestrial phenomena he ridiculed as the conceptions of the insane theory.

His learning in the curious art of alchemy was equally sublime. He laughed at the fancy of an immortal elixir, and his notion of the mythology of the philosopher's stone was the very essence and spirituality of ethics. The elixir of immortality he described to me as an allegory, which, from its component parts, emblems of talents and virtues, only showed that perseverance, industry, goodwill, and a gift from God were the requisite ingredients necessary to attain renown.

His knowledge of the philosopher's stone was still more beautiful. He referred to the writings of the Rosicrucians, whose secrets were couched in artificial symbols, to prove that the sages of that sect were not the fools that the lesser wise of later days would represent them. The self-denial, the patience, the humility, the trusting in God, the treasuring of time by lamp and calculation which the venerable alchemists recommended, he used to say, were only the elements which constitute the conduct of the youth that would attain to riches and honour; and these different stages which are illuminated in the alchemical volumes as descriptive of stages in the process of making the stone were but hieroglyphical devices to explain the effects of well-applied human virtue and industry.

To me it was amazing to what clear simplicity he reduced all things, and on what a variety of subjects his bright and splendid fancy threw a fair and effecting light. All those demi-sciences — physiognomy — palmistry — scaileology, etc., even magic and witchcraft, obtained from his interpretations a philosophical credibility.

In disquisitions on these subjects we spent the anniversary. He had by them enlarged the periphery of my comprehension; he had added to my knowledge, and inspired me with a profounder respect for himself.

He was an accomplished musician, in the remotest, if I may use the expression, depths of the art. His performance on the pianoforte was simple, heavy, and seemingly the labour of an unpractised hand, but his expression was beyond all epithet exquisite and solemn; his airs were grave, devotional, and pathetic, consisting of the simplest harmonic combinations; but they were wonderful; every note was a portion of an invocation; every melody the voice of a passion or a feeling supplied with elocution.

We had spent the day in the fields, where he illustrated his astrological opinions by appeals to plants, and leaves, and flowers, and other attributes of the season, with such delightful perspicuity that no time can efface from the registers of my memory the substance of his discourses. In the evening he delighted me with his miraculous music, and, as the night advanced, I was almost persuaded that he was one of those extraordinary men who are said sometimes to acquire communion with spirits and dominion over demons.

Just as we were about to sit down to our frugal supper, literally or philosophically so, as if it had been served for Zeno himself, Dick, the son of the old ferryman, who by this time was some years dead, came to the door, and requested to speak with me in private. Of course I obeyed, when he informed me that he had brought across the ferry that night a gentleman officer, from a far country, who was in bad health, and whom he could not accommodate properly in the ferry-house.

'The inn,' said Dick, 'is too far off, for he is lame, and has an open wound in the thigh. I have therefore ventured to bring him here, sure that you will be glad to give him a bed for the night. His servant tells me that he was esteemed the bravest officer in all the service in the Mysore of India.'

It was impossible to resist this appeal. I went to the door where the gentleman was waiting, and with true-heartedness expressed how great my satisfaction would be if my house could afford him any comfort.

I took him in with me to the room where my German friend was sitting. I was much pleased with the gentleness and unaffected simplicity of his manners.

He was a handsome middle-aged man — his person was robust and well formed — his features had been originally handsome, but they were disfigured by a scar, which had materially changed their symmetry. His conversation was not distinguished by any remarkable intelligence, but after the high intellectual excitement which I had enjoyed all day with my philosophical companion, it was agreeable and gentlemanly.

Several times during supper, something came across my mind as if I had seen him before, but I could neither recollect when nor where; and I observed that more than once he looked at me as if under the influence of some research in his memory. At last, I observed that his eyes were dimmed with tears, which assured me that he then recollected me. But I considered it a duty of hospitality not to inquire aught concerning him more than he was pleased to tell himself.

In the meantime, my German friend, I perceived, was watching us both, but suddenly he ceased to be interested, and appeared absorbed in thought, while good manners required me to make some efforts to entertain my guest. This led on to some inquiry concerning the scene of his services, and he told us that he had been many years in India.

'On this day eight years ago,' said he, 'I was in the battle of Borupknow, where I received the wound which has so disfigured me in the face.'

At that moment I accidentally threw my eyes upon my German friend — and look which he gave me in answer caused me to shudder from head to foot, and I began to ruminate on Nocton the recruit, and Mary Blake, while my friend continued the conversation in a light desultory manner, as it would have seemed to any stranger, but to me it was awful and oracular. He spoke to the stranger on all manner of topics, but ever and anon he brought him back, as if without design, to speak of the accidents of fortune which had befallen him on the anniversary of that day, giving it as a reason for his curious remarks that most men observed anniversaries, time and experience having taught them to notice that there were curious coincidences with respect to times, and places, and individuals — things which of themselves form part of the great demonstration of the wisdom and skill displayed in the construction, not only of the mechanical, but the mortal world, showing that each was a portion of one and the same thing.

'I have been,' said he to the stranger, 'an observer and recorder of such things. I have my book of registration here in this house; I will fetch it from my bed-chamber, and we shall see in what other things, as far as your fortunes have been concerned, how it corresponds with the accidents of your life on this anniversary.'

I observed that the stranger paled a little at this proposal, and said, with an affectation of carelessness while he was evidently disturbed, that he would see it in the morning. But the philosopher was too intent upon his purpose to forbear. I know not what came upon me, but I urged him to bring the book. This visibly disconcerted the stranger still more, and his emotion became, as it were, a motive which induced me, in a peremptory manner, to require the production of the book, for I felt that strange horror, so often experienced, returning upon me; and was constrained, by an irresistible impulse, to seek an explanation of the circumstances by which I had for so many years suffered such an eclipse of mind.

The stranger seeing how intent both of us were, desisted from his wish to procrastinate the curious disclosure which my friend said he could make; but it was evident he was not at ease. Indeed he was so much the reverse, that when the German went for his book, he again proposed to retire, and only consented to abide at my jocular entreaty, until he should learn what his future fortunes were to be, by the truth of what would be told him of the past.

My friend soon returned with the book. It was a remarkable volume, covered with vellum, shut with three brazen clasps, secured by a lock of curious construction. Altogether it was a strange, antique, and necromantic-looking volume. The corner was studded with knobs of brass, with a small mirror in the centre, round which were inscribed in Teutonic characters words to the effect, 'I WILL SHOW THEE THYSELF'. Before unlocking the clasp, my friend gave the book to the stranger, explained some of the emblematic devices which adorned the cover, and particularly the words of the motto that surrounded the little mirror.

Whether it was from design, or that the symbols required it, the explanations of my friend were mystical and abstruse; and I could see that they produced an effect on the stranger, so strong that it was evident he could with difficulty maintain his self-possession. The colour entirely faded from his countenance; he became wan and cadaverous, and his hand shook violently as he returned the volume to the philosopher, who, on receiving it back, said:

'There are things in this volume which may not be revealed to every eye, yet to those who may not discover to what they relate, they will seem trivial notations.'

He then applied the key to the lock, and unclosed the volume. My stranger guest began to breathe hard and audibly. The German turned over the vellum leaves searchingly and carefully. At last he found the record and description of my last vision, which he read aloud. It was not only minute in the main circumstances in which I had seen Nocton, but it contained an account of many things, the still life, as it is called, of the picture, which I had forgotten, and among other particulars a picturesque account of the old General whom I saw standing at the bedside.

'By all that's holy,' cried the stranger, 'it is old Cripplington himself — the queue of his hair was, as you say, always crooked, owing to a habit he had of pulling it when vexed — where could you find the description of all this?'

I was petrified; I sat motionless as a statue, but a fearful vibration thrilled through my whole frame.

My friend looked back in his book, and found the description of my sixth vision. It contained the particulars of the crisis of battle in which, as the stranger described, he had received the wound in his face. It affected him less than the other, but still the effect upon him was impressive.

The record of the fifth vision produced a more visible alarm. The description was vivid to an extreme degree — the appearance of Nocton, sword in hand, on the rampart — the animation of the assault, and the gorgeous landscape of domes and pagodas, was limned with words as vividly as a painter could have made the scene. The stranger seemed to forget his anxiety, and was delighted with the reminiscences which the description recalled.

But when the record of the fourth vision was read, wherein Nocton was described as sitting in the regimentals of an aide-de-camp, at a convivial table, he exclaimed, as if unconscious of his words:

'It was on that night I had first the honour of dining with the German general.'

The inexorable philosopher proceeded, and read what I had told him of Nocton, stretched pale and wounded on a bed, with new epaulettes spread on the coverlet, as if just unfolded from a paper. The stranger started from his seat, and cried with a hollow and fearful voice:

'This is the book of life.'

The German turned over to the second vision, which he read slowly and mournfully, especially the description of my own feelings, when I beheld the charnel visage of Mary Blake. The stranger, who had risen from his seat, and was panting with horror, cried out with a shrill howl, as it were:

'On that night as I was sitting in my tent, methought her spirit came and reproached me.'

I could not speak, but my German friend rose from his seat, and holding the volume in his left hand, touched it with his right, and looked sternly at the stranger, said:

'In this volume, and in your own conscience, are the evidences which prove that you are Ralph Nocton, and that on this night, twice seven years ago, you murdered Mary Blake.'

The miserable stranger lost all self-command, and cried in consternation:

'It is true, the waters raged; the rain and the hail came; she bitterly upbraided me; I flung her from the boat; the lightning flashed, and the thunder — Oh! it was not so dreadful as her drowning execrations.'

Before any answer could be given to this confession, he staggered from the spot, and almost in the same instant fell dead upon the floor.

IX

MS Found in a Bottle

Edgar Allan Poe

That master of the macabre, Edgar Allan Poe, made, not surprisingly, a lasting impression on many authors of this type of story and was long acknowledged as the master, a place he holds no less strongly today. His ability to create those brooding and festering landscapes remains unchallenged. This story is a particularly fine example of his work, elaborating as it does the ancient theme of the ship on an eternal voyage. But under Poe's guidance the horror of this situation takes on an even greater dimension and ends with yet a darker and more profound mystery.

Poe was to take this theme further in his story The Mystery of Arthur Gordon Pym, *to which, unfortunately, Jules Verne added a weak and silly appendage many years later. However, this same thread was taken up with far greater skill by H.P. Lovecraft, with his* At the Mountains of Madness. *The polar icecaps, like the very seas themselves, remain the last great unknown tracts of our planet. For this reason perhaps Poe's story still hold fast the element of mystery and the unknown.*

> Qui n'a plus qu-un moment à vivre
> N'a plus rien à dissimuler.
>
> —Quinault—ATYS.

Of my country and of my family I have little to say. Ill usage and length of years have driven me from the one, and estranged me from the other. Hereditary wealth afforded me an education of no common order, and a contemplative turn of mind enabled me to methodize the stores which early study very diligently garnered up. Beyond all things, the study of the German moralists gave me great delight; not from any ill-advised admiration of their eloquent madness, but from the ease with which my habits of rigid thought enabled me to detect their falsities. I have often been reproached with the aridity of my genius; a deficiency of imagination has been imputed to me as a crime; and the Pyrrhonism of my opinions has at all times rendered me notorious. Indeed, a strong relish for physical philosophy has, I fear, tinctured my mind with a very common error of this age — I mean the habit of referring occurrences, even the last susceptible of such reference, to the principles of that science. Upon the whole, no person could be less liable than myself to be led away from the severe precincts of truth by the *ignes fatui* of superstition. I have thought proper to premise thus much, lest the incredible tale I have to tell should be considered rather the raving of a crude imagination, than the positive experience of a mind to which the reveries of fancy have been a dead letter and a nullity.

After many years spent in foreign travel, I sailed in the year 18—, from the port of Batavia, in the rich and populous island of Java, on a voyage to the Archipelago of the Sunda islands. I went as passenger — having no other inducement than a kind of nervous restlessness which haunted me as a fiend.

Our vessel was a beautiful ship of about four hundred tons, copper-fastened, and built at Bombay of Malabar teak. She was freighted with cotton-wool and oil, from the Lachadive islands. We had also on board coir, jaggeree, ghee, cocoa-nuts, and a few cases of opium. The stowage was clumsily done, and the vessel consequently crank.

We got under way with a mere breath of wind, and for many days stood along the eastern coast of Java, without any other incident to beguile the monotony of our course than the occasional meeting with some of the small grabs of the Archipelago to which we were bound.

One evening, leaning over the taffrail, I observed a very singular, isolated cloud, to the N.W. It was remarkable, as well for its colour, as from its being the first we had seen since our departure from Batavia. I watched it attentively until sunset, when it spread all at once to the eastward and westward, girting in the horizon with a narrow strip of vapour, and looking like a long line of low beach. My notice was soon afterwards attracted by the dusky-red appearance of the moon, and the peculiar character of the sea. The latter was undergoing a rapid change, and the water seemed more than usually transparent. Although I could distinctly see the bottom, yet heaving the lead, I found the ship in fifteen fathoms. The air now became intolerably hot, and was loaded with spiral exhalations similar to those arising from heated iron. As night came on, every breath of wind died away, and a more entire calm it is impossible to conceive. The flame of a candle burned upon the poop without the least perceptible motion, and a long hair, held between the finger and thumb, hung without the possibility of detecting a vibration.

However, as the captain said he could perceive no indication of danger, and as we were drifting in bodily to shore, he ordered the sails to be furled, and the anchor let go. No watch was set, and the crew, consisting principally of Malays, stretched themselves deliberately upon the deck. I went below — not without a full presentiment of evil. Indeed, every appearance warranted me in apprehending a Simoom. I told the captain my fears; but he paid no attention to what I said, and left me without deigning to give a reply. My uneasiness, however, prevented me from sleeping, and about midnight I went up on deck. As I placed my foot upon the upper step of the companion-ladder, I was startled by a loud, humming noise, like that occasioned by the rapid revolution of a mill-wheel, and before I could ascertain its meaning, I found the ship quivering to its centre. In the next instant, a wildness of foam hurled us upon our beam-ends, and rushing over us fore and aft, swept the entire decks from stem to stern.

The extreme fury of the blast proved, in a great measure, the salvation of the ship. Although completely water-logged, yet, as her masts had gone by the board, she rose, after a minute, heavily from the sea, and staggering awhile beneath the immense pressure of the tempest, finally righted.

By what miracle I escaped destruction, it is impossible to say. Stunned by the shock of the water, I found myself, upon recovery, jammed in between the stern-post and rudder. With great difficulty I gained my feet, and looking dizzily around, was, at first, struck with the idea of our being among breakers; so terrific, beyond the wildest imagination, was the whirlpool of mountainous and foaming ocean within which we were engulfed. After a while, I heard the voice of an old Swede, who had shipped with us at the moment of our leaving port. I hallooed to him with all my strength, and presently he came reeling aft. We soon discovered that we were the sole survivors of the accident. All on deck, with the exception of ourselves, had been swept overboard; the captain and mates must have perished as they slept, for the cabins were deluged with water. Without assistance, we could expect to do little for the security of the ship, and our exertions were at first paralyzed by the momentary expectation of going down. Our cable had, of course, parted like pack-thread, at the first breath of the hurricane, or we should have been instantaneously over-whelmed. We scudded with frightful velocity before the sea, and the water made clear breaches over us. The frame-work of our stern was shattered excessively, and, in almost every respect, we had received considerable injury; but to our extreme joy we found the pumps unchoked, and that we had made no great shifting of our ballast. The main fury of the blast had already blown over, and we apprehended little danger from the violence of the wind; but we looked forward to its total cessation with dismay; well believing, that, in our shattered condition, we should inevitably perish in the tremendous swell which would ensue. But this very just apprehension seemed by no means likely to be soon verified.

For five entire days and nights — during which our only subsistence was a small quantity of jaggeree, procured with great difficulty from the forecastle — the hulk flew at a rate defying computation, before rapidly succeeding flaws of wind, which, without equalling the first violence of the Simoom, were still more terrific than any tempest I had before encountered. Our course for the first four days was, with trifling variations, S.E. and by S.; and we must have run down the coast of New Holland.

On the fifth day the cold became extreme, although the wind had hauled round a point more to the northward. The sun arose with a sickly yellow lustre, and clambered a very few degrees above the horizon — emitting no decisive light. There were no clouds apparent, yet the wind was upon the increase, and blew with a fitful and unsteady fury. About noon, as nearly as we could guess, our attention was again arrested by the appearance of the sun. It gave out no light, properly so called, but a dull and sullen glow without reflection, as if all its rays were polarized. Just before sinking within the turgid sea, its central fires suddenly went out, as if hurriedly extinguished by some unaccountable power. It was a dim, silver-like rim, alone, as it rushed down the unfathomable ocean.

We waited in vain for the arrival of the sixth day — that day to me has not arrived — to the Swede, never did arrive. Thenceforward we were enshrouded in pitchy darkness, so that we could not have seen an object at twenty paces from the ship. Eternal night continued to envelop us, all unrelieved by the phosphoric sea-brilliancy to which we had been accustomed in the tropics. We observed too, that, although the tempest continued to rage with unabated violence, there was no longer to be discovered the usual appearance of surf, or foam, which had hitherto attended us. All around were horror, and thick gloom, and a black sweltering desert of ebony. Superstitious terror crept by degrees into the spirit of the old Swede, and my own soul was wrapped up in silent wonder. We neglected all care of the ship, as worse than useless, and securing ourselves, as well as possible, to the stump of the mizzen-mast, looked out bitterly into the world of ocean. We had no means of calculating time, nor could we form any guess of our situation. We were, however, well aware of having made farther to the southward than any previous navigators, and felt great amazement at not meeting with the usual impediments of ice. In the meantime every moment threatened to be our last — every mountainous billow hurried to overwhelm us. The swell surpassed anything I had imagined possible, and that we were not instantly buried is a miracle. My companion spoke of the lightness of our cargo, and reminded me of the excellent qualities of our ship; but I could not help feeling the utter hopelessness of hope itself, and prepared myself gloomily for that death which I thought nothing could defer beyond an hour, as, with every knot of way the ship made, the swelling of the black stupendous seas became more dismally appalling. At time we gasped for breath at an elevation beyond the albatross — at times became dizzy with the velocity of our descent into some watery hell, where the air grew stagnant, and no sound disturbed the slumbers of the kraken.

We were at the bottom of one of these abysses, when a quick scream from my companion broke fearfully upon the night. 'See! see!' cried he, shrieking in my ears, 'Almighty God! see! see!' As he spoke, I became aware of a dull, sullen glare of red light which streamed down the sides of the vast chasm where we lay, and threw a fitful brilliancy upon our deck. Casting my eyes upwards, I beheld a spectacle which froze the current of my blood.

At a terrific height directly above us, and upon the very verge of the precipitous descent, hovered a gigantic ship, of perhaps four thousand tons. Although upreared upon the summit of a wave more than a hundred times her own altitude, her apparent size still exceeded that of any ship of the line or East Indiaman in existence. Her huge hull was of a deep dingy black, unrelieved by any of the customary carvings of a ship. A single row of brass cannon protruded from her open ports, and dashed from their polished surfaces the fires of innumerable battle-lanterns, which swung to and fro about her rigging. But what mainly inspired us with horror and astonishment, was that she bore up under a press of sail in the very teeth of that supernatural sea, and of that ungovernable hurricane. When we first discovered her, her bows were alone to be seen, as she rose slowly from the dim and horrible gulf beyond her. For a moment of intense terror she paused upon the giddy pinnacle, as if in contemplation of her own sublimity, then trembled and tottered, and — came down.

At this instant, I know not what sudden self-possession came over my spirit. Staggering as far aft as I could, I awaited fearlessly the ruin that was to overwhelm. Our own vessel was at length ceasing from her struggles, and sinking with her head to the sea. The shock of the descending mass struck her, consequently, in that portion of her frame which was already under water, and the inevitable result was to hurl me, with irresistible violence, upon the rigging of the stranger.

As I fell, the ship hove in stays, and went about; and to the confusion ensuing I attributed my escape from the notice of the crew. With little difficulty I made my way unperceived to the main hatchway, which was partially open, and soon found an opportunity of secreting myself in the hold. Why I did so I can hardly tell. An indefinite sense of awe, which at first sight of the navigators of the ship had taken hold of my mind, was perhaps the principle of my concealment. I was unwilling to trust myself with a race of people who had offered, to the cursory glance I had taken, so many points of vague novelty, doubt, and apprehension. I therefore thought proper to contrive a hiding-place in the hold. This I did by removing a small portion of the shifting-boards, in such a manner as to afford me a convenient retreat between the huge timbers of the ship.

I had scarcely completed my work, when a footstep in the hold forced me to make use of it. A man passed by my place of concealment with a feeble and unsteady gait. I could not see his face, but had an opportunity of observing his general appearance. There was about it an evidence of great age and infirmity. His knees tottered beneath a load of years, and his entire frame quivered under the burthen. He muttered to himself, in a low broken tone, some words of a language which I could not understand, and groped in a corner among a pile of singular-looking instruments, and decayed charts of navigation. His manner was a wild mixture of the peevishness of second childhood, and the solemn dignity of a God. He at length went on deck, and I saw him no more.

A feeling, for which I have no name, has taken possession of my soul — a sensation which will admit of no analysis, to which the lessons of by-gone times are inadequate, and for which I fear futurity itself will offer me no key. To a mind constituted like my own, the latter consideration is an evil. I shall never — I know that I shall never — be satisfied with regard to the nature of my conceptions. Yet it is not wonderful that these conceptions are indefinite, since they have their origin in sources so utterly novel. A new sense — a new entity is added to my soul.

It is long since I first trod the deck of this terrible ship, and the rays of my destiny are, I think, gathering to a focus. Incomprehensible men! Wrapped up in meditations of a kind which I cannot divine, they pass me by unnoticed. Concealment is utter folly on my part, for the people *will not* see. It was but just now that I passed directly before the eyes of the mate — it was no long while ago that I ventured into the captain's own private cabin, and took thence the materials with which I write, and have written. I shall from time to time continue this journal. It is true that I may not find an opportunity of transmitting it to the world, but I will not fail to make the endeavour. At the last moment I will enclose the MS. in a bottle, and cast it within the sea.

An incident has occurred which has given me new room for meditation. Are such things the operation of ungoverned Chance? I had ventured upon deck and thrown myself down, without attracting any notice, among a pile of ratlin-stuff and old sails, in the bottom of the yawl. While musing upon the singularity of my fate, I unwittingly daubed with a tar-brush the edges of a neatly-folded studding-sail which lay near me on a barrel. The studding-sail is now bent upon the ship, and the thoughtless touches of the brush are spread out into the word DISCOVERY.

I have made many observations lately upon the structure of the vessel. Although well armed, she is not, I think, a ship of war. Her rigging, build, and general equipment, all negative a supposition of this kind. What she *is not*, I can easily perceive — what she *is* I fear it is impossible to say. I know not how it is, but in scrutinizing her strange model and singular cast of spars, her huge size and overgrown suits of canvas, her severely simple bow and antiquated stern, there will occasionally flash across my mind a sensation of familiar things, and there is always mixed up with such indistinct shadows of recollection, an unaccountable memory of old foreign chronicles and ages long ago.

I have been looking at the timbers of the ship. She is built of a material to which I am a stranger. There is a peculiar character about the wood which strikes me as rendering it unfit for the purpose to which it has been applied. I mean its extreme *porousness*, considered independently of the worm-eaten condition which is a consequence of navigation in these seas, and apart from the rottenness attendant upon age. It will appear perhaps an observation somewhat over-curious, but this wood would have every characteristic of Spanish oak, if Spanish oak were distended by any unnatural means.

In reading the above sentence a curious apothegm of an old weather-beaten Dutch navigator comes full upon my recollection. 'It is as sure,' he was wont to say, when any doubt was entertained of his veracity, 'as sure as there is a sea where the ship itself will grow in bulk like the living body of the seaman.'

About an hour ago, I made bold to thrust myself among a group of the crew. They paid me no manner of attention, and, although I stood in the very midst of them all, seemed utterly unconscious of my presence. Like the one I had at first seen in the hold, they all bore about them the marks of a hoary old age. Their knees trembled with infirmity; their shoulders were bent double with decrepitude; their shrivelled skins rattled in the wind; their voices were low, tremulous and broken; their eyes glistened with the rheum of years; and their grey hairs streamed terribly in the tempest. Around them, on every part of the deck, lay scattered mathematical instruments of the most quaint and obsolete construction.

I mentioned some time ago the bending of a studding-sail. From that period the ship, being thrown dead off the wind, has continued her terrific course due south, with every rag of canvas packed upon her, from her trucks to her lower studding-sail booms, and rolling every moment her top-gallant yardarms into the most appalling hell of water which it can enter into the mind of man to imagine. I have just left the deck, where I find it impossible to maintain a footing, although the crew seem to experience little inconvenience. It appears to me a miracle of miracles that our enormous bulk is not swallowed up at once and forever. We are surely doomed to hover continually upon the brink of Eternity, without taking a final plunge into the abyss. From billows a thousand times more stupendous than any I have ever seen, we glide away with the facility of the arrow sea-gull; and the colossal waters rear their heads above us like demons of the deep, but like demons confined to simple threats and forbidden to destroy. I am led to attribute these frequent escapes to the only natural cause which can account for such effect. I must suppose the ship to be within the influence of some strong current, or impetuous under-tow.

I have seen the captain face to face, and in his own cabin — but, as I expected, he paid me no attention. Although in his appearance there is, to a casual observer, nothing which might bespeak him more or less than man — still a feeling of irrepressible reverence and awe mingled with the sensation of wonder with which I regarded him. In stature he is nearly my own height; that is, about five feet eight inches. He is of a well-knit and compact frame of body, neither robust nor remarkably otherwise. But it is the singularity of the expression which reigns upon the face — it is the intense, the wonderful, the thrilling evidence of old age, so utter, so extreme, which excites within my spirit a sense — a sentiment ineffable. His forehead, although little wrinkled, seems to bear upon it the stamp of a myriad of years. His grey hairs are records of the past, and his greyer eyes are Sybils of the future. The cabin floor was thickly strewn with strange, iron-clasped folios, and mouldering instruments of science, and obsolete long-forgotten charts. His head was bowed down upon his hands, and he pored, with a fiery unquiet eye, over a paper which I took to be a commission, and which, at all events, bore the signature of a monarch. He muttered to himself, as did the first seaman whom I saw in the hold, some low peevish syllables of a foreign tongue, and although the speaker was close at my elbow, his voice seemed to reach my ears from the distance of a mile.

The ship and all in it are imbued with the spirit of Eld. The crew glide to and fro like the ghosts of buried centuries; their eyes have an eager and uneasy meaning; and when their fingers fall athwart my path in the wild glare of the battle-lanterns, I feel as I have never felt before, although I have been all my life a dealer in antiquities, and have imbibed the shadows of fallen columns at Balbec, and Tadmor, and Persepolis, until my very soul has become a ruin.

When I look around me I feel ashamed of my former apprehensions. If I trembled at the blast which has hitherto attended us, shall I not stand aghast at a warring of wind and ocean, to convey any idea of which the words tornado and simoom are trivial and ineffective? All in the immediate vicinity of the ship is the blackness of eternal night, and a chaos of foamless water; but, about a league on either side of us, may be seen, indistinctly and at intervals, stupendous ramparts of ice, towering away into the desolate sky, and looking like the walls of the universe.

As I imagined, the ship proves to be in a current; if that appellation can properly be given to a tide which, howling and shrieking by the white ice, thunders on to the southward with a velocity like the headlong dashing of a cataract.

To conceive the horror of my sensations is, I presume, utterly impossible; yet a curiosity to penetrate the mysteries of these awful regions, predominates even over my despair, and will reconcile me to the most hideous aspect of death. It is evident that we are hurrying onwards to some exciting knowledge — some never-to-be imparted secret, whose attainment is destruction. Perhaps this current leads us to the southern pole itself. It must be confessed that a supposition apparently so wild has every probability in its favour.

The crew pace the deck with unquiet and tremulous step; but there is upon their countenances an expression more of the eagerness of hope than of the apathy of despair.

In the meantime the wind is still in our poop, and, as we carry a crowd of canvas, the ship is at times lifted bodily from out the sea — Oh, horror upon horror! the ice opens suddenly to the right, and to the left, and we are whirling dizzily, in immense concentric circles, round and round the borders of a gigantic amphitheatre, the summit of whose walls is lost in the darkness and the distance. But little time will be left me to ponder upon my destiny — the circles rapidly grow small — we are plunging madly within the grasp of the whirlpool — and amid a roaring, and bellowing, and thundering of ocean and of tempest, the ship is quivering, oh God! and — going down.

Note: The 'MS. Found in a Bottle' was originally published in 1831, and it was not until many years afterwards that I became acquainted with the maps of Mercator, in which the ocean is represented as rushing, by four months, into the (northern) Polar Gulf, to be absorbed into the bowels of the earth; the Pole itself being represented by a black rock, towering to a prodigious height. (The Author)

X

The Lagoon

Joseph Conrad

This Polish master of both the English language and of stories of the sea has in this short story instilled his own special brand of magic mixture to bring to life a tale of death and disaster with the adds to the atmosphere of betrayal. Although the conventional Conrad situation, this tale is one that is worth preserving for that very reason, a masterpiece by the master, set in an exotic framework.

The white man, leaning with both arms over the roof of the little house in the stern of the boat, said to the steersman —
'We will pass the night in Arsat's clearing. It is late.'

The Malay only grunted, and went on looking fixedly at the river. The white man rested his chin on his crossed arms and gazed at the wake of the boat. At the end of the straight avenue of forests cut by the intense glitter of the river, the sun appeared unclouded and dazzling, poised low over the water that shone smoothly like a band of metal. The forests, sombre and dull, stood motionless and silent on each side of the broad stream. At the foot of big, towering trees, trunkless nipa palms rose from the mud of the bank, in bunches of leaves enormous and heavy, that hung unstirring over the brown swirl of eddies. In the stillness of the air every tree, every leaf, every bough, every tendril of creeper and every petal of minute blossoms seemed to have been bewitched into an immobility perfect and final. Nothing moved on the river but the eight paddles that rose flashing regularly, dipped together with a single splash; while the steersman swept right and left with a periodic and sudden flourish of his blade describing a glinting semicircle above his head. The churned-up water frothed alongside with a confused murmur. And the white man's canoe, advancing up stream in the short-lived disturbance of its own making, seemed to enter the portals of a land from which the very memory of motion had for ever departed.

The white man, turning his back upon the setting sun, looked along the empty and broad expanse of the sea-reach. For the last three miles of its course the wandering, hesitating river, as if enticed irresistibly by the freedom of an open horizon, flows straight into the sea, flows straight to the east — to the east that harbours both light and darkness. Astern of the boat the repeated call of some bird, a cry discordant and feeble, skipped along over the smooth water and lost itself, before it could reach the other shore, in the breathless silence of the world.

The steersman dug his paddle into the stream, and held hard with stiffened arms, his body thrown forward. The water gurgled aloud; and suddenly the long straight reach seemed to pivot on its centre, the forests swung in a semicircle, and the slanting beams of sunset touched the broadside of the canoe with a fiery glow, throwing the slender and distorted shadows of its crew upon the streaked glitter of the river. The white man turned to look ahead. The course of the boat had been altered at right-angles to the stream, and the carved dragon-head of its prow was pointing now at a gap in the fringing bushes of the bank. It glided through, brushing the overhanging twigs, and disappeared from the river like some slim and amphibious creature leaving the water for its lair in the forests.

The narrow creek was like a ditch: tortuous, fabulously deep; filled with gloom under the thin strip of pure and shining blue of the heaven. Immense trees soared up, invisible behind the festooned draperies of creepers. Here and there, near the glistening blackness of the water, a twisted root of some tall tree showed amongst the tracery of small ferns, black and dull, writhing and motionless, like an arrested snake. The short words of the paddlers reverberated loudly between the thick and sombre walls of vegetation. Darkness oozed out from between the trees, through the tangled maze of the creepers, from behind the great fantastic and unstirring leaves; the darkness, mysterious and invincible; the darkness scented and poisonous of impenetrable forests.

The men poled in the shoaling water. The creek broad-
ened, opening out into a wide sweep of a stagnant lagoon.
The forests receded from the marshy bank, leaving a level
strip of bright green, reedy grass to frame the reflected
blueness of the sky. A fleecy pink cloud drifted high above,
trailing the delicate colouring of its image under the floating
leaves and the silvery blossoms of the lotus. A little house,
perched on high piles, appeared black in the distance. Near it,
two tall nibong palms, that seemed to have come out of the
forests in the background, leaned slightly over the ragged
roof, with a suggestion of sad tenderness and care in the
droop of their leafy and soaring heads.

The steersman, pointing with his paddle, said, 'Arsat is
there. I see his canoe fast between the piles.'

The polers ran along the sides of the boat glancing over
their shoulders at the end of the day's journey. They would
have preferred to spend the night somewhere else than on
this lagoon of weird aspect and ghostly reputation. Moreover,
they disliked Arsat, first as a stranger, and also because he
who repairs a ruined house, and dwells in it, proclaims that
he is not afraid to live amongst the spirits that haunt the
places abandoned by mankind. Such a man can disturb the
course of fate by glances or words; while his familiar ghosts
are not easy to propitiate by wayfarers upon whom they long
to wreak the malice of their human master. White men care
not for such things, being unbelievers and in league with the
Father of Evil, who leads them unharmed through the
invisible dangers of this world. To the warnings of the
righteous they oppose an offensive pretence of disbelief.
What is there to be done?

So they thought, throwing their weight on the end of their
long poles. The big canoe glided on swiftly, noiselessly, and
smoothly, towards Arsat's clearing, till, in a great rattling of
poles thrown down, and the loud murmurs of 'Allah be
praised!' it came with a gentle knock against the crooked
piles below the house.

The boatmen with uplifted faces shouted discordantly,
'Arsat! O Arsat!' Nobody came. The white man began to
climb the rude ladder giving access to the bamboo platform
before the house. The juragan of the boat said sulkily, 'We

will cook in the sampan, and sleep on the water'.

'Pass my blankets and basket,' said the white man curtly. He knelt on the edge of the platform to receive the bundle. Then the boat shoved off, and the white man, standing up, confronted Arsat, who had come out through the low door of his hut. He was a young man, powerful, with a broad chest and muscular arms. He had nothing on but his sarong. His head was bare. His big, soft eyes stared eagerly at the white man, but his voice and demeanour were composed as he asked, without any words of greeting —

'Have you medicine, Tuan?'

'No,' said the visitor in a startled tone. 'No. Why? Is there sickness in the house?'

'Enter and see,' replied Arsat, in the same calm manner, and turning short round, passed again through the small doorway. The white man, dropping his bundles, followed.

In the dim light of the dwelling he made out on a couch of bamboos a woman stretched on her back under a broad sheet of red cotton cloth. She lay still, as if dead; but her big eyes, wide open, glittered in the gloom, staring upwards at the slender rafters, motionless and unseeing. She was in a high fever, and evidently unconscious. Her cheeks were sunk slightly, her lips were partly open, and on the young face there was the ominous and fixed expression — the absorbed, contemplating expression — of the unconscious who are going to die. The two men stood looking at her in silence.

'Has she been long ill?' asked the traveller.

'I have not slept for five nights,' answered the Malay, in a deliberate tone. 'At first she heard voices calling her from the water and struggled against me who held her. But since the sun of today rose she hears nothing — she hears not me. She sees nothing. She sees not me — me!'

He remained silent for a minute, then asked softly —

'Tuan, will she die?'

'I fear so,' said the white man sorrowfully. He had known Arsat years ago, in a far country in times of trouble and danger, when no friendship is to be despised. And since his Malay friend had come unexpectedly to dwell in the hut on the lagoon with a strange woman, he had slept many times there, in his journeys up and down the river. He liked the man who knew how to keep faith in council and how to fight without fear by the side of his white friend. He liked him — not so much perhaps as a man likes his favourite dog — but still he liked him well enough to help and ask no questions, to think sometimes vaguely and hazily in the midst of his own pursuits, about the lonely man and the long-haired woman with audacious face and triumphant eyes, who lived together hidden by the forests — alone and feared.

The white man came out of the hut in time to see the enormous conflagration of sunset put out by the swift and stealthy shadows that, rising like a black and impalpable vapour above the tree-tops, spread over the heaven, extinguishing the crimson glow of floating clouds and the red brilliance of departing daylight. In a few moments all the stars came out above the intense blackness of the earth, and the great lagoon gleaming suddenly with reflected lights resembled an oval patch of night sky flung down in the hopeless and abysmal night of the wilderness. The white man had some supper out of the basket, then collecting a few sticks that lay about the platform, made up a small fire, not for warmth, but for the sake of the smoke, which would keep off the mosquitoes. He wrapped himself in his blankets and sat with his back against the reed wall of the house, smoking thoughtfully.

Arsat came through the doorway with noiseless steps and squatted down by the fire. The white man moved his outstretched legs a little.

'She breathes,' said Arsat in a low voice, anticipating the expected question. 'She breathes and burns as if with a great fire. She speaks not; she hears not — and burns!'

He paused for a moment, then asked in a quiet, incurious tone —

'Tuan . . . will she die?'

The white man moved his shoulders uneasily, and muttered in a hesitating manner — 'If such is her fate.'

'No, Tuan,' said Arsat calmly. 'If such is my fate. I hear, I see, I wait. I remember . . . Tuan, do you remember the old days? Do you remember my brother?'

'Yes,' said the white man. The Malay rose suddenly and went in. The other, sitting still outside, could hear the voice in the hut. Arsat said: 'Hear me! Speak!' His words were succeeded by a complete silence. 'O Diamelen!' he cried suddenly. After that cry there was a deep sigh. Arsat came out and sank down again in his old place.

They sat in silence before the fire. There was no sound within the house, there was no sound near them; but far away on the lagoon they could hear the voices of the boatmen ringing fitful and distinct on the calm water. The fire in the bows of the sampan shone faintly in the distance with a hazy red glow. Then it died out. The voices ceased. The land and the water slept invisible, unstirring and mute. It was as though there had been nothing left in the world but the glitter of stars streaming, ceaseless and vain, through the black stillness of the night.

The white man gazed straight before him into the darkness with wide-open eyes. The fear and fascination, the inspiration and the wonder of death — of death near, unavoidable, and unseen — soothed the unrest of his race and stirred the most indistinct, the most intimate of his thoughts. The ever-ready suspicion of evil, the gnawing suspicion that lurks in our hearts, flowed out into the stillness round him — into the stillness profound and dumb, and made it appear untrustworthy and infamous, like the placid and impenetrable mask of an unjustifiable violence. In that fleeting and powerful disturbance of his being the earth enfolded in the starlight peace became a shadowy country of inhuman strife, a battlefield of phantoms terrible and charming, august or ignoble, struggling ardently for the possession of our helpless hearts. An unquiet and mysterious country of inextinguishable desires and fears.

A plaintive murmur rose in the night; a murmur saddening and startling, as if the great solitudes of surrounding woods had tried to whisper into his ear the wisdom of their immense and ofty indifference. Sounds hesitating and vague floated in the air round him, shaped themselves slowly into words; and at last flowed on gently in murmuring stream of soft and monotonous sentences. He stirred like a man waking up and changed his position slightly. Arsat, motionless and shadowy, sitting with bowed head under the stars, was speaking in a low and dreamy tone —

'. . . For where can we lay down the heaviness of our trouble but in a friend's heart? A man must speak of war and of love. You, Tuan, know what war is, and you have seen me in time of danger seek death as other men seek life! A writing may be lost; a lie may be written; but what the eye has seen is truth and remains in the mind!'

'I remember,' said the white man quietly. Arsat went on with mournful composure —

'Therefore I shall speak to you of love. Speak in the night. Speak before both night and love are gone — and the eyes of day look upon my sorrow and my shame; upon my blackened face; upon my burnt-up heart.'

A sigh, short and faint, marked an almost imperceptible pause, and then his words flowed on, without a stir, without a gesture.

'After the time of trouble and war was over and you went away from my country in the pursuit of your desires, which we, men of the islands, cannot understand, I and my brother became again, as we had been before, the sword-bearers of the Ruler. You know we were men of family, belonging to a ruling race, and more fit than any to carry on our right shoulder the emblem of power. And in the time of prosperity Si Dendring showed us favour, as we, in time of sorrow, had showed to him the faithfulness of our courage. It was a time of peace. A time of deer-hunts and cock-fights; of idle talks and foolish squabbles between men whose bellies are full and weapons are rusty. But the sower watched the young rice-shoots grow up without fear, and the traders came and went, departed lean and returned fat into the river of peace. They brought news, too. Brought lies and truth mixed together, so that no man knew when to rejoice and when to be sorry. We heard from them about you also. They had seen you here and had seen you there. And I was glad to hear, for I remembered the stirring times, and I always remembered you, Tuan, till the time came when my eyes could see nothing in the past, because they had looked upon the one who is dying there — in the house.'

He stopped to exclaim in an intense whisper, 'O Mara bahia! O Calamity!' then went on speaking a little louder.

'There's no worse enemy and no better friend than a

brother, Tuan, for one brother knows another, and in perfect knowledge is strength for good or evil. I loved my brother. I went to him and told him that I could see nothing but one face, hear nothing but one voice. He told me: "Open your heart so that she can see what is in it — and wait. Patience is wisdom. Inchi Midah may die or our Ruler may throw off his fear of a woman!" . . . I waited! . . . You remember the lady with the veiled face, Tuan, and the fear of our Ruler before her cunning and temper. And if she wanted her servant, what could I do? But I fed the hunger of my heart on short glances and stealthy words. I loitered on the path to the bath-houses in the daytime, and when the sun had fallen behind the forest I crept along the jasmine hedges of the women's courtyard. Unseeing, we spoke to one another through the scent of flowers, through the veil of leaves, through the blades of long grass that stood still before our lips; so great was our prudence, so faint was the murmur of our great longing.

'The time passed swiftly . . . and there were whispers amongst women — and our enemies watched — my brother was gloomy, and I began to think of killing and of a fierce death. . . . We are of a people who take what they want — like you whites. There is a time when a man should forget loyalty and respect. Might and authority are given to rulers, but to all men is given love and strength and courage. My brother said, "You shall take her from their midst. We are two who are like one." And I answered, "Let it be soon, for I find no warmth in sunlight that does not shine upon her."

'Our time came when the Ruler and all the great people went to the mouth of the river to fish by torchlight. There were hundreds of boats, and on the white sand, between the water and the forests, dwellings of leaves were built for the households of the Rajahs. The smoke of cooking-fires was like a blue mist of the evening, and many voices rang in it joyfully. While they were making the boats ready to beat up the fish, my brother came to me and said, "Tonight!"

'I looked to my weapons, and when the time came our canoe took its place in the circle of boats carrying the torches. The lights blazed on the water, but behind the boats there was darkness. When the shouting began and the excitement made them like mad, we dropped out. The water swallowed our fire, and we floated back to the shore that was dark with only here and there the glimmer of embers. We could hear the talk of slave-girls amongst the sheds. Then we found a place deserted and silent. We waited there. She came. She came running along the shore, rapid and leaving no trace, like a leaf driven by the wind into the sea. My brother said gloomily, "Go and take her; carry her into our boat." I lifted her in my arms. She panted. Her heart was beating against my breast. I said, "I take you from those people. You came to the cry of my heart, but my arms take you into my boat against the will of the great!" "It is right," said my brother. "We are men who take what we want and can hold it against many. We should have taken her in daylight." I said, "Let us be off"; for since she was in my boat I began to think of our Ruler's many men. "Yes. Let us be off," said my brother. "We are cast out and this boat is our country now — the sea is our refuge."

'He lingered with his foot on the shore, and I entreated him to hasten, for I remembered the strokes of her heart against my breast and thought that two men cannot withstand a hundred. We left, paddling downstream close to the bank; and as we passed by the creek where they were fishing, the great shouting had ceased, but the murmur of voices was loud like the humming of insects flying at noonday. The boats floated, clustered together, in the red light of torches, under a black roof of smoke, and the men talked of their sport. Men that boasted, and praised, and jeered — men that would have been our friends in the morning, but on that night we already were enemies. We paddled swiftly past. We had no more friends in the country of our birth. She sat in the middle of the canoe with covered face; silent as she is now; unseeing as she is now — and I had no regret at what I was leaving because I could hear her breathing close to me — as I can hear her now.'

He paused, listened with his ear turned to the doorway, then shook his head and went on.

'My brother wanted to shout the cry of challenge — one cry only — to let the people know we were freeborn robbers who trusted our arms and the great sea. And again I begged him in the name of our love to be silent. Could I not hear her breathing close to me? I knew the pursuit would come quick enough. My brother loved me. He dipped his paddle without a splash. He only said, "There is half a man in you now — the other half is in that woman. I can wait. When you are a whole man again, you will come back with me here to shout defiance. We are sons of the same mother."

'I made no answer. All my strength and all my spirit were in my hands that held the paddle — for I longed to be with her in a safe place beyond the reach of men's anger and of women's spite. My love was so great, that I thought it could guide me to a country where death was unknown, if I could only escape from Inchi Midah's fury and from our Ruler's sword. We paddled with haste, breathing through our teeth. The blades bit deep into the smooth water. We passed out of the river; we flew in clear channels amongst the shallows. We skirted the black coast; we skirted the sand beaches where the sea speaks in whispers to the land; and the gleam of white sand flashed back past our boat, so swiftly she ran upon the water. We spoke not. Only once I said, "Sleep, Diamelen, for soon you may want all your strength." I heard the sweetness of her voice but I never turned my head.

'The sun rose and still we went on. Water fell from my face like rain from a cloud. We flew in the light and heat. I never looked back, but I knew that my brother's eyes, behind me, were looking steadily ahead, for the boat went as straight as a bushman's dart, when it leaves the end of the sumpitan. There was no better paddler, no better steersman than my brother. Many times, together, we had won races in that canoe. But we never had put out our strength as we did then — then, when for the last time we paddled together! There was no braver or stronger man in our country than my brother. I could not spare the strength to turn my head and look at him, but every moment I heard the hiss of his breath getting louder behind me. Still he did not speak. The sun was high. The heat clung to my back like the flame of fire. My ribs were ready to burst, but I could no longer get enough air into my chest. And then I felt I must cry out with my last breath, "Let us rest!"... "Good!" he answered; and his voice was firm. He was strong. He was brave. He knew not fear and no fatigue.... My brother!'

A murmur powerful and gentle, a murmur vast and faint;
the murmur of trembling leaves, of stirring boughs, ran
through the tangled depths of the forest, ran over the starry
smoothness of the lagoon, and the water between the piles
lapped the slimy timber once with a sudden splash. A breath
of warm air touched the two men's faces and passed on with
a mournful sound — a breath loud and short like an uneasy
sigh of the dreaming earth.

Arsat went on in an even, low voice.

'We ran our canoe on the white beath of a little bay close
to a long tongue of land that seemed to bar our road; a long,
wooded cape going far into the sea. My brother knew that
place. Beyond the cape a river has its entrance, and through
the jungle of that land there is a narrow path. We made a fire
and cooked rice. Then we lay down to sleep on the soft sand
in the shade of our canoe, while she watched. No sooner had
I closed my eyes than I heard her cry of alarm. We leaped up.

'The sun was halfway down the sky already, and coming in
sight in the opening of the bay we saw a prau manned by
many paddlers. We knew it at once: it was one of our Rajah's
praus. They were watching the shore, and saw us. They beat
the gong, and turned the head of the prau into the bay. I felt
my heart become weak within my breast. Diemelen sat on
the sand and covered her face. There was no escape by sea.
My brother laughed. He had the gun you had given him,
Tuan, before you went away, but there was only a handful of
powder. He spoke to me quickly: "Run with her along the
path. I shall keep them back, for they have no firearms, and
landing in the face of a man with a gun is certain death for
some. Run with her. On the other side of that wood there is a
fisherman's house — and a canoe. When I have fired all the
shots, I will follow. I am a great runner, and before they can
come up we shall be gone. I will hold out as long as I can, for
she is but a woman — that can neither run nor fight, but she
has your heart in her hands." He dropped behind the canoe.

'The prau was coming. She and I ran, and as we rushed
along the path I heard shots. My brother fired — once —
twice — and the booming of the gong ceased. There was
silence behind us. That neck of land is narrow. Before I heard
my brother fire the third shot I saw the shelving shore, and I

saw the water again: the mouth of a broad river. We crossed a glassy glade. We ran down to the water. I saw a low hut above the black mud, and a small canoe hauled up. I heard another shot behind me. I thought, "That is his last charge." We rushed down to the canoe; a man came running from the hut, but I leaped on him, and we rolled together in the mud. Then I got up, and he lay still at my feet. I don't know whether I had killed him or not. I and Diamelen pushed the canoe afloat. I heard yells behind me, and I saw my brother run across the glade. Many men were bounding after him. I took her in my arms and threw her into the boat, then leaped in myself. When I looked back I saw that my brother had fallen. He fell and was up again, but the men were closing round him. He shouted, "I am coming!" The men were close to him. I looked. Many men. Then I looked at her. Tuan, I pushed the canoe! I pushed it into the deep water. She was kneeling forward looking at me, and I said, "Take your paddle," while I struck the water with mine. Tuan, I heard him cry. I heard him cry my name twice; and I heard voices shouting, "Kill! Strike!" I never turned back. I heard him calling my name again with a great shriek, as when life is going out together with the voice — and I never turned my head. My own name! ... My brother! Three times he called — but I was not afraid of life. Was she not there in that canoe? And could I not with her find a country where death is forgotten — where death is unknown!'

The white man sat up. Arsat rose and stood, an indistinct and silent figure above the dying embers of the fire. Over the lagoon a mist drifting and low had crept, erasing slowly the glittering images of the stars. And now a great expanse of white vapour covered the land: it flowed cold and grey in the darkness, eddied in noiseless whirls round the tree-trunks and about the platform of the house, which seemed to float upon a restless and impalpable illusion of a sea. Only far away the tops of the trees stood outlined on the twinkle of heaven, like a sombre and forbidding shore — a coast deceptive, pitiless and black.

Arsat's voice vibrated loudly in the profound peace.

'I had her there! I had her! To get her I would have faced all mankind. But I had her — and — '

His words went out ringing into the empty distances. He paused, and seemed to listen to them dying away very far — beyond help and beyond recall. Then he said quietly —

'Tuan, I loved my brother.'

A breath of wind made him shiver. High above his head, high above the silent sea of mist the drooping leaves of the palms rattled together with a mournful and expiring sound. The white man stretched his legs. His chin rested on his chest, and he murmured sadly without lifting his head —

'We all love our brothers.'

Arsat burst out with an intense whispering violence —

'What did I care who died? I wanted peace in my own heart.'

He seemed to hear a stir in the house — listened — then stepped in noiselessly. The white man stood up. A breeze was coming in fitful puffs. The stars shone paler as if they had retreated into the frozen depths of immense space. After a chill gust of wind there were a few seconds of perfect calm and absolute silence. Then from behind the black and wavy line of the forests a column of golden light shot up into the heavens and spread over the semi-circle of the eastern horizon. The sun had risen. The mist lifted, broke into drifting patches, vanished into thin flying wreaths; and the unveiled lagoon lay, polished and black, in the heavy shadows at the foot of the wall of trees. A white eagle rose over it with a slanting and ponderous flight, reached the clear sunshine and appeared dazzlingly brilliant for a moment, then soaring higher, became a dark and motionless speck before it vanished into the blue as if it had left the earth for ever. The white man, standing gazing upwards before the doorway, heard in the hut a confused and broken murmur of distracted words ending with a loud groan. Suddenly Arsat stumbled out with outstretched hands, shivered, and stood still for some time with fixed eyes. Then he said —

'She burns no more.'

Before his face the sun showed its edge upon the tree-tops, rising steadily. The breeze freshened; a great brilliance burst upon the lagoon, sparkled on the rippling water. The forests came out of the clear shadows of the morning, became distinct, as if they had rushed nearer — to stop short in a great stir of leaves, of nodding boughs, of swaying branches. In the merciless sunshire the whisper of unconscious life grew louder, and speaking in an incomprehensible voice round the dumb darkness of that human sorrow. Arsat's eyes wandered slowly, then stared at the rising sun.

'I can see nothing,' he said half aloud to himself.

'There is nothing,' said the white man, moving to the edge of the platform and waving his hand to his boat. A shout came faintly over the lagoon and the sampan began to glide towards the abode of the friend of ghosts.

'If you want to come with me, I will wait all the morning,' said the white man, looking away upon the water.

'No, Tuan,' said Arsat softly. 'I shall not eat or sleep in this house, but I must first see my road. Now I can see nothing — see nothing! There is no light and no peace in the world; but there is death — death for many. We were sons of the same mother — and I left him in the midst of enemies; but I am going back now.'

He drew a long breath and went on in a dreamy tone.

'In a little while I shall see clear enough to strike — to strike. But she has died, and . . . now . . . darkness.'

He flung his arms wide open, let them fall along his body, then stood still with unmoved face and stony eyes, staring at the sun. The white man got down into his canoe. The polers ran smartly along the sides of the boat, looking over their shoulders at the beginning of a weary journey. High in the stern, his head muffled up in white rags, the juragan sat moody, letting his paddle trail in the water. The white man, leaning with both arms over the grass roof of the little cabin, looked back at the shining ripple of the boat's wake. Before the sampan passed out of the lagoon into the creek he lifted his eyes. Arsat had not moved. He stood lonely in the searching sunshine; and he looked beyond the great light of a cloudless day into the darkness of a world of illusions.

XI

In the Abyss

H.G. Wells

That remarkable prophet H.G. Wells, who foresaw the tank, the rise of dictatorships and much, much more, so much more in fact that it led him from supreme confidence in the inventiveness of man, to black despair at his twisted use of everything good, could hardly have guessed that even today, after man has actually landed on the moon, he still knows little more of the deep ocean depths of his own planet than he did when this story was written. Although the grim pylons of the Electricity Boards have conquered and defiled the countryside in a more complete and permanent manner than did Well's Martians in their tripod fighting machines, still the sea beds remain unknown.

Perhaps then the fate of Elstead in this story, a forerunner of the Kraken Awakes, *perhaps, still holds some lessons for us in the depths.*

The lieutenant stood in front of the steel sphere and gnawed a piece of pine splinter. 'What do you think of it, Steevens?' he asked.

'It's an idea,' said Steevens, in the tone of one who keeps an open mind.

'I believe it will smash — flat,' said the lieutenant.

'He seems to have calculated it all out pretty well,' said Steevens, still impartial.

'But think of the pressure,' said the lieutenant. 'At the surface of the water it's fourteen pounds to the inch, thirty feet down it's double that; sixty, treble; ninety, four times; nine hundred, forty times; five thousand, three hundred — that's a mile — it's two hundred and forty times fourteen pounds; that's — let's see — thirty hundredweight — a ton and a half, Steevens; *a ton and a half* to the square inch. And the ocean where he's going is five miles deep. That's seven and a half' —

'Sounds a lot,' said Steevens, 'but it's jolly thick steel.'

The lieutenant made no answer, but resumed his pine splinter. The object of their conversation was a huge ball of steel, having an exterior diameter of perhaps nine feet. It looked like the shot for some Titanic piece of artillery. It was elaborately nested in a monstrous scaffolding built into the framework of the vessel, and the gigantic spars that were presently to sling it overboard gave the stern of the ship an appearance that had raised the curiosity of every decent sailor who had sighted it, from the Pool of London to the Tropic of Capricorn. In two places, one above the other, the steel gave place to a couple of circular windows of enormously thick glass, and one of these, set in a steel frame of great solidity, was now partially unscrewed. Both the men had seen the interior for the first time that morning.

It was elaborately padded with air cushions, with little studs sunk between bulging pillows to work the simple mechanism of the affair. Everything was elaborately padded, even the Myers apparatus which was to absorb carbonic acid and replace the oxygen inspired by its tenant, when he had crept in by the glass manhole, and had been screwed in. It was so elaborately padded that a man might have been fired from a gun in it with perfect safety. And it had need to be, for presently a man was to crawl in through that glass manhole, to be screwed up tightly, and to be flung overboard, and to sink down — down — down, for five miles, even as the lieutenant said. It had taken the strongest hold of his imagination; it made him a bore at mess; and he found Steevens, the new arrival aboard, a godsend to talk to about it, over and over again.

'It's my opinion,' said the lieutenant, 'that that glass will simply bend in and bulge and smash, under a pressure of that sort. Daubrée has made rocks run like water under big pressures — and, you mark my words' —

'If the glass did break in,' said Steevens, 'what then?'

'The water would shoot in like a jet of iron. Have you ever felt a straight jet of high pressure water? It would hit as hard as a bullet. It would simply smash him and flatten him. It would tear down his throat, and into his lungs; it would blow in his ears' —

'What a detailed imagination you have!' protested

Steevens, who saw things vividly.

'It's a simple statement of the inevitable,' said the lieutenant.

'And the globe?'

'Would just give out a few little bubbles, and it would settle down comfortably against the day of judgment, among the oozes and the bottom clay — with poor Elstead spread over his own smashed cushions like butter over bread.'

He repeated this sentence as though he liked it very much. 'Like butter over bread,' he said.

'Having a look at the jigger?' said a voice, and Elstead stood behind them, spick and span in white, with a cigarette between his teeth, and his eyes smiling out of the shadow of his ample hat-brim. 'What's that about bread and butter, Weybridge? Grumbling as usual about the insufficient pay of naval officers? It won't be more than a day now before I start. We are to get the slings ready today. This clean sky and gentle swell is just the kind of thing for swinging off a dozen tons of lead and iron, isn't it?'

'It won't affect you much,' said Weybridge.

'No. Seventy or eighty feet down, and I shall be there in a dozen seconds, there's not a particle moving, though the wind shriek itself hoarse up above, and the water lifts halfway to the clouds. No. Down there' — He moved to the side of the ship and the other two followed him. All three leant forward on their elbows and stared down into the yellow-green water.

'*Peace*,' said Elstead, finishing his thought aloud.

'Are you dead certain that clockwork will act?' asked Weybridge presently.

'It has worked thirty-five times,' said Elstead. 'It's bound to work.'

'But if it doesn't?'

'Why shouldn't it?'

'I wouldn't go down in that confounded thing,' said Weybridge, 'for twenty thousand pounds.'

'Cheerful chap you are,' said Elstead, and spat sociably at a bubble below.

'I don't understand yet how you mean to work the thing,' said Steevens.

'In the first place, I'm screwed into the sphere,' said Elstead, 'and when I've turned the electric light off and on three times to show I'm cheerful, I'm swung out over the stern by that crane, with all those big lead sinkers slung below me. The top lead weight has a roller carrying a hundred fathoms of strong cord rolled up, and that's all that joins the sinkers to the sphere, except the slings that will be cut when the affair is dropped. We use cord rather than wire rope because it's easier to cut and more buoyant — necessary points, as you will see.

'Through each of these lead weights you notice there is a hole, and an iron rod will be run through that and will project six feet on the lower side. If that rod is rammed up from below, it knocks up a lever and sets the clockwork in motion at the side of the cylinder on which the cord winds.

'Very well. The whole affair is lowered gently into the water, and the slings are cut. The sphere floats — with the air in it, it's lighter than water — but the lead weights go down straight and the cord runs out. When the cord is all paid out, the sphere will go down too, pulled down by the cord.'

'But why the cord?' asked Steevens. 'Why not fasten the weights directly to the sphere?'

'Because of the smash down below. The whole affair will go rushing down, mile after mile, at a head-long pace at last. It would be knocked to pieces on the bottom if it wasn't for that cord. But the weights will hit the bottom, and directly they do, the buoyancy of the sphere will come into play. It will go on sinking slower and slower; come to a stop at last, and then begin to float upward again.

'That's where the clockwork comes in. Directly the weights smash against the sea bottom, the rod will be knocked through and will kick up the clockwork, and the cord will be rewound on the reeel. I shall be lugged down to the sea bottom. There I shall stay for half an hour, with the electric light on, looking about me. Then the clockwork will release a spring knife, the cord will be cut, and up I shall rush again, like a soda-water bubble. The cord itself will help the flotation.'

'And if you should chance to hit a ship?' said Weybridge.

'I should come up at such a pace, I should go clean

through it,' said Elstead, 'like a cannon ball. You needn't worry about that.'

'And suppose some nimble crustacean should wriggle into your clockwork' —

'It would be a pressing sort of invitation for me to stop,' said Elstead, turning his back on the water and staring at the sphere.

They had swung Elstead overboard by eleven o'clock. The day was serenely bright and calm, with the horizon lost in haze. The electric glare in the little upper compartment beamed cheerfully three times. Then they let him down slowly to the surface of the water, and a sailor in the stern chains hung ready to cut the tackle that held the lead weights and the sphere together. The globe, which had looked so large on deck, looked the smallest thing conceivable under the stern of the ship. It rolled a little, and its two dark windows, which floated uppermost, seemed like eyes turned up in round wonderment at the people who crowded the rail. A voice wondered how Elstead liked the rolling. 'Are you ready?' sang out the commander. 'Ay, ay, sir!' 'Then let her go!'

The rope of the tackle tightened against the blade and was cut, and an eddy rolled over the globe in a grotesquely helpless fashion. Someone waved a handkerchief, someone else tried an ineffectual cheer, a middy was counting slowly, 'Eight, nine, ten!' Another roll, then with a jerk and a splash the thing righted itself.

It seemed to be stationary for a moment, to grow rapidly smaller, and then the water closed over it, and it became visible, enlarged by refraction and dimmer, below the surface. Before one could count three it had disappeared. There was a flicker of white light far down in the water, that diminished to a speck and vanished. Then there was nothing but a depth of water going down into blackness, through which a shark was swimming.

Then suddenly the screw of the cruiser began to rotate, the water was crickled, the shark disappeared in a wrinkled confusion, and a torrent of foam rushed across the crystalline clearness that had swallowed up Elstead. 'What's the idea?' said one A.B. to another.

'We're going to lay off about a couple of miles, 'fear he should hit us when he comes up,' said his mate.

The ship steamed slowly to her new position. Aboard her almost everyone who was unoccupied remained watching the breathing swell into which the sphere had sunk. For the next half-hour it is doubtful if a word was spoken that did not bear directly or indirectly on Elstead. The December sun was now high in the sky, and the heat very considerable.

'He'll be cold enough down there,' said Weybridge. 'They say that below a certain depth sea water's always just about freezing.'

'Where'll he come up?' asked Steevens. 'I've lost my bearings.'

'That's the spot,' said the commander, who prided himself on his omniscience. He extended a precise finger south-east-ward. 'And this, I reckon, is pretty nearly the moment,' he said. 'He's been thirty-five minutes.'

'How long does it take to reach the bottom of the ocean?' asked Steevens.

'For a depth of five miles, and reckoning — as we did — an acceleration of two feet per second, both ways, is just about three-quarters of a minute.'

'Then he's overdue,' said Weybridge.

'Pretty nearly,' said the commander. 'I suppose it takes a few minutes for that cord of his to wind in.'

'I forgot that,' said Weybridge, evidently relieved.

And then began the suspense. A minute slowly dragged itself out, and no sphere shot out of the water. Another followed, and nothing broke the low oily swell. The sailors explained to one another that little point about the winding-in of the cord. The rigging was dotted with expectant faces. 'Come up, Elstead!' called one hairy-chested salt impatiently, and the others caught it up, and shouted as though they were waiting for the curtain of a theatre to rise.

The commander glanced irritably at them.

'Of course, if the acceleration's less than two,' he said, 'he'll be all the longer. We aren't absolutely certain that was the proper figure. I'm no slavish believer in calculations.'

Steevens agreed concisely. No one spoke for a couple of minutes. Then Steevens' watchcase clicked.

When, twenty-one minutes after, the sun reached the zenith, they were still waiting for the globe to reappear, and not a man aboard had dared to whisper that hope was dead. It was Weybridge who first gave expression to that realisation. He spoke while the sound of eight bells still hung in the air. 'I always distrusted that window,' he said quite suddenly to Steevens.

'Good God!' said Steevens, 'you don't think — ?'

'Well!' said Weybridge, and left the rest to his imagination.

'I'm no great believer in calculations myself,' said the commander dubiously, 'so that I'm not altogether hopeless yet.' And at midnight the gunboat was steaming slowly in a spiral round the spot where the globe had sunk, and the white beam of the electric light fled and halted and swept discontentedly onward again over the waste of phosphorescent waters under the little stars.

'If his window hasn't burst and smashed him,' said Weybridge, 'then it's a cursed sight worse, for his clockwork has gone wrong, and he's alive now, five miles under our feet, down there in the cold and dark, anchored in that little bubble of his, where never a ray of light has shone or a human being lived, since the waters were gathered together. He's there without food, feeling hungry and thirsty and scared, wondering whether he'll starve or stifle. Which will it be? The Myers apparatus is running out, I suppose. How long do they last?'

'Good heavens!' he exclaimed; 'what little things we are! What daring little devils! Down there, miles and miles of water — all water, and all this empty water about us and this sky. Gulfs!' He threw his hands out, and as he did so, a little white streak swept noiselessly up the sky, travelled more slowly, stopped, became a motionless dot, as though a new star had fallen up into the sky. Then it went sliding back again and lost itself amidst the reflections of the stars and the white haze of the sea's phosphorescence.

At the sight he stopped, arm extended and mouth open. He shut his mouth, opened it again, and waved his arms with an impatient gesture. Then he turned, shouted 'El-stead ahoy!' to the first watch, and went at a run to Lindley and the search-light. 'I saw him,' he said. 'Starboard there! His light's on, and he's just shot out of the water. Bring the light round. We ought to see him drifting, when he lifts on the swell.'

But they never picked up the explorer until dawn. Then they almost ran him down. The crane was swung out and a boat's crew hooked the chain to the sphere. When they had shipped the sphere, they unscrewed the manhole and peered into the darkness of the interior (for the electric light chamber was intended to illuminate the water about the sphere, and was shut off entirely from its general cavity).

The air was very hot within the cavity, and the indiarubber at the lip of the manhole was soft. There was no answer to their eager questions and no sound of movement within. Elstead seemed to be lying motionless, crumpled up in the bottom of the globe. The ship's doctor crawled in and lifted him out to the men outside. For a moment or so they did not know whether Elstead was alive or dead. His face, in the yellow light of the ship's lamps, glistened with perspiration. They carried him down to his own cabin.

He was not dead, they found, but in a state of absolute nervous collapse, and besides cruelly bruised. For some days he had to lie perfectly still. It was a week before he could tell his experiences.

Almost his first words were that he was going down again. The sphere would have to be altered, he said, in order to allow him to throw off the cord if need be, and that was all. He had had the most marvellous experience. 'You thought I should find nothing but ooze,' he said. 'You laughed at my explorations, and I've discovered a new world!' He told his story in disconnected fragments, and chiefly from the wrong end, so that it is impossible to re-tell it in his words. But what follows is the narrative of his experience.

It began atrociously, he said. Before the cord ran out, the thing kept rolling over. He felt like a frog in a football. He could see nothing but the crane and the sky overhead, with an occasional glimpse of the people on the ship's rail. He couldn't tell a bit which way the thing would roll next. Suddenly he would find his feet going up, and try to step, and over he went rolling, head over heels, and just anyhow, on the padding. Any other shape would have been more comfortable, but no other shape was to be relied upon under the huge pressure of the nethermost abyss.

Suddenly the swaying ceased; the globe righted, and when he had picked himself up, he saw the water all about him greeny-blue, with an attenuated light filtering down from above, and a shoal of little floating things went rushing up past him, as it seemed to him, towards the light. And even as he looked, it grew darker and darker, until the water above was as dark as the midnight sky, albeit of a greener shade, and the water below black. And little transparent things in the water developed a faint glint of luminosity, and shot past him in faint greenish streaks.

And the feeling of falling! It was just like the start of a lift, he said, only it kept on. One has to imagine what that means, that keeping on. It was then of all times that Elstead repented of his adventure. He saw the chances against him in an altogether new light. He thought of the big cuttle-fish people knew to exist in the middle waters, the kind of things they find half digested in whales at times, or floating dead and rotten and half eaten by fish. Suppose one caught hold and wouldn't let go. And had the clockwork really been sufficiently tested? But whether he wanted to go on or to go back mattered not the slightest now.

In fifty seconds everything was as black as night outside, except where the beam from his light struck through the waters, and picked out every now and then some fish or scrap of sinking matter. They flashed by too fast for him to see what they were. Once he thinks he passed a shark. And then the sphere began to get hot by friction against the water. They had underestimated this, it seems.

The first thing he noticed was that he was perspiring, and then he heard a hissing growing louder under his feet, and saw a lot of little bubbles — very little bubbles they were — rushing upward like a fan through the water outside. Steam! He felt the window, and it was hot. He turned on the minute glow-lamp that lit his own cavity, looked at the padded watch by the studs, and saw he had been travelling now for two minutes. It came into his head that the window would crack through the conflict of temperatures, for he knew the bottom water is very near freezing.

Then suddenly the floor of the sphere seemed to press against his feet, the rush of bubbles outside grew slower and slower, and the hissing diminished. The sphere rolled a little. The window had not cracked, nothing had given, and he knew that the dangers of sinking, at any rate, were over.

In another minute or so he would be on the floor of the abyss. He thought, he said, of Steevens and Weybridge and the rest of them five miles overhead, higher to him than the very highest clouds that ever floated over land are to us, steaming slowly and staring down and wondering what had happened to him.

He peered out of the window. There were no more bubbles now, and the hissing had stopped. Outside there was a heavy blackness — as black as black velvet — except where the electric light pierced the empty water and showed the colour of it — a yellow-green. Then three things like shapes of fire swam into sight, following each other through the water. Whether they were little and near or big and far off he could not tell.

Each was outlined in a bluish light almost as bright as the lights of a fishing smack, a light which seemed to be smoking greatly, and all along the sides of them were specks of this, like the lighter portholes of a ship. Their phosphorescence seemed to go out as they came into the radiance of his lamp, and he saw then that they were little fish of some strange sort, with huge heads, vast eyes, and dwindling bodies and tails. Their eyes were turned towards him, and he judged they were following him down. He supposed they were attracted by his glare.

Presently others of the same sort joined them. As he went on down, he noticed that the water became of a pallid colour, and that little specks twinkled in his ray like motes in a sunbeam. This was probably due to the clouds of ooze and mud that the impact of his leaden sinkers had distrubed.

By the time he was drawn down to the lead weights he was in a dense fog of white that his electric light failed altogether to pierce for more than a few yards, and many minutes elapsed before the hanging sheets of sediment subsided to any extent. Then, lit by his light and by the transient phosphorescence of a distant shoal of fishes, he was able to see under the huge blackness of the super-incumbent water an undulating expanse of greyish-white ooze, broken here and there by tangled thickets of a growth of sea lilies, waving hungrey tentacles in the air.

Farther away were the graceful, translucent outlines of a group of gigantic sponges. About this floor there were scattered a number of bristling flattish tufts of rich purple and black, which he decided must be some sort of sea-urchin, and small, large-eyed or blind things having a curious resemblance, some to woodlice, and others to lobsters, crawled sluggishly across the track of the light and vanished into the obscurity again, leaving furrowed trails behind them.

Then suddenly the hovering swarm of little fishes veered about and came towards him as a flight of starlings might do. They passed over him like a phosphorescent snow, and then he saw behind them some larger creature advancing towards the sphere.

At first he could see it only dimly, a faintly moving figure remotely suggestive of a walking man, and then it came into the spray of light that the lamp shot out. As the glare struck it, it shut its eyes, dazzled. He stared in rigid astonishment.

It was a strange vertebrated animal. Its dark purple head was dimly suggestive of a chameleon, but it had such a high forehead and such a braincase as no reptile ever displayed before; the vertical pitch of its face gave it a most extraordinary resemblance to a human being.

Two large and protruding eyes projected from sockets in chameleon fashion, and it had a broad reptilian mouth with horny lips beneath its little nostrils. In the position of the ears were two huge gill-covers, and out of these floated a branching tree of coralline filaments, almost like the tree-like gills that very young rays and sharks possess.

But the humanity of the face was not the most extraordinary thing about the creature. It was a biped; its almost globular body was poised on a tripod of two frog-like legs and a long thick tail, and its fore limbs, which grotesquely caricatured the human hand, much as a frog's do, carried a long shaft of bone, tipped with copper. The colour of the creature was variegated; its head, hands, and legs were purple; but its skin, which hung loosely upon it, even as clothes might do, was a phosphorescent grey. And it stood there blinded by the light.

At last this unknown creature of the abyss blinked its eyes open, and, shading them with its disengaged hand, opened its mouth and gave vent to a shouting noise, articulate almost as speech might be, that penetrated even the steel case and padded jacket of the sphere. How a shouting may be accomplished without lungs Elstead does not profess to explain. It then moved sideways out of the glare into the mystery of shadow that bordered it on either side, and Elstead felt rather than saw that it was coming towards him. Fancying the light had attracted it, he turned the switch that cut off the current. In another moment something soft dabbed upon the steel, and the globe swayed.

Then the shouting was repeated, and it seemed to him that a distant echo answered it. The dabbing recurred, and the globe swayed and ground against the spindle over which the wire was rolled. He stood in the blackness and peered out into the everlasting night of the abyss. And presently he saw, very faint and remote, other phosphorescent quasi-human forms hurrying towards him.

Hardly knowing what he did, he felt about in his swaying prison for the stud of the exterior electric light, and came by accident against his own small glow-lamp in its padded recess. The sphere twisted, and then threw him down; he heard shouts like shouts of surprise, and when he rose to his feet, he saw two pairs of stalked eyes peering into the lower window and reflecting his light.

In another moment hands were dabbing vigorously at his steel casing, and there was a sound, horrible enough in his position, of the metal protection of the clockwork being vigorously hammered. That, indeed, sent his heart into his mouth, for if these strange creatures succeeded in stopping that, his release would never occur. Scarcely had he thought as much when he felt the sphere sway violently, and the floor of it press hard against his feet. He turned off the small glow-lamp that lit the interior, and sent the ray of the large light in the separate compartment out into the water. The sea-floor and the man-like creatures had disappeared, and a couple of fish chasing each other dropped by the window.

He thought at once that these strange denizens of the deep sea had broken the rope, and that he had escaped. He drove up faster and faster, and then stopped with a jerk that sent him flying against the padded roof of his prison. For half a minute, perhaps, he was too astonished to think.

Then he felt that the sphere was spinning slowly, and rocking, and it seemed to him that it was also being drawn through the water. By crouching close to the window, he managed to make his weight effective and roll that part of the sphere downward, but he could see nothing save the pale ray of his light striking down ineffectively into the darkness. It occurred to him that he would see more if he turned the lamp off, and allowed his eyes to grow accustomed to the profound obscurity.

In this he was wise. After some minutes the velvety blackness became a translucent blackness, and then, far away, and as faint as the zodiacal light of an English summer evening, he saw shapes moving below. He judged these creatures had detached his cable, and were towing him along the sea bottom.

And then he saw something faint and remote across the undulations of the submarine plain, a broad horizon of pale luminosity that extended this way and that way as far as the range of his little window permitted him to see. To this he was being towed, as a balloon might be towed by men out of the open country into a town. He approached it very slowly, and very slowly the dim irradiation was gathered together into more definite shapes.

It was nearly five o'clock before he came over this luminous area, and by that time he could make out an arrangement suggestive of streets and houses grouped about a vast roofless erection that was grotesquely suggestive of a ruined abbey. It was spread out like a map below him. The houses were all roofless enclosures of walls, and their substance being, as he afterwards saw, of phosphorescent bones, gave the place an appearance as if it were built of drowned moonshine.

Among the inner caves of the place waving trees of crinoid stretched their tentacles, and tall, slender, glassy sponges shot like shining minarets and lilies of filmy light out of the general glow of the city. In the open spaces of the place he could see a stirring movement as of crowds of people, but he was too many fathoms above them to distinguish the individuals in those crowds.

Then slowly they pulled him down, and as they did so, the details of the place crept slowly upon his apprehension. He saw that the courses of the cloudy buildings were marked out with beaded lines of round objects, and then he perceived that at several points below him, in broad open spaces, were forms like the encrusted shapes of ships.

Slowly and surely he was drawn down, and the forms below him became brighter, clearer, more distinct. He was being pulled down, he perceived, towards the large building in the centre of the town, and he could catch a glimpse ever and again of the multitudinous forms that were tugging at his cord. He was astonished to see that the rigging of one of the ships, which formed such a prominent feature of the place, was crowded with a host of gesticulating figures regarding him, and then the walls of the great building rose about him silently, and hid the city from his eyes.

And such walls they were, of water-logged wood, and twisted wire-rope, and iron spars, and copper, and the bones and skulls of dead men. The skulls ran in zigzag lines and spirals and fantastic curves over the building; and in and out of their eye-sockets, and over the whole surface of the place, lurked and played a multitude of silver little fishes.

Suddenly his ears were filled with a low shouting and a noise like the violent blowing of horns, and this gave place to a fantastic chant. Down the sphere sank, past the huge pointed windows, through which he saw vaguely a great number of these strange, ghostlike people regarding him, and at last he came to rest, as it seemed, on a kind of altar that stood in the centre of the place.

And now he was at such a level that he could see these strange people of the abyss plainly once more. To his astonishment, he perceived that they were prostrating themselves before him, all save one, dressed as it seemed in a robe of placoid scales, and crowned with a luminous diadem, who stood with his reptilian mouth opening and shutting, as though he led the chanting of the worshippers.

A curious impulse made Elstead turn on his small glow-lamp again, so that he became visible to these creatures of the abyss, albeit the glare made them disappear forthwith into night. At this sudden sight of him, the chanting gave place to a tumult of exultant shouts; and Elstead, being anxious to watch them, turned his light off again, and vanished from before their eyes. But for a time he was too blind to make out what they were doing, and when at last he could distinguish them, they were kneeling again. And thus they continued worshipping him, without rest or intermission, for a space of three hours.

Most circumstantial was Elstead's account of this astounding city and its people, these people of perpetual night, who have never seen sun or moon or stars, green vegetation, nor any living, air-breathing creatures, who know nothing of fire, nor any light but the phosphorescent light of living things.

Startling as is his story, it is yet more startling to find that scientific men, of such eminence as Adams and Jenkins, find nothing incredible in it. They tell me they see no reason why intelligent, water-breathing, vertebrated creatures, inured to a low temperature and enormous pressure, and of such a heavy structure, that neither alive nor dead would they float, might not live upon the bottom of the deep sea, and quite unsuspected by us, descendants like ourselves of the great Theriomorpha of the New Red Sandstone age.

We should be known to them, however, as strange, meteoric creatures, wont to fall catastrophically dead out of the mysterious blackness of their watery sky. And not only we ourselves, but our ships, our metals, our appliances, would come raining down out of the night. Sometimes sinking things would smite down and crush them, as if it were the judgment of some unseen power above, and sometimes would come things of the utmost rarity or utility, or shapes of inspiring suggestion. One can understand, perhaps, something of their behaviour at the descent of a living man, if one thinks what a barbaric people might do, to whom an enhaloed, shining creature came suddenly out of the sky.

At one time or another Elstead probably told the officers of the *Ptarmigan* every detail of his strange twelve hours in the abyss. That he also intended to write them down is certain, but he never did, and so unhappily we have to piece together the discrepant fragments of his story from the reminiscences of Commander Simmons, Weybridge, Steevens, Lindley, and the others.

We see the thing darkly in fragmentary glimpses — the huge ghostly building, the bowing, chanting people, with their dark chameleon-like heads and faintly luminous clothing, and Elstead, with his light turned on again, vainly trying to convey to their minds that the cord by which the sphere was held was to be severed. Minute after minute slipped away, and Elstead, looking at his watch, was horrified to find that he had oxygen only for four hours more. But the chant in his honour kept on as remorselessly as if it was the marching song of his approaching death.

The manner of his release he does not understand, but to judge by the end of cord that hung from the sphere, it had been cut through by rubbing against the edge of the altar. Abruptly the sphere rolled over, and he swept up, out of their world, as an ethereal creature clothed in a vacuum would sweep through our own atmosphere back to its native ether again. He must have torn out of their sight as a hydrogen bubble hastens upward from our air. A strange ascension it must have seemed to them.

The sphere rushed up with even greater velocity than, when weighted with the lead sinkers, it had rushed down. It became exceedingly hot. It drove up with the windows uppermost, and he remembers the torrent of bubbles frothing against the glass. Every moment he expected this to fly. Then suddenly something like a huge wheel seemed to be released in his head, the padded compartment began spinning about him, and he fainted. His next recollection was of his cabin, and of the doctor's voice.

But that is the substance of the extraordinary story that Elstead related in fragments to the officers of the *Ptarmigan*. He promised to write it all down at a later date. His mind was chiefly occupied with the improvement of his apparatus, which was effected at Rio.

It remains only to tell that on February 2, 1896, he made his second descent into the ocean abyss, with the improvements his first experience suggested. What happened we shall probably never know. He never returned. The *Ptarmigan* beat about over the point of his submersion, seeking him in vain for thirteen days. Then she returned to Rio, and the news was telegraphed to his friends. So the matter remains for the present. But it is hardly probable that no further attempt will be made to verify his strange story of these hitherto unsuspected cities of the deep sea.

XII

Mrs Scarr

Elinor Mordaunt

Women and the sea do not mix. An old adage this, which would be vehemently disputed today but one which, in the superstitious world of the seaman, still is held as very valid. Although of course women have proven to everyone's satisfaction that they are as at home on the seas as any man, those who read this cautionary tale, written by a woman let me hasten to add, will see why many an old salt would uphold this saying today, no matter what.

There was only one thing in heaven or earth that Captain John Scarr cared for, and that was his wife. He feared nothing and nobody besides. For he both feared and reverenced her. Not with that fear that a blustering woman may instil into a man as the result of a mere craving for peace, but the fear of a stronger personality, a something exquisite and pure beyond the comprehension of his coarsened mind. The fear which dogs an elderly man — who through many experiences in which he had picked away all the fineness and restraint from his victims, as a vulture picks the flesh from the bones of its prey, and reaching the common brute, grown to believe that he had fathomed the entire feminine sex — when he at last encounters a woman of whose heart and body he is for the first time absolutely sure, and yet realizes that there is some elusive quality in her that he has never touched — something subtle and intangible as a perfume, a mist.

For years Scarr had been mate of a Yankee Hell-ship trading from San Francisco, round by the Horn to New York, with one of the shanghaied crews which are usually all that can be picked up on the west coast of America, and probably the experience had brutalized him. For brutal he certainly was, with the hard, swaggering brutality of a handsome animal, possessing nerves of iron and absolutely no conscience of any sort. /

Leaving the American trade, he had run between Spain and the Philippines; then knocked about the China Sea for a time; got himself into trouble over some affair of opium-running in Sydney, in which his character suffered only with the more scrupulous owners, and his pockets not at all. Lastly, at the time of which I write he was part-owner and captain of a cattle boat which ran between the Island and Madagascar, an old South Sea whaler, of which the best part of the deck — flush fore and aft — had been built up with wooden stalls for the cattle, wild-eyed, hump-backed creatures, which were as lean and tough as Scarr himself by the time they reached the Island.

Scarr and his wife had made their home in Tamatave. The houses there are two-storeyed, with balconies all round them; the unpaved streets are deep to the knees in sand; the shops — with no frontage — run far back into a dim mystery of dirt and disorder and stench. You may shop by your nose in Tamatave; while there is no knowing what you will buy in your keg of salt butter or barrel of herrings — things get so easily mixed, and there are always flies and cockroaches, and sickly-white lizards that drop from the beams into whatever stands beneath them.

All day blinds of split bamboo are down round the houses. But in the evening they are drawn up, and the women come out and sit in the upper verandas. They do not walk in the streets because of the sand and the sandflies — which will distort the prettiest foot into a shapeless mass within an hour; but as they are for the most part half-caste women, they have no taste for exercise.

They all wear black — nothing else. Black unrelieved by any touch of white, save for the rice-powder with which they coat their faces; only some — and those are the ones who lean their bare arms along the rail and smile down into the street below, ogling any new men who may plough their way up the sandy streets from their ships — stick a crimson hybiscus-blossom behind one ear. But the men of the town, the French soldiers and clerks and Government officials, go out each evening to the end of the tiny pier, and with white faces and eyes that are bright — not only with fever but with the intolerable nostalgia for home that only a Frenchman knows — gaze out over the sea, smoke innumerable cigarettes and sniff up the wash of steamy vapour which passes between Tamatave and the Island, and is all the coast-dwellers know of fresh air.

People in Madagascar count the hours of the day by events. Towards the evening there is the 'sun-flush', then 'sun-dead'; then 'fowls come in', 'edge of cooking-pen obscured', 'people begin to cook rice', 'people eat rice', 'finish eating', 'go to bed', 'everyone asleep', 'the gunfire', 'midnight'.

At the time of which I write it was Samámbisámby — dusk or twilight — and the last lighter was being unloaded at the side of the *Mary Anna*, Scarr's ship that lay in the bay.

The main deck was a billowing, surging mass of perspiring, blaspheming men and terrified cattle; the engines were being started, and out of the guts of the hideous abortion that called herself a ship were pouring clouds of thick yellowish smoke too heavy to rise higher than the tops of the funnels; while the anchor was being catted, and the first mate — a half-caste Malagasy — was up on the bridge, signalling furiously to the two men in the gig, which was hanging against the pier-side, to go up to town and see what the something-something could have become of the Captain.

Scarr and his wife rented the upper storey of a house, the lower part of which was used as a store, and they were sitting now either side of the table at which they had just finished eating their supper.

Mrs. Scarr called herself French, and it was certainly true that her father had been a French officer. So had her maternal grandfather — and that's as far back as one need go in Madagascar. Anyhow, she was as fair as any white woman, fairer than many, with a clear, fine skin the colour of an almond, glossy, blue-black hair, and — a noticeable fact in that land of anaemic whites — brilliantly red, full lips. She was very small, very slender, very quiet; she never raised her voice, and she but seldom raised her eyes, but when she did so one realized that one had not even begun to know anything about women.

Another peculiarity — apart from her red lips — which distinguished Mrs. Scarr was that she always dressed in white. She had been born on a Saturday, and it is well known that — according to the belief of the Malagasy — the 'Sanandro' of all such people is white. But that does not explain why, when Mrs. Scarr was not a native, she should comply with native superstitions; unless she simply regarded white as being the most becoming wear, in such the same fashion as was the native 'lamba', or mantle, in which she so often enfolded herself, a garment of infinite, subtle possibilities.

All the true Malagasy people, men and women alike, wear the lamba, women of ill-repute covering their faces with it as they walk through the streets — like the harlots of whom it is spoken in the Book of Genesis — for the Malagasy is of Arabian origin, his signs of the Zodiac and many of his beliefs being almost precisely similar. No half-castes, however, will be seen in a lamba, for fear of being taken for people of pure blood, which is curious; while the fact that Mrs. Scarr wore it constantly was perhaps more proof than anything else of her assertions that her people were entirely French, though it was an undoubted fact that she had been born in the Island.

Only there were things. She had learnt less and knew more than most European women. Then she wore her lamba with such an air — nay, more, an expression! Sometimes tightly folded round her, showing every curve of her delicate form. Sometimes flying like wings at either side of her. Then again — and this is the crowning peculiarity of all — she was not frightened of the outside world as were the half-castes or few travelling French-women. She was at one with the country, so much so that she did what few of the natives ever ventured upon — she went out alone at night. Not in a filánjana, or carrying-chair, or at twilight; but alone at the 'tapi-mandry ólona', or 'everyone-in-bed' time, which was very suspicious.

Some said that she was so white because she had drunk of milk in which there were ghosts. Others — and this was a graver accusation — that she was actually an Angalápona; going down into the water at night — unwetted by the element through which she passed — to her secret cave, whose door opened and shut at her voice. As everyone knows, an Angalápona is small as a child, with very long hair; for it is thus that the diviners call upon it when working their oracle, saying: 'Arise, for thou hast come from the long-haired one!'

Now, Mrs. Scarr scarcely reached to Scarr's heart, and — as her maid could bear witness — her hair, when it was loosed from its coils, hung to below her knees. She was not an Angalápòna, however, though she knew what the native people said of her, and took a sort of mischievous pleasure in encouraging their beliefs. She was simply one of those people whose souls are bigger than their bodies, who need quiet and wide, open spaces as others need air. And in this she was right. For in silent, lonely places is to be found the ultimate testing of souls. I would never register a friendship until I knew my friend away from cities, companionship, and artificial light. The cowardly, the brutal, the false, fear loneliness, darkness and silence more than they fear the devil himself, while their souls are in their stomachs and by no means separable from their bodies.

Now in Tamatave, despite the depth of the sandy streets, there is no peace or quietness; for people talk loudly as if quarrelling, and pedlars and street-sellers cry their wares. Besides, during the daytime — when it is really too hot to be out of doors at all — Mrs. Scarr was a busy little housekeeper, sober-minded and practical, a creature adapted to the beads of four walls. The explanation was very simple; and yet, as I said, there were things and women must not dare to trespass outside of the ordinary.

At night it seemed to her as, wending her way through the low scrub and mysterious windings of the baynian-trees, she reached the seashore, and seated herself on the hard white sand, that here was her real self — an intimate, delightful thing of fairy fancies, quite untrammelled, capable of any flights. She would pretend — and this at first in a spirit of purest fancy — to call to her soul; to take it — always, as she seemed to see it, in the form of a velvety white moth — between her finger and thumb; to hold it aloft, poised for a moment with an airy gesture; then, with a flick of her hand, a puff of her breath, release it, let it go where it would; usually, so curiously are women constituted, to Scarr — Scarr, awake and recklessly dissipated, or drunk, or asleep. For, oddly enough, she loved her husband as much as he loved her, only in a different way.

A lamp, with two branching flames, stood on the table where Scarr and his wife sat, and across which she leant, with his great hands laid between her small white ones, while she looked in his face, her head still a little bent, her eyes raised.

'I hold you,' she said, with the passionate certainty that acknowledges doubt — for of late mischief-makers had been busy in the Island, and scraps of gossip had drifted across to her, in what was written, or even more significant, what was left unwritten: 'I hold you all, and why should I let you go? Leave a little bit of yourself behind. I am sad tonight because Anna told me my Vitana, and said it was ordained that I should die first. John' — she laughed, though her lips trembled and her eyes filled with sudden tears — 'if that should happen, and you ever belong to any other woman, I shall come back and haunt you.'

Scarr laughed loudly and awkwardly. He had belonged to many other women, though, as he said, she was the only one that he ever cared a twopenny damn about. After all, what the eye does not see the heart does not grieve over, and a man is not a milk-and-water saint. Still, he did not care to meet his wife's clear gaze, and, moving uneasily, loosed his hands and made a snatch at a white moth which just at that moment fluttered across the table between them.

'That confounded thing again!'

'Why do you say "again"? I have not seen it before.'

Mrs. Scarr's lips were parted; it seemed as if her life might be hanging on a sudden hope, an unrealized possibility. How her whole being had yearned to him at that moment, longing to follow; and here —

'Of course it's not the same,' and Scarr laughed uneasily. 'But I seem to be haunted by the damned things. In the Island it is the same. A wo—— someone I knew said they must take me for a bloomin' lamp — and always one at a time, that's the odd thing about it. Look, there it is again.' And springing to his feet, he made another scooping dash with his hands. But Mrs. Scarr, whiter than ever by now, had risen too, and, leaning over the table, caught at his great wrists.

'Don't, John — oh, John, don't!' Her voice had risen almost to a shriek; then, as the frail creature fluttered away in safety, she, too, laughed and dropped her voice to its usual low tones. 'Don't ever kill a white moth, dear love. I have a sort of superstition about them. It might be me — you don't know.

Look' — and, laughing again, she spread her lamba wing-like on either side of her — 'look, and remember that the white moth is my emblem. You know the Tangéna — ah, no, you have not lived here as long as I have, but by the Tangéna ordeal you may kill an insect, bird, or animal, and kill at the same time the human being to whom it belongs. Remember this, husband mine: the white moth is fàrdy — forbidden to you. It is my soul.'

'Leave your soul alone. What possesses you to be always muddling about with that silly native rot?'

Scarr's voice was sharp with irritation as he picked up his cap and pulled on his coat.

'No man on God's earth cares a damn about a woman's soul; there's enough for him without that.' He laughed again, and, taking her by the shoulders, shook her gently; she was such a little thing, so fine and sweet, so altogether his. 'Look here, kid, what you've got to do is to eat and drink a little more, and get a little more flesh on your bones; then you'll forget all this twaddle, and I shall have a real wife to hold in my arms in place of this piece of cotton-down.' And he lifted her, one big hand at either side of her waist, held her up like a doll for a minute, kissed her soundly then set her on her feet again.

'There's that whistle again! I must be going; they were getting up steam an hour ago, and there'll be a hell of a lot to see to. They're born muddlers, the lot of them. So long, old girl'; and he flung his arms round her, kissed her again and swung out of the room, clattering down the wooden stairs while Mrs. Scarr slipped to the veranda, and from the shelter of one of the posts watched the tall figure vanish into the dusky vista which led to the pier.

Re-entering the room, she turned out the lamp, and sat silent, with her hands folded in her lap, thinking. Then, as the darkness thickened to an impenetrable wall of velvety blackness, she closed the shutters, folded her lamba round her, and slipped out of the house.

Reaching the shore, Mrs. Scarr sat down on the sand, still wet and hard from the outgoing tide. The town was quite hidden by a jutting neck of land, while at the back of her lay thick trees and a rising mass of undulating country, and in front the sea — pure silver in the moonlight — and the narrow strip of wet sand, its smoothness unbroken save by a small round object which lay just at her feet, and which, as she leaned forward and picked it up, she found to be the perfect shell of a sea-urchin, delicately tinted, fine as porcelain, and empty.

The woman turned it round and round in her hands and looked at it, a wise, sad smile growing on her face. Then, placing it gently on the sand at her side, and clasping her arms round her knees, she drew a long, deep breath.

Gradually it seemed, as she drew herself in upon herself, that all material surrounding things vanished; that the moonlight was spun into a shimmering crystal bowl upturned above her; that then, as a rose unfolds, petal by petal, her body unfolded; turning back tissue upon tissue, till her soul, the source of her life, lay bare. And she put out her hand — the left hand, all of her that remained tangibly the same — and taking this vital thing between her finger and thumb, held it aloft, a palpitating creature of velvety whiteness.

And, lastly, the hand, having done its work, folded back with the other discarded petals of the body, while, spreading its wings, a white moth fluttered forth across the moonlight with the wash of the outgoing tide — Island-wards.

At dawn, trembling with utter weariness, and yet with a glory of fulfilment transfiguring her white face, Mrs. Scarr let herself into her house. And an hour later, when her maid came across from her *cas*, prepared the coffee and took it up to her mistress, she found her curled up in bed, sleeping like a wearied child, one hand curled up under her chin, and a pile of dew-drenched garments on the floor at the bedside.

The *Mary Anna* lay up against the quay of St. Julian. The cattle were gone, and with them the plague of flies. But she was loading up with sugar now, and the sugar had brought the cockroaches, swarming over everything, heaping to the brim any glass in which a few drops of liquor or sweet wine had been left overnight; to add to which, the heat was so intense that the pitch in the deck seams fairly boiled, while the paint on the bulwarks rose in simmering blisters, and it may be well imagined that the *Mary Anna* — lying tucked under the smells of St. Julian as under a frowzy blanket — was not the pleasantest spot on earth, and that Scarr was glad to be away out of it, up in the hills, as soon as ever the day's work was over. As long as there had been any light to see by, however, Scarr had stuck to his ship, for a part-owner makes a conscientious captain — or slavedriver — it all depends from whose point of view you look at it.

It had been a bad day, however. The crew, storing away bags of sugar in the hold, had smuggled down a keg of arrack with them, and there had been several in irons, mad-drunk, and several more incapacitated by knife-wounds; whilst the first mate, who was keeping tally, had his arm broken by a badly slung bag. All this in addition to the heat, which is quite enough in itself. It was no wonder that Scarr had a thirst on him that you could have cut with a knife by the time that he stepped out of the little train into the scented twilight of Bellair, and made for Affan-Wen's shop.

It was the usual Chinaman's shop, littered with a medley of salt fish, fly-spotted raw meat, withered vegetables, herbs, medicines, silks, and pots and pans of all sorts, indiscriminately mixed; while Affan-Wen was the usual Chinese shopkeeper — indifferent and aloof, mysterious as the country which had bred him.

But passing through a little door at the back and along a narrow, dark passage, one passed also into another world. A large room, with several smaller ones opening into it; a table in one corner, at which sat, or stood, a group of Celestials, playing fan-tan under the direction of two seraphic-looking croupiers in heavenly blue, the whole crew hanging like one over the small greenish-white counters; while upon a raised platform, others — Chinese, Europeans, and half-castes — lounged upon couches covered with Manchester saddle-bags, either smoking opium with a feverish longing for the dream-world it evokes, or sleeping with open mouths, and eyes that showed a ghastly thread of white between the lids.

The main floor of the room, however, and the other little tables — at which people played cards or drank — was occupied by quite a different species of humanity: Frenchmen, young Government clerks for the most part, hysterical with a delirium of joy; half-castes of every shade, silent and watchful; an English planter or two, haggard with fever or dissipation; a distorted cripple with stumps in the place of arms, and a face that looked as if it were overgrown with blue mould: the captain of another tramp, who nodded to Scarr as he entered — and women!

One Englishwoman, gross beyond any words — known in Aden, known in Bombay, tolerated only in the Island — sat with her arm round the neck of a French boy of eighteen; and there were half-caste women of all grades, some almost pure negress, others as nearly pure French; some in the sombre black draperies of the creole women, their faces livid with rice-powder; others with evening dresses half slipping off their voluptuous shoulders.

For once Scarr was in no mood for feminine amenities. He noticed nobody except his fellow-captain as he came in, and, sitting down heavily at a small corner table, ordered rum from Affan's obsequious aide; literally kicking aside a girl who came sidling up to him, and scowling savagely upon the rest.

'*Le pauvre peti*' Scarr, he is thirsty *comme les esprits dans enfer!*' laughed the woman to whom the other had run whimpering. 'Wait a little — *un peti' moment*, and he will once more be the Scarr we all love.' And she patted her friend consolingly on the shoulder.

Scarr was possessed of a pair of brilliant blue eyes, quite undimmed by the life which he had led, fringed with thick black lashes, and set under straight black brows. But on this particular evening, when he had first entered the room, brightly illuminated with hanging kerosene lamps, they had been light in colour, the pupils contracted to a pin-point. As he sat staring in front of him, however, and drinking the green rum which he had ordered, the pupils expanded, rimmed with brilliant sapphire, and the colour rose to his face.

Half-defiantly the girl — Rose — who had been watching him from beneath lowered lids, as a cat watches a mouse, got up and swished her scarlet silk shirts across the floor just in front of him; pretending to look the other way, smiling archly and significantly at a man in the opposite corner.

Scarr laughed, and again stretched out his foot, but this time only to bar her progress, while he caught her by her bare arm.

'Hulloo, youngster! Sulking, eh?'

'You are not nice, Meester Scarr; you do not love me any more. I am not used to being treated save as a lady.' And she pouted, at the same time allowing herself to be drawn upon his knee and roughly caressed.

The next moment, however, Scarr had pushed her aside, and risen to his feet. 'What's the matter with you all tonight? You all seem half dead-and-alive. Strike me silly! but you're enough to give a fellow the pip! Here, Barratt!' — and he beckoned to his fellow-captain — 'come over here and let's get up a game of poker. And you, La Fèvre; and you — what's your name? — you, Johnny, with a wall-eye. That's right — eh, what? All right, Rose; you can sit on my knee; only, mind, no hands in my pockets, or you'll get hell. Now, you cut, Barratt. Wait a jiffy, though — Jaldi, you boy there, bring us some more drinks before we start; make haste, now; get a move on you!'

Scarr's luck was out, as it had been all day; he lost steadily, he drank as steadily, and his pockets were nearly emptied of loose change, when he felt Rose — who had curled up like a cat on his knees, and appeared to have dropped asleep — slip one hand into his inner breast-pocket, where lay a wad of rupee-notes.

'No, you don't!' His voice was a snarl, scarcely raised, as he caught her hand through his coat and held it there. The girl laughed; she was very pretty, and she had grown used to having men take all her depredations merely as artful tricks.

'La-la! That's enough; let me go, Scarr. I was only playing. Nom de peti' Bonhomme, drop it! Do you hear? You hurt me! Clare! — Bella! You devil! Stop him! Stop him, I say!' And she shrieked, for Scarr had deliberately taken the cigar from his mouth and pressed the burning edge against the bare flesh of her wrist, passing it round so that she was burnt in the form of a bracelet.

'Stop him, stop him, you curs! Do you hear? My God! he'll kill me!' And she screamed again.

But the men only laughed — all save the French boy, who made an ineffectual attempt to escape from the Englishwoman, fallen asleep now with her arm round his neck, and so come to the rescue; while the other women gathered together, screaming. But only as Scarr shifted his grasp, declaring that he would give her a necklace also, did the girl drag herself free, and, taking refuge among the others of her own sex, break out into a torrent of wild sobs and imprecations.

Scarr took up his cards again, and leant forward across the table, challenging the other men with his hard stare.

'Now then, it's my deal; come on!' And he commenced to play out the cards. Then, as the others hung back, and a sulky undercurrent of growls sounded from among the half-castes, broken only by Rose's gulping sobs, his hand slid into his hip-pocket.

'Play, you devils — play — or, by God, you'll be in hell before you can say Jack-knife! What?' And he raised his revolver to his line of vision. 'You won't, won't you?'

His finger was actually on the trigger — for the three other men, the two creoles stupid with drink, and the English captain laughing in reckless defiance, had made no effort to pick up their cards — when a large white moth fluttered between Scarr's hand and eyes, almost touching his face.

'Damn that thing! Where did that come from? What the — '

'It's been here all the evening,' put in a voice from among the women.

'It's your familiar, Capitaine. I saw Rose whisk it away with her handkerchief,' cried another.

With a visible effort and hunching movement of his great shoulders, Scarr pulled himself together.

'Play, do you hear! Play!'

'There's nothing to play for; I guess we've pretty well cleaned you out this trip, Scarr.' And Barratt laughed.

With an oath, Scarr pulled out the wad of notes from his pocket — his share of the profits on the last cargo of cattle — and flung them upon the table.

'Now will you play? Eh, you white-livered curs — will you play now? Play or rot, eh? Take your chance, once and for all.'

'Scarr, you're a devil! I believe you'd gamble away anything in heaven or earth — your own wife, for the matter of that.'

'*Et qui ci ca?*' interposed a mocking voice from the knot of women; while one, separating herself from the rest, stole forward, and, leaning her arm on Scarr's shoulder, gazed hungrily at the notes.

Scarr laughed — a mad laugh ugly to hear. 'The notes first — then we'll play for wives, eh, Barratt? I don't know what yours is like, but mine's a white-faced — There, there it is again! I won't have it! I tell you, I won't have it!' And his voice rose to a bellow, as once more the white moth fluttered in front of him, and then hovered; returned again as he brushed it aside, and yet again; till, maddened by the insistence of the creature and the loud laughter of the people around him, Scarr darted out his curved hand and caught it in his palm, staggered, rocking, to his feet, and, opening his hand, laid it flat, knuckles downward, on the table.

'Good God!' Oddly enough, the laughter ceased, and a sudden silence fell over the room at Scarr's exclamation; while the crowd, extraordinarily sensitive, as are all such degenerate creatures to any phase of the emotions, fathered round him, staring at his livid face, then at the crushed white moth he held in his palm, upon which his gaze was fixed in a sort of stony horror.

Suddenly someone laughed — it was Rose — a high-pitched, malicious laugh, at the sound of which Scarr lifted his face for a moment, stared round upon them all with a look which made the women cross themselves, and then, capless as he was, with his hand closed gently round the dead moth, turned and stalked out of the room.

Rose spat. 'Ach! the devils go with you! For me — Martin! *mais je me fou de vous!*'

A fortnight later, the *Mary Anna* once again swung heavily into the bay outside Tamatave. In the savage silence which had characterized him through the entire voyage Scarr went through the necessary formalities with the Health and Customs officers; who, in their turn, glanced at him askance, moistening their lips with their tongues, half-opening their mouths as if to say something, and then, after another glance at the captain's face, falling silent over all save business matters.

As soon as possible Scarr ordered the gig to be lowered, and was rowed to the pier. There had been some talk among the sailors and the men on the Customs boat, and they eyed him now much as the others had done, though they volunteered no remark and Scarr asked no questions.

It was the same when the pier was reached, and passing up the sandy street. Men nodded to him with averted eyes; then, when he had passed, turned round and stared after him.

The blinds were still down all round the house above the

store — though by now it was the 'miditra-akòko', the 'fowls-come-in' time — while even the door was shut; and it was only after long knocking that Scarr heard the creole servant clattering, with her loose-heeled slippers, down the wooden stairs; and the bolts were drawn, the door opened a crack.

'Ah, ben! It is you, Captain — it is you; ah, well!' And the little old creature, flinging the door wide, leant forward on the step, and peered up at him in the thickening gloom. 'Ah, ben! — you have heard?'

'I have heard nothing,' said Scarr. Even since that night at Affan-Wen's his heart had felt like an open wound; but at the old woman's words it seemed as if an ice-cold hand had clutched it, squeezing it hard in the grip of certainty.

'I have heard nothing.'

'But you know, all the same. I told her she would be first; it was her Vitana; no one can go against that. It was on the night of Alarobia (Wednesday), two weeks back. When I came in the morning, she was not here. I searched for her all day, and could not find her, and towards evening I made a 'Sikidy', and cast a spell by my *cas*, the North and the South being the ends, and the East and the West being the sides, and the twelve months with the twelve points of the compass — four at either end, and two by the door, and two by the window. It was a good "Sikidy".' The old woman spoke with pride. 'For I found her.'

'I will go indoors and sit down,' said Scarr. And climbing the steep stairs heavily, he sat himself at the table where he and his wife had supped the night before the last voyage, and signed to the old woman to continue.

'She was on the seashore to the South, laid just above the water–line. There was neither mark nor stratch upon her. But when I went to raise her, knowing that she was dead, lo! both her arms were broken. And I called for men and we carried her home; and I washed her and combed her long black hair, and we buried her that day. The Vitana of her soul was too strong for her, O Captain! For, behold, it broke both her arms before it left her. She was a child of Asabòtsy (Saturday); I know — I — for I nursed her at my heart from her birth upwards. And to the children of Saturday is youth and whiteness. It was her Vitana; she could not have lived to an old age.'

Scarr's elbows were on the table, his hands clasped, his chin resting upon them, while he gazed in front of him with unseeing eyes. The old crone stared at him doubtfully. She had never liked him, but it troubled her to see one of the dominant sex so broken — of a sudden, like an old, old man — and after the manner of her kind she essayed to comfort him.

'Even now, O Captain, I have been out to turn her in her grave, that she may not weary with long lying on one side. She is at rest. And are there not other women yet in the world?'

'Of a sort,' said Scarr.

XIII

The Voice in the Night

William Hope Hodgson

One of the most tragic losses to the ranks of the great writers of fantasy was the death, during the Great War, of William Hope Hodgson. His published works were few and he has been sadly neglected since his demise but there is a growing realisation of his great depth of imagination today that is bringing his work back into favour. His classic novel, The House of the Borderland, *pre-empts some aspects of* 2001 *by over fifty years while the brooding nightmare landscape he created in* The Night Lands *is chilling and unforgettable. A seaman for many years, this yarn gives some indication of his worth, and our loss.*

It was a dark, starless night. We were becalmed in the Northern Pacific. Our exact position I do not know; for the sun had been hidden during the course of a weary, breathless week, by a thin haze which had seemed to float above us, about the height of our mastheads, at whiles descending and shrouding the surrounding sea.

With there being no wind, we had steadied the tiller, and I was the only man on deck. The crew, consisting of two men and a boy, were sleeping forrard in their den; while Will — my friend, and the master of our little craft — was aft in his bunk on the port side of the little cabin.

Suddenly, from out of the surrounding darkness, there came a hail:

'Schooner, ahoy!'

The cry was so unexpected that I gave no immediate answer, because of my surprise.

It came again — a voice curiously throaty and inhuman, calling from somewhere upon the dark sea away on our port broadside:

'Schooner, ahoy!'

'Hullo!' I sung out, having gathered my wits somewhat. 'What are you? What do you want?'

'You need not be afraid,' answered the queer voice, having probably noticed some trace of confusion in my tone. 'I am only an old — man.'

The pause sounded oddly; but it was only afterwards that it came back to me with any significance.

'Why don't you come alongside, then?' I queried somewhat snappishly; for I liked not his hinting at my having been a trifle shaken.

'I — I — can't. It wouldn't be safe. I — ' The voice broke off, and there was silence.

'What do you mean?' I asked, growing more and more astonished. 'Why not safe? Where are you?'

I listened for a moment; but there came no answer. And then, a sudden indefinite suspicion, of I knew not what, coming to me, I stepped swiftly to the binnacle, and took out the lighted lamp. At the same time, I knocked on the deck with my heel to waken Will. Then I was back at the side, throwing the yellow funnel of light out into the silent immensity beyond our rail. As I did so, I heard a slight, muffled cry, and then the sound of a splash as though some one had dipped oars abruptly. Yet I cannot say that I saw anything with certainty; save, it seemed to me, that with the first flash of light, there had been something upon the waters, where now there was nothing.

'Hullo, there!' I called. 'What foolery is this!'

But there came only the indistinct sounds of a boat being pulled away into the night.

Then I heard Will's voice, from the direction of the after scuttle:

'What's up, George?'

'Come here, Will!' I said.

'What is it?' he asked, coming across the deck.

I told him the queer thing which had happened. He put several questions; then, after a moment's silence, he raised his hands to his lips, and hailed:

'Boat, ahoy!'

From a long distance away there came back to us a faint reply, and my companion repeated his call. Presently, after a short period of silence, there grew on our hearing the muffled sound of oars; at which Will hailed again.

This time there was a reply:

'Put away the light.'

'I'm damned if I will,' I muttered; but Will told me to do as the voice bade, and I shoved it down under the bulwarks.

'Come nearer,' he said, and the oar-strokes continued. Then, when apparently some half dozen fathoms distant, they again ceased.

'Come alongside,' exclaimed Will. 'There's nothing to be frightened of aboard here!'

'Promise that you will not show the light?'

'What's to do with you,' I burst out, 'that you're so infernally afraid of the light?'

'Because — ' began the voice, and stopped short.

'Because what?' I asked quickly.

Will put his hand on my shoulder.

'Shut up a minute, old man,' he said, in a low voice. 'Let me tackle him.'

He leant more over the rail.

'See here, mister,' he said, 'this is a pretty queer business, you coming upon us like this, right out in the middle of the blessed Pacific. How are we to know what sort of a hanky-panky trick you're up to? You say there's only one of you. How are we to know, unless we get a squint at you — eh? What's your objection to the light, anyway?'

As he finished, I heard the noise of the oars again, and then the voice came; but now from a greater distance, and sounding extremely hopeless and pathetic.

'I am sorry — sorry! I would not have troubled you, only I am hungry, and — so is she.'

The voice died away, and the sound of the oars, dipping irregularly, was borne to us.

'Stop!' sung out Will. 'I don't want to drive you away. Come back! We'll keep the light hidden, if you don't like it.'

He turned to me:

'It's a damned queer rig, this; but I think there's nothing to be afraid of?'

There was a question in his tone, and I replied.

'No, I think the poor devil's been wrecked around here, and gone crazy.'

The sound of the oars drew nearer.

'Shove the lamp back in the binnacle,' said Will; then he

leaned over the rail and listened. I replaced the lamp, and came
back to his side. The dipping of the oars ceased some dozen
yards distant.

'Won't you come alongside now?' asked Will in an even
voice. 'I have had the lamp put back in the binnacle.'

'I — I cannot,' replied the voice. 'I dare not come nearer. I
dare not even pay you for the — the provisions.'

'That's all right,' said Will, and hesitated. 'You're welcome to
as much grub as you can take — ' Again he hesitated.

'You are very good,' exclaimed the voice. 'May God, Who
understands everything, reward you — ' It broke off huskily.

'The — the lady?' said Will abruptly. 'Is she — '

'I have left her behind upon the island,' came the voice.

'What island?' I cut in.

'I know not its name,' returned the voice. 'I would to
God — !' it began, and checked itself as suddenly.

'Could we not send a boat for her?' asked Will at this point.

'No!' said the voice, with extraordinary emphasis. 'My God!
No!' There was a moment's pause; then it added, in a tone
which seemed a merited reproach:

'It was because of our want I ventured — because her agony
tortured me.'

'I am a forgetful brute,' exclaimed Will. 'Just wait a minute,
whoever you are, and I will bring you up something at once.'

In a couple of minutes he was back again, and his arms were
full of various edibles. He paused at the rail.

'Can't you come alongside for them?' he asked.

'No — I *dare not*,' replied the voice, and it seemed to me that
in its tones I detected a note of stifled craving — as though the
owner hushed a mortal desire. It came to me then in a flash,
that the poor old creature out there in the darkness, was
suffering for actual need of that which Will held in his arms; and
yet, because of some unintelligible dread, refraining from
dashing to the side of our little schooner, and receiving it. And
with the lightning-like conviction, there came the knowledge
that the Invisible was not mad; but sanely facing some
intolerable horror.

'Damn it, Will!' I said, full of many feelings, over which
predominated a vast sympathy. 'Get a box. We must float off
the stuff to him in it.'

This we did — propelling it away from the vessel, out into the darkness, by means of a boathook. In a minute, a slight cry from the Invisible came to us, and we knew that he had secured the box.

A little later, he called out a farewell to us, and so heartful a blessing, that I am sure we were the better for it. Then, without more ado, we heard the ply of oars across the darkness.

'Pretty soon off,' remarked Will, with perhaps just a little sense of injury.

'Wait,' I replied. 'I think somehow he'll come back. He must have been badly needing that food.'

'And the lady,' said Will. For a moment he was silent; then he continued:

'It's the queerest thing ever I've tumbled across, since I've been fishing.'

'Yes,' I said, and fell to pondering.

And so the time slipped away — an hour, another, and still Will stayed with me; for the queer adventure had knocked all desire for sleep out of him.

The third hour was three parts through, when we heard again the sound of oars across the silent ocean.

'Listen!' said Will, a low note of excitement in his voice.

'He's coming, just as I thought,' I muttered.

The dipping of the oars grew nearer, and I noted that the strokes were firmer and longer. The food had been needed.

They came to a stop a little distance off the broadside, and the queer voice came again to us through the darkness:

'Schooner, ahoy!'

'That you?' asked Will.

'Yes,' replied the voice. 'I left you suddenly; but — there was great need.'

'The lady?' questioned Will.

'The — lady is grateful now on earth. She will be more grateful soon in — in heaven.'

Will began to make some reply, in a puzzled voice; but became confused, and broke off short. I said nothing. I was wondering at the curious pauses, and, apart from my wonder, I was full of a great sympathy.

The voice continued: 'We — she and I, have talked, as we shared the result of God's tenderness and yours —'

Will interposed; but without coherence.

'I beg of you not to – to belittle your deed of Christian charity this night,' said the voice. 'Be sure that it has not escaped His notice.'

It stopped, and there was a full minute's silence. Then it came again:

'We have spoken together upon that which – which has befallen us. We had thought to go out, without telling any, of the terror which has come into our – lives. She is with me in believing that tonight's happenings are under a special ruling, and that it is God's wish that we should tell to you all that we have suffered since – since – '

'Yes?' said Will softly.

'Since the sinking of the *Albatross*.'

'Ah!' I exclaimed involuntarily. 'She left Newcastle for 'Frisco some six months ago, and hasn't been heard of since.'

'Yes,' answered the voice. 'But some few degrees to the North of the line she was caught in a terrible storm, and dismasted. When the day came, it was found that she was leaking badly, and, presently, it falling to a calm, the sailors took to the boats, leaving – leaving a young lady – my fiancée – and myself upon the wreck.

'We were below, gathering together a few of our belongings, when they left. They were entirely callous, through fear, and when we came upon the decks, we saw them only as small shapes afar off upon the horizon. Yet we did not despair, but set to work and constructed a small raft. Upon this we put such few matters as it would hold, including a quantity of water and some ship's biscuit. Then, the vessel being very deep in the water, we got ourselves on to the raft, and pushed off.

'It was later, when I observed that we seemed to be in the way of some tide or current, which bore us from the ship at an angle; so that in the course of three hours, by my watch, her hull became invisible to our sight, her broken masts remaining in view for a somewhat longer period. Then, towards evening, it grew misty, and so through the night. The next day we were still encompassed by the mist, the weather remaining quiet.

'For four days we drifted through this strange haze, until, on the evening of the fourth day, there grew upon our ears the murmur of breakers at a distance. Gradually it became plainer, and, somewhat after midnight, it appeared to sound upon either hand at no very great space. The raft was raised upon a swell several times, and then we were in smooth water, and the noise of the breakers were behind.

'When the morning came, we found that we were in a sort of great lagoon; but of this we noticed little at the time; for close before us, through the enshrouding mist, looked the hull of a large sailing-vessel. With one accord, we fell upon our knees and thanked God; for we thought that here was an end to our perils. We had much to learn.

'The raft drew near to the ship, and we shouted on them to take us aboard; but none answered. Presently the raft touched against the side of the vessel, and, seeing a rope hanging downwards, I seized it and began to climb. Yet I had much ado to make my way up, because of a kind of grey, lichenous fungus which had seized upon the rope, and which blotched the side of the ship lividly.

'I reached the rail and clambered over it, on to the deck. Here I saw that the decks were covered, in great patches, with the grey masses, some of them rising into nodules several feet in height; but at the time I thought less of this matter than of the possibility of there being people aboard the ship. I shouted; but none answered. Then I went to the door below the poop deck. I opened it, and peered in. There was a great smell of staleness, so that I knew in a moment that nothing living was within, and with the knowledge, I shut the door quickly; for I felt suddenly lonely.

'I went back to the side where I had scrambled up. My — my sweetheart was still sitting quietly upon the raft. Seeing me look down she called up to know whether there were any aboard of the ship. I replied that the vessel had the appearance of having been long deserted; but that if she would wait a little I would see whether there was anything in the shape of a ladder by which she could ascend to the deck. Then we would make a search through the vessel together. A little later, on the opposite side of the decks, I found a rope side-ladder. This I carried across, and a minute afterwards she was beside me.

'Together we explored the cabins and apartments in the after part of the ship; but nowhere was there any sign of life. Here and there, within the cabins themselves, we came across odd patches of that queer fungus; but this, as my sweetheart said, could be cleaned away.

'In the end, having assured ourselves that the after portion of the vessel was empty, we picked our ways to the bows, between the ugly grey nodules of that strange growth; and here we made a further search, which told us that there was indeed none aboard but ourselves.

'This being now beyond any doubt, we returned to the stern of the ship and proceeded to make ourselves as comfortable as possible. Together we cleared out and cleaned two of the cabins; and after that I made examination whether there was anything eatable in the ship. This I soon found was so, and thanked God in my heart for His goodness. In addition to this I discovered the whereabouts of the fresh-water pump, and having fixed it I found the water drinkable, though somewhat unpleasant to the taste.

'For several days we stayed aboard the ship, without attempting to get to the shore. We were busily engaged in making the place habitable. Yet even thus early we became aware that our lot was even less to be desired than might have been imagined; for though, as a first step, we scraped away the odd patches of growth that studded the floors and walls of the cabins and saloon, yet they returned almost to their original size within the space of twenty-four hours, which not only discouraged us, but gave us a feeling of vague unease.

'Still we would not admit ourselves beaten, so set to work afresh, and not only scraped away the fungus, but soaked the places where it had been, with carbolic, a can-full of which I had found in the pantry. Yet by the end of the week the growth had returned in full strength, and, in addition, it had spread to other places, as though our touching it had allowed germs from it to travel elsewhere.

'On the seventh morning, my sweetheart woke to find a small patch of it growing on her pillow, close to her face. At that, she came to me, so soon as she could get her garments upon her. I was in the galley at the time lighting the fire for breakfast.

' "Come here, John," she said, and led me aft. When I saw the thing upon her pillow I shuddered, and then and there we agreed to go right out of the ship and see whether we could not fare to make ourselves more comfortable ashore.

'Hurriedly we gathered together our few belongings, and even among these I found that the fungus had been at work; for one of her shawls had a little lump of it growing near one edge. I threw the whole thing over the side, without saying anything to her.

'The raft was still alongside, but it was too clumsy to guide, and I lowered down a small boat that hung across the stern, and in this we made our way to the shore. Yet, as we drew near to it, I became gradually aware that here the vile fungus, which had driven us from the ship, was growing riot. In places it rose into horrible, fantastic mounds, which seemed almost to quiver, as with a quiet life, when the wind blew across them. Here and there it took on the forms of vast fingers, and in others it just spread out flat and smooth and treacherous. Odd places, it appeared as grotesque stunted trees, seeming extraordinarily kinked and gnarled. The whole quaking vilely at times.

'At first, it seemed to us that there was no single portion of the surrounding shore which was not hidden beneath the masses of the hideous lichen; yet, in this, I found we were mistaken; for somewhat later, coasting along the shore at a little distance, we descried a smooth white patch of what appeared to be fine sand, and there were landed. It was not sand. What it was I do not know. All that I have observed is that upon it the fungus will not grow; while everywhere else, save where the sand-like earth wanders oddly, pathwise, amid the grey desolation of the lichen, there is nothing but the loathsome greyness.

'It is difficult to make you understand how cheered we were to find one place that was absolutely free from the growth, and here we deposited our belongings. Then we went back to the ship for such things as it seemed to us we should need. Among other matters, I managed to bring ashore with me one of the ship's sails, with which I constructed two small tents, which, though exceedingly rough-shaped, served the purposes for which they were intended. In these we lived and stored our various necessities, and thus for a matter of some four weeks all went smoothly and without particular unhappiness. Indeed, I may say with much of happiness — for — for we were together.

'It was on the thumb of her right hand that the growth first showed. It was only a small circular spot, much like a little grey mole. My God! how the fear leapt to my heart when she showed me the place. We cleansed it, between us, washing it with carbolic and water. In the morning of the following day she showed her hand to me again. The grey warty thing had returned. For a little while, we looked at one another in silence. Then, still wordless, we started again to remove it. In the midst of the operation she spoke suddenly.

' "What's that on the side of your face, dear?" Her voice was sharp with anxiety. I put my hand up to feel.

' "There! Under the hair by your ear. A little to the front a bit." My finger rested upon the place, and then I knew.

' "Let us get your thumb done first," I said. And she submitted, only because she was afraid to touch me until it was cleansed. I finished washing and disinfecting her thumb, and then she turned to my face. After it was finished we sat together and talked awhile of many things; for there had come into our lives sudden, very terrible thoughts. We were, all at once afraid of something worse than death. We spoke of loading the boat with provisions and water and making our way out on to the sea; yet we were helpless, for many causes, and — and the growth had attacked us already. We decided to stay. God would do with us what was His will. We would wait.

'A month, two months, three months passed and the places grew somewhat, and there had come others. Yet we fought so strenuously with the fear that its headway was but slow, comparatively speaking.

'Occasionally we ventured off to the ship for such stores as we needed. There we found that the fungus grew persistently. One of the nodules on the maindeck became soon as high as my head.

'We had now given up all thought or hope of leaving the island. We had realized that it would be unallowable to go among healthy humans, with the things from which we were suffering.

'With this determination and knowledge in our minds we knew that we should have to husband our food and water; for we did not know, at that time, but that we should possibly live for many years.

'This reminds me that I have told you that I am an old man.

Judged by years this is not so. But — but — '

He broke off; then continued somewhat abruptly:

'As I was saying, we knew that we should have to use care in the matter of food. But we had no idea then how little food there was left, of which to take care. It was a week later that I made the discovery that all the other bread tanks — which I had supposed full — were empty, and that (beyond odd tins of vegetables and meat, and some other matters) we had nothing on which to depend, but the bread in the tank which I had already opened.

'After learning this I bestirred myself to do what I could, and set to work at fishing in the lagoon; but with no success. At this I was somewhat inclined to feel desperate until the thought came to me to try outside the lagoon, in the open sea.

'Here, at times, I caught odd fish; but so infrequently that they proved of but little help in keeping us from the hunger which threatened. It seemed to me that our deaths were likely to come by hunger, and not by the growth of the thing which had seized upon our bodies.

'We were in this state of mind when the fourth month wore out. Then I made a very horrible discovery. One morning, a little before midday, I came off from the ship with a portion of the biscuits which were left. In the mouth of her tent I saw my sweetheart sitting, eating something.

' "What is it, my dear?" I called out as I leapt ashore. Yet, on hearing my voice, she seemed confused, and, turning slyly threw something towards the edge of the little clearing. It fell short, and a vague suspicion having arisen within me, I walked across and picked it up. It was a piece of the grey fungus.

'As I went to her with it in my hand, she turned deadly pale; then a rose red. I felt strangely dazed and frightened.

' "My dear! My dear!" I said, and could say no more. Yet at my words she broke down and cried bitterly. Gradually, as she calmed, I got from her the news that she had tried it the preceding day, and — and liked it. I got her to promise on her knees not to touch it again, however great our hunger. After she had promised she told me that the desire for it had come suddenly, and that, until the moment of desire, she had experienced nothing towards it but the most extreme repulsion.

'Later in the day, feeling strangely restless, and much shaken with the thing which I had discovered, I made my way along one of the twisted paths — formed by the white, sand-like substance — which led among the fungoid growth. I had, once before, ventured along there; but not to any great distance. This time, being involved in perplexing thought, I went much further than hitherto.

'Suddenly I was called to myself by a queer hoarse sound on my left. Turning I saw that there was movement among an extraordinary shaped mass of fungus, close to my elbow. It was swaying uneasily, as though it possessed life of its own. Abruptly, as I stared, the thought came to me that the thing had a grotesque resemblance to the figure of a distorted human creature. Even as the fancy flashed into my brain, there was a slight, sickening noise of tearing, and I saw that one of the branch-like arms was detaching itself from the surrounding grey masses, and coming towards me. The head of the thing — shapeless grey ball, inclined in my direction. I stood stupidly, and the vile arm brushed across my face. I gave out a frightened cry, and ran back a few paces. There was a sweetish taste upon my lips where the thing had touched me. I licked them, and was immediately filled with an inhuman desire. I turned and seized a mass of the fungus. Then more, and — more. I was insatiable. In the midst of devouring, the remembrance of the morning's discovery swept into my mazed brain. It was sent by God. I dashed the fragment I held to the ground. Then, utterly wretched and feeling a dreadful guiltiness, I made my way back to the little encampment.

'I think she knew, by some marvellous intuition which love must have given, so soon as she set eyes on me. Her quiet sympathy made it easier for me, and I told her of my sudden weakness; yet omitted to mention the extraordinary thing which had gone before. I desired to spare her all unnecessary terror.

'But, for myself, I had added an intolerable knowledge, to breed an incessant terror in my brain; for I doubted not but that I had seen the end of one of those men who had come to the island in the ship in the lagoon; and in that monstrous ending I had seen our own.

'Thereafter we kept from the abominable food, though the

desire for it had entered into our blood. Yet our dear punishment was upon us; for, day by day, with monstrous rapidity, the fungoid growth took hold of our poor bodies. Nothing we could do would check it materially, and so — and so — we who had been human, became — Well it matters less each day. Only — only we had been man and maid!

'And day by day the fight is more dreadful, to withstand the hunger-lust for the terrible lichen.

'A week ago we ate the last of the biscuit, and since that time I have caught three fish. I was out here fishing tonight when your schooner drifted upon me out of the mist. I hailed you. You know the rest, and may God, out of His great heart, bless you for your goodness to a — a couple of poor outcast souls.'

There was the dip of an oar — another. Then the voice came again, and for the last time, sounding through the slight surrounding mist, ghostly and mournful.

'God bless you! Good-bye!'

'Good-bye,' we shouted, together, hoarsely, our hearts full of many emotions.

I glanced about me. I became aware that the dawn was upon us.

The sun flung a stray beam across the hidden sea; pierced the mist dully, and lit up the receding boat with a gloomy fire. Indistinctly I saw something nodding between the oars. I thought of a sponge — a great, grey nodding sponge. The oars continued to ply. They were grey — as was the boat — and my eyes searched a moment vainly for the conjunction of hand and oar. My gaze flashed back to the — head. It nodded forward as the oars went backward for the stroke. Then the oars were dipped, the boat shot out of the path of light, and the — the thing went nodding into the mist.

XIV

The Screaming Skull

F. Marion Crawford

F. Marion Crawford was a classic teller of mysteries and in The Screaming Skull *he combines a perfectly good ghost story, told as a narrative, with a vague legend, which he may have added for the sake of flavour, as Conan Doyle was alleged to have done with* The Hound of the Baskervilles. *The reader might reflect on some similarity between this story and that told earlier by 'Sea-Wrack', but they both hold up to comparison and both are worthy of inclusion.*

I have often heard it scream. No, I am not nervous, I am not imaginative, and I never believed in ghosts, unless that thing is one. Whatever it is, it hates me almost as much as it hated Luke Pratt, and it screams at me.

If I were you, I would never tell ugly stories about ingenious ways of killing people, for you never can tell but that some one at the table may be tired of his or her nearest and dearest. I have always blamed myself for Mrs. Pratt's death, and I suppose I was responsible for it in a way, though heaven knows I never wished her anything but long life and happiness. If I had not told that story she might be alive yet. That is why the thing screams at me, I fancy.

She was a good little woman, with a sweet temper, all things considered, and a nice gentle voice; but I remember hearing her shriek once when she thought her little boy was killed by a pistol that went off, though every one was sure that it was not loaded. It was the same scream; exactly the same, with a sort of rising quaver at the end; do you know what I mean? Unmistakable.

The truth is, I had not realized that the doctor and his wife were not on good terms. They used to bicker a bit now and then when I was here, and I often noticed that little Mrs. Pratt got very red and bit her lip hard to keep her temper, while Luke grew pale and said the most offensive things. He was that sort when he was in the nursery, I remember, and afterwards at school. He was my cousin, you know; that is how I came by this house; after he died, and his boy Charley was killed in South Africa, there were no relations left. Yes, it's pretty little property, just the sort of thing for an old sailor like me who has taken to gardening.

One always remembers one's mistakes much more vividly than one's cleverest things, doesn't one? I've often noticed it. I was dining with the Pratts one night, when I told them the story that afterwards made so much difference. It was a wet night in November, and the sea was moaning. Hush! – if you don't speak you will hear it now. . . .

Do you hear the tide? Gloomy sound, isn't it? Sometimes, about this time of year – hallo! – there it is! Don't be frightened, man – it won't eat you – it's only a noise, after all! But I'm glad you've heard it, because there are always people who think it's the wind, or my imagination, or something. You won't hear it again tonight, I fancy, for it doesn't often come more than once. Yes – that's right. Put another stick on the fire, and a little more stuff into that weak mixture you're so fond of. Do you remember old Blauklot the carpenter, on that German ship that picked us up when the *Clontarf* went to the bottom? We were hove to in a howling gale one night, as snug as you please, with no land within five hundred miles, and the ship coming up and falling off as regularly as clockwork – 'Biddy te boor beebles ashore tis night, poys!' old Blauklot sang out, as he went off to his quarters with the sail-maker. I often think of that, now that I'm ashore for good and all.

Yes, it was on a night like this, when I was at home for a spell, waiting to take the *Olympia* out on her first trip – it was on the next voyage that she broke the record, you remember – but that dates it. Ninety-two was the year, early in November.

The weather was dirty, Pratt was out of temper, and the dinner was bad, very bad indeed, which didn't improve matters, and cold, which made it worse. The poor little lady was very unhappy about it, and insisted on making a Welsh rarebit on the table to counteract the raw turnips and the half-boiled mutton. Pratt must have had a hard day. Perhaps he had lost a patient. At all events, he was in a nasty temper.

'My wife is trying to poison me, you see!' he said. 'She'll succeed some day.' I saw that she was hurt, and I made believe to laugh, and said that Mrs. Pratt was much too clever to get rid of her husband in such a simple way; and then I began to tell them about Japanese tricks with spun glass and chopped horsehair and the like.

Pratt was a doctor, and knew a lot more than I did about such things, but that only put me on my mettle, and I told a story about a woman in Ireland who did for three husbands before any one suspected foul play.

Did you never hear that tale? The fourth husband managed to keep awake and caught her, and she was hanged. How did she do it? She drugged them, and poured melted lead into their ears, through a little horn funnel when they were asleep.

. . . No — that's the wind whistling. It's backing up to the southward again. I can tell by the sound. Besides, the other thing doesn't often come more than once in an evening at this time of year — when it happened. Yes, it was in November. Poor Mrs. Pratt died suddenly in her bed not long after I dined here. I can fix the date, because I got the news in New York by the steamer that followed the *Olympia* when I took her out on her first trip. You had the *Leofric* the same year? Yes, I remember. What a pair of old buffers we are coming to be, you and I. Nearly fifty years since were apprentices together on the *Clontarf*. Shall you ever forget old Blauklot? 'Biddy te boor beebles ashore, poys!' Ha, ha! Take a little more, with all that water. It's the old Hulstkamp I found in the cellar when this house came to me, the same I brought Luke from Amsterdam five-and-twenty years ago. He had never touched a drop of it. Perhaps he's sorry now, poor fellow.

Where did I leave off? I told you that Mrs. Pratt died suddenly — yes. Luke must have been lonely here after she was dead, I should think; I came to see him now and then, and he looked worn and nervous, and told me that his practice was growing too heavy for him, though he wouldn't take an assistant on any account. Years went on, and his son was killed in South Africa, and after that he began to be queer. There was something about him not like other people. I believe he kept his senses in his profession to the end; there was no complaint of his having made bad mistakes in cases, or anything of that sort, but he had a look about him —

Luke was a red-headed man with a pale face when he was young, and he was never stout; in middle age he turned a sandy grey, and after his son died he grew thinner and thinner, till his head looked like a skull with parchment stretched over it very tight, and his eyes had a sort of glare in them that was very disagreeable to look at.

He had an old dog that poor Mrs. Pratt had been fond of, and that used to follow her everywhere. He was a bull-dog, and the sweetest tempered beast you ever saw, though he had a way of hitching his upper lip behind one of his fangs that frightened strangers a good deal. Sometimes, of an evening, Pratt and Bumble — that was the dog's name — used to sit and look at each other a long time, thinking about old times, I suppose, when Luke's wife used to sit in that chair you've got. That was always her place, and this was the doctor's, where I'm sitting. Bumble used to climb up by the footstool — he was old and fat by that time, and could not jump much, and his teeth were getting shaky. He would look steadily at Luke, and Luke looked steadily at the dog, his face growing more and more like a skull with two little coals for eyes; and after about five minutes or so, though it may have been less, old Bumble would suddenly begin to shake all over, and all on a sudden he would set up an awful howl, as if he had been shot, and tumble out of the easy-chair and trot away, and hide himself under the sideboard, and lie there making odd noises.

Considering Pratt's looks in those last months, the thing is not surprising, you know. I'm not nervous or imaginative, but I can quite believe he might have sent a sensitive woman into hysterics — his head looked so much like a skull in parchment.

At last I came down one day before Christmas, when my ship was in dock and I had three weeks off. Bumble was not about, and I said casually that I supposed the old dog was dead.

'Yes,' Pratt answered, and I thought there was something odd in his tone even before he went on after a little pause. 'I killed him,' he said presently. 'I could not stand it any longer.'

I asked what it was that Luke could not stand, though I guessed well enough.

'He had a way of sitting in her chair and glaring at me, and then howling.' Luke shivered a little, as if he thought I might imagine he had been cruel. 'I put iodine into his drink to make him sleep soundly, and then I chloroformed him gradually, so that he could not have felt suffocated even if he was dreaming. It's been quieter since then.'

I wondered what he meant, for the words slipped out as if he could not help saying them. I've understood since. He meant that he did not hear that noise so often after the dog was out of the way. Perhaps he thought at first that it was old Bumble in the yard howling at the moon, though it's not that kind of noise, is it? Besides, I know what it is, if Luke didn't. It's only a noise, after all, and a noise never hurt anybody yet. But he was much more imaginative than I am. No doubt there really is something about this place that I don't understand; but when I don't understand a thing, I call it a phenomenon, and I don't take it for granted that it's going to kill me, as he did. I don't understand everything, by long odds, nor do you, nor does any man who has been to sea. We used to talk of tidal waves, for instance, and we could not account for them; now we account for them by calling them submarine earthquakes, and we branch off into fifty theories, anyone of which might make earthquakes quite comprehensible if we only knew what they are. I fell in with one of them once, and the inkstand flew straight up from the table against the ceiling of my cabin. The same thing happened to Captain Lecky — I dare-say you've read about it in his *Wrinkles*. Very good. If that sort of thing took place ashore, in this room for instance, a nervous person would talk about spirits and levitation and fifty things that mean nothing, instead of just quietly setting it down as a 'phenomenon' that has not been explained yet. My view of that voice, you see.

Besides, what is there to prove that Luke killed his wife? I would not even suggest such a thing to any one but you. After all, there was nothing but the coincidence that poor little Mrs. Pratt died suddenly in her bed a few days after I told that story at dinner. She was not the only woman who ever died like that. Luke got the doctor over from the next parish, and they agreed that she had died of something the matter with her heart. Why not? It's common enough.

Of course, there was the ladle. I never told anybody about that, and it made me start when I found it in the cupboard in the bedroom. It was new, too — a little tinned iron ladle that had not been in the fire more than once or twice, and there was some lead in it that had been melted, and stuck to the bottom of the bowl, all grey, with hardened dross on it. But that proves nothing. A country doctor is generally a handy man, who does everything for himself, and Luke may have had a dozen reasons for melting a little lead in a ladle. He was fond of sea-fishing, for instance, and he may have cast a sinker for a night-line; perhaps it was a weight for the hall clock, or something like that. All the same, when I found it I had a rather queer sensation, because it looked so much like the thing I had described when I told them the story. Do you understand? It affected me unpleasantly, and I threw it away; it's at the bottom of the sea a mile from the Spit, and it will be jolly well rusted beyond recognizing if it's ever washed up by the tide.

You see, Luke must have bought it in the village, years ago, for the man sells just such ladles still. I suppose they are used in cooking. In any case, there was no reason why an inquisitive housemaid should find such a thing lying about, with lead in it, and wonder what it was, and perhaps talk to the maid who heard me tell the story at dinner — for that girl married the plumber's son in the village, and may remember the whole thing.

You understand me, don't you? Now that Luke Pratt is dead and gone, and lies buried beside his wife, with an honest man's tombstone at his head, I should not care to stir up anything that could hurt his memory. They are both dead and their son, too. There was trouble enough about Luke's death, as it was.

How? He was found dead on the beach one morning, and there was a coroner's inquest. There were marks on his throat, but he had not been robbed. The verdict was that he had come to his end 'by the hands or teeth of some person or animal unknown,' for half the jury thought it might have been a big dog that had thrown him down and gripped his windpipe, though the skin of his throat was not broken. No one knew at what time he had gone out, nor where he had been. He was found lying on his back above high-water mark, and an old cardboard bandbox that had belonged to his wife lay under his hand, open. The lid had fallen off. He seemed to have been carrying home a skull in the box — doctors are fond of collecting such things. It had rolled out and lay near his head, and it was a remarkably fine skull, rather small, beautifully shaped and very white, with perfect teeth. That is to say, the upper jaw was perfect, but there was no lower one at all, when I first saw it.

Yes, I found it here when I came. You see, it was very white and polished, like a thing meant to be kept under a glass case, and the people did not know where it came from, nor what to do with it; so they put it back into the bandbox and set it on the shelf of the cupboard in the best bedroom, and of course they showed it to me when I took possession. I was taken down to the beach, too, to be shown the place where Luke was found, and the old fisherman explained just how he was lying, and the skull beside him. The only point he could not explain was why the skull had rolled up the sloping sand towards Luke's head instead of rolling downhill to his feet. It did not seem odd to me at the time, but I have often thought of it since, for the place is rather steep. I'll take you tomorrow if you like — I made a sort of cairn of stones there afterwards.

When he fell down, or was thrown down — whichever happened — the bandbox struck the sand, and the lid came off, and the thing came out and ought to have rolled down. But it didn't. It was close to his head, almost touching it, and turned with the face towards it. I say it didn't strike me as odd when the man told me; but I could not help thinking about it afterwards, again and again, till I saw a picture of it all when I closed my eyes; and then I began to ask myself why the plaguey thing had rolled up instead of down, and why it had stopped near Luke's head, instead of a yard away, for instance.

You naturally want to know what conclusion I reached, don't you? None that at all explained the rolling, at all events. But I got something else into my head, after a time, that made me feel downright uncomfortable.

Oh, I don't mean as to anything supernatural! There may be ghosts, or there may not be. If there are, I'm not inclined to believe that they can hurt living people except by frightening them, and, for my part, I would rather face any shape of ghost than a fog in the Channel when it's crowded. No. What bothered me was just a foolish idea, that's all, and I cannot tell how it began, nor what made it grow till it turned into a certainty.

I was thinking about Luke and his poor wife one evening over my pipe and a dull book, when it occurred to me that the skull might possibly be hers, and I have never got rid of the thought since. You'll tell me there's no sense in it, no doubt; that Mrs. Pratt was buried like a Christian and is lying in the churchyard where they put her, and that it's perfectly monstrous to suppose her husband kept her skull in her old bandbox in his bedroom. All the same, in the face of reason, and common sense, and probability, I'm convinced that he did. Doctors do all sorts of queer things that would make men like you and me feel creepy, and those are just the things that don't seem probable, nor logical, nor sensible to us.

Then, don't you see? — if it really was her skull, poor woman, the only way of accounting for his having it is that he really killed her, and did it in that way, as the woman killed her husbands in the story, and that he was afraid there might be an examination some day which would betray him. You see, I told that too, and I believe it had really happened some fifty or sixty years ago. They dug up the three skulls, you know, and there was a small lump of lead rattling about in each one. That was what hanged the woman. Luke remembered that, I'm sure. I don't want to know what he did when he thought of it; my taste never ran in the direction of horrors, and I don't fancy you care for them either, do you? No. If you did, you might supply what is wanting to the story.

It must have been rather grim, eh? I wish I did not see the whole thing so distinctly, just as everything must have happened. He took it the night before she was buried, I'm sure, after the coffin had been shut, and when the servant girl was asleep. I would bet anything, that when he'd got it, he put something under the sheet in its place, to fill up and look like it. What do you suppose he put there, under the sheet?

I don't wonder you take me up on what I'm saying! First I tell you that I don't want to know what happened, and that I hate to think about horrors, and then I describe the whole thing to you as if I had seen it. I'm quite sure that it was her work-bag that he put there. I remember the bag very well, for she always used it of an evening; it was made of brown plush, and when it was stuffed full it was about the size of — you understand. Yes, there I am, at it again! You may laugh at me, but you don't live here alone, where it was done, and you didn't tell Luke the story about the melted lead. I'm not nervous, I tell you, but sometimes I begin to feel that I understand why some people are. I dwell on all this when I'm alone, and I dream of it, and when that thing screams — well, frankly, I don't like the noise any more than you do, though I should be used to it by this time.

I ought not to be nervous. I've sailed in a haunted ship. There was a Man in the Top, and two-thirds of the crew died of the West Coast fever inside of ten days after we anchored; but I was all right, then and afterwards. I have seen some ugly sights, too, just as you have, and all the rest of us. But nothing ever stuck in my head in the way this does.

You see, I've tried to get rid of the thing, but it doesn't like that. It wants to be there in its place, in Mrs. Pratt's bandbox in the cupboard in the best bedroom. It's not happy anywhere else. How do I know that? Because I've tried it. You don't suppose that I've not tried, do you? As long as it's there it only screams now and then, generally at this time of year, but if I put it out of the house it goes on all night, and no servant will stay here twenty-four hours. As it is, I've often been left alone and have been obliged to shift for myself for a fortnight at a time. No one from the village would ever pass a night under the roof now, and as for selling the place, or even letting it, that's out of the question. The old women say that if I stay here I shall come to a bad end myself before long.

I'm not afraid of that. You smile at the mere idea that any one could take such nonsense seriously. Quite right. It's utterly blatant nonsense, I agree with you. Didn't I tell you that it's only a noise after all when you started and looked round as if you expected to see a ghost standing behind your chair?

I may be all wrong about the skull, and I like to think that I am — when I can. It may be just a fine specimen which Luke got somewhere long ago and what rattles about inside when you shake it may be nothing but a pebble, or a bit of hard clay, or anything. Skulls that have lain long in the ground generally have something inside them that rattles, don't they? No, I've never tried to get it out, whatever it is; I'm afraid it might be lead, don't you see? And if it is, I don't want to know the fact, for I'd much rather not be sure. If it really is lead, I killed her quite as much as if I had done the deed myself. Anybody must see that, I should think. As long as I don't know for certain, I have the consolation of saying that it's all utterly ridiculous nonsense, that Mrs. Pratt died a natural death and that the beautiful skull belonged to Luke when he was a student in London. But if I were quite sure, I believe I should have to leave the house; indeed I do, most certainly. As it is, I had to give up trying to sleep in the best bedroom where the cupboard is.

You ask me why I don't throw it into the pond — yes, but please don't call it a 'confounded bugbear' — it doesn't like being called names.

There! Lord, what a shriek! I told you so! You're quite pale, man. Fill up your pipe and draw your chair nearer to the fire, and take some more drink. Old Hollands never hurt anybody yet. I've seen a Dutchman in Java drink half a jug of Hulstkamp in a morning without turning a hair. I don't take much rum myself, because it doesn't agree with my rheumatism, but you are not rheumatic and it won't damage you. Besides, it's a very damp night outside. The wind is howling again, and it will soon be in the south-west; do you hear how the windows rattle? The tide must have turned too, by the moaning.

We should not have heard the thing again if you had not said that. I'm pretty sure we should not. Oh yes, if you choose to describe it as a coincidence, you are quite welcome, but I would rather that you should not call the thing names again, if you don't mind. It may be that the poor little woman hears, and perhaps it hurts her, don't you know? Ghost? No! You don't call anything a ghost that you can take in your hands and look at in broad daylight, and that rattles when you shake it. Do you now? But it's something that hears and understands; there's no doubt about that.

I tried sleeping in the best bedroom when I first came to the house, just because it was the best and the most comfortable, but I had to give it up. It was their room, and there's the big bed she died in, and the cupboard is in the thickness of the wall, near the head, on the left. That's where it likes to be kept, in its bandbox. I only used the room for a fortnight after I came, and then I turned out and took the little room downstairs, next to the surgery, where Luke used to sleep when he expected to be called to a patient during the night.

I was always a good sleeper ashore; eight hours is my dose, eleven to seven when I'm alone, twelve to eight when I have a friend with me. But I could not sleep after three o'clock in the morning in that room — a quarter past, to be accurate — as a matter of fact, I timed it with my old pocket chronometer, which still keeps good time, and it was always at exactly seventeen minutes past three. I wonder whether that was the hour when she died?

It was not what you have heard. If it had been that I could not have stood it two nights. It was just a start and a moan and hard breathing for a few seconds in the cupboard, and it could never have waked me under ordinary circumstances, I'm sure. I suppose you are like me in that, and we are just like other people who have been to sea. No natural sounds disturb us at all, not all the racket of a square-rigger hove to in a heavy gale, or rolling on her beam ends before the wind. But if a lead pencil gets adrift and rattles in the drawer of your cabin table you are awake in a moment. Just so — you always understand. Very well, the noise in the cupboard was no louder than that, but it waked me instantly.

I said it was like a 'start'. I know what I mean, but it's hard to explain without seeming to talk nonsense. Of course you cannot exactly 'hear' a person 'start'; at the most, you might hear the quick drawing of the breath between the parted lips and closed teeth, and the almost imperceptible sound of clothing moving suddenly though very slightly. It was like that.

You know how one feels what a sailing vessel is going to do, two or three seconds before she does it, when one has the wheel. Riders say the same of a horse, but that's less strange, because the horse is a live animal with feelings of its own, and only poets and landsmen talk about a ship being alive, and all that. But I have always felt somehow that besides being a steaming machine or a sailing machine for carrying weights, a vessel at sea is a sensitive instrument, and a means of communication between nature and man, and most particularly the man at the wheel, if she is steered by hand. She takes her impressions directly from wind and sea, tide and stream, and transmits them to the man's hand, just as the wireless telegraph picks up the interrupted currents aloft and turns them out below in the form of a message.

You see what I am driving at; I felt that something started in the cupboard, and I felt it so vividly that I heard it, though there may have been nothing to hear, and the sound inside my head waked me suddenly. But I really heard the other noise. It was as if it were muffled inside a box, as far away as if it came through a long-distance telephone; and yet I knew that it was inside the cupboard near the head of my bed. My hair did not bristle and my blood did not run cold that time. I simply resented being waked up by something that had no business to make a noise, any more than a pencil should rattle in the drawer of my cabin table on board ship. For I did not understand; I just supposed that the cupboard had some communication with the outside air, and that the wind had got in and was moaning through it with a sort of very faint screech. I struck a light and looked at my watch, and it was seventeen minutes past three. Then I turned over and went to sleep on my right ear. That's my good one; I'm pretty deaf with the other, for I struck the water with it when I was a lad in diving from the foretopsail yard. Silly thing to do, it was, but the result is very convenient when I want to go to sleep when there's a noise.

That was the first night, and the same thing happened again and several times afterwards, but not regularly, though it was always at the same time, to a second; perhaps I was sometimes sleeping on my good ear, and sometimes not. I overhauled the cupboard and there was no way by which the wind could get in, or anything else, for the door makes a good fit, having been meant to keep out moths, I suppose; Mrs. Pratt must have kept her winter things in it, for it still smells of camphor.

After about a fortnight I had had enough of the noises. So far I had said to myself that it would be silly to yield to it and take the skull out of the room. Things always look differently by daylight, don't they? But the voice grew louder — I suppose one may call it a voice — and it got inside my deaf ear, too, one night. I realized that when I was wide awake, for my good ear was jammed down on the pillow, and I ought not to have heard a fog-horn in that position. But I heard that, and it made me lose my temper, unless it scared me, for sometimes the two are not far apart. I struck a light and got up, and I opened the cupboard, grabbed the bandbox and threw it out of the window, as far as I could.

Then my hair stood on end. The thing screamed in the air, like a shell from a twelve-inch gun. It fell on the other side of the road. The night was very dark, and I could not see it fall, but I know it fell beyond the road. The window is just over the front door, it's fifteen yards to the fence, more or less, and the road is ten yards wide. There's a quickset hedge beyond, along the glebe that belongs to the vicarage.

I did not sleep much more that night. It was not more than half an hour after I had thrown the bandbox out when I heard a shriek outside — like what we've had tonight, but worse, more despairing, I should call it; and it may have been my imagination, but I could have sworn that the screams came nearer and nearer each time. I lit a pipe, and walked up and down for a bit, and then took a book and sat up reading, but I'll be hanged if I can remember what I read nor even what the book was, for every now and then a shriek came up that would have made a dead man turn in his coffin.

A little before dawn someone knocked at the front door. There was no mistaking that for anything else, and I opened my window and looked down, for I guessed that someone wanted the doctor, supposing that the new man had taken Luke's house. It was rather a relief to hear a human knock after that awful noise.

You cannot see the door from above, owing to the little porch. The knocking came again, and I called out, asking who was there, but nobody answered, though the knock was repeated. I sang out again, and said that the doctor did not live here any longer. There was no answer, but it occurred to me that it might be some old countryman who was stone deaf. So I took my candle and went down to open the door. Upon my word, I was not thinking of the thing yet, and I had almost forgotten the other noises. I went down convinced that I should find somebody outside, on the doorstep, with a message. I set the candle on the hall table, so that the wind should not blow it out when I opened. While I was drawing the old-fashioned bolt I heard the knocking again. It was not loud, and it had a queer, hollow sound, now that I was close to it, I remember, but I certainly thought it was made by some person who wanted to get in.

It wasn't. There was nobody there, but as I opened the door

inward, standing a little on one side, so as to see out at once, something rolled across the threshold and stopped against my foot.

I drew back as I felt it, for I knew what it was before I looked down. I cannot tell you how I knew, and it seemed unreasonable, for I am still quite sure that I had thrown it across the road. It's a French window, that opens wide, and I got a good swing when I flung it out. Besides, when I went out early in the morning, I found the bandbox beyond the thickset hedge.

You may think it opened when I threw it and that the skull dropped out; but that's impossible, for nobody could throw an empty cardboard box so far. It's out of the question; you might as well try to fling a ball of paper twenty-five yards, or a blown bird's egg.

To go back, I shut and bolted the hall door, picked the thing up carefully, and put it on the table beside the candle. I did that mechanically, as one instinctively does the right thing in danger without thinking at all — unless one does the opposite. It may seem odd, but I believe my first thought had been that somebody might come and find me there on the threshold while it was resting against my foot, lying a little on its side, and turning one hollow eye up at my face, as if it meant to accuse me. And the light and shadow from the candle played in the hollows of the eyes as it stood on the table, so that they seemed to open and shut at me. Then the candle went out quite unexpectedly, though the door was fastened and there was not the least draught; and I used up at least half a dozen matches before it would burn again.

I sat down rather suddenly, without quite knowing why. Probably I had been badly frightened, and perhaps you will admit there was no great shame in being scared. The thing had come home, and it wanted to go upstairs, back to its cupboard. I sat still and stared at it for a bit, till I began to feel very cold; then I took it and carried it up and set it in its place, and I remember that I spoke to it, and promised that it should have its bandbox again in the morning.

You want to know whether I stayed in the room till daybreak? Yes, but I kept a light burning, and sat up smoking and reading, most likely out of fright; plain, undeniable fear, and you need not call it cowardice either, for that's not the same thing. I could not have stayed alone with that thing in the cupboard; I should have been scared to death, though I'm not more timid than other people. Confound it all, man, it had crossed the road alone, and had got up the doorstep, and had knocked to be let in.

When the dawn came, I put on my boots and went out to find the bandbox. I had to go a good way round, by the gate near the highroad, and I found the box open and hanging on the other side of the hedge. It had caught on the twigs by the string, and the lid had fallen off and was lying on the ground below it. That shows that it did not open till it was well over; and if it had not opened as soon as it left my hand, what was inside it must have gone beyond the road too.

That's all. I took the box upstairs to the cupboard, and put the skull back and locked it up. When the girl brought me my breakfast she said she was sorry, but that she must go, and she did not care if she lost her month's wages. I looked at her, and her face was a sort of greenish, yellowish white. I pretended to be surprised, and asked what was the matter; but that was of no use, for she just turned on me and wanted to know whether I meant to stay in a haunted house, and how long I expected to live if I did, for though she noticed I was sometimes a little hard of hearing, she did not believe that even I could sleep through those screams again — and if I could, why had I been moving about the house and opening and shutting the front door, between three and four in the morning? There was no answering that since she had heard me, so off she went, and I was left to myself. I went down to the village during the morning and found a woman who was willing to come and do the little work there is and cook my dinner, on condition that she might go home every night. As for me, I moved downstairs that day, and I have never tried to sleep in the best bedroom since. After a while I got a brace of middle-aged Scots servants from London, and things were quiet enough for a long time. I began by telling them that the house was in a very exposed position, and that the wind whistled round it a good deal in the autumn and winter, which had given it a bad name in the village, the Cornish people being inclined to superstition and telling ghost stories. The two hard-faced, sandy-haired sisters almost smiled, and they answered with great contempt that they had no great opinion of any Southern bogey whatever, having been in service in two English haunted houses, where they had never seen so much as the Boy in Gray, whom they reckoned no very particular rarity in Forfarshire.

They stayed with me several months, and while they were in the house we had peace and quiet. One of them is here again now, but she went away with her sister within the year. This one — she was the cook — married the sexton, who works in my garden. That's the way of it. It's a small village and he has not much to do, and he knows enough about flowers to help me nicely, besides doing most of the hard work; for though I'm fond of exercise, I'm getting a little stiff in the hinges. He's a sober, silent sort of fellow, who minds his own business, and he was a widower when I came here — Trehearn is his name, James Trehearn. The Scots sisters would not admit that there was anything wrong about the house, but when November came they gave me warning that they were going, on the ground that the chapel was such a long walk from here, being in the next parish, and that they could not possibly go to our church. But the younger one came back in the spring, and as soon as the banns could be published she was married to James Trehearn by the vicar, and she seems to have had no scruples about hearing him preach since then. I'm quite satisfied, if she is! The couple live in a small cottage that looks over the churchyard.

I suppose you are wondering what all this has to do with what I was talking about. I'm alone so much that when an old friend comes to see me, I sometimes go on talking just for the sake of hearing my own voice. But in this case there is really a connection of ideas. It was James Trehearn who buried poor Mrs. Pratt, and her husband after her in the same grave, and it's not far from the back of his cottage. That's the connection in my mind, you see. It's plain enough. He knows something; I'm quite sure that he does, by his manner, though he's such a reticent beggar.

Yes, I'm alone in the house at night now, for Mrs. Trehearn does everything herself, and when I have a friend the sexton's niece comes in to wait on the table. He takes his wife home every evening in winter, but in summer, when there's light, she goes by herself. She's not a nervous woman, but she's less sure

than she used to be that there are no bogies in England worth a
Scots woman's notice. Isn't it amusing, the idea that Scotland
has a monopoly of the supernatural? Odd sort of national
pride, I call that, don't you?

That's a good fire, isn't it? When driftwood gets started at
last there's nothing like it, I think. Yes, we get lots of it, for I'm
sorry to say there are still a great many wrecks about here. It's a
lonely coast, and you may have all the wood you want for the
trouble of bringing it in. Trehearn and I borrow a cart now and
then, and load it between here and the Spit. I hate a coal fire
when I can get wood of any sort. A log is company, even if it's
only a piece of deck-beam or timber sawn off, and the salt in it
makes pretty sparks. See how they fly, like Japanese
hand-fireworks! Upon my word, with an old friend and a good
fire and a pipe, one forgets all about that thing upstairs,
especially now that the wind has moderated. It's only a lull,
though, and it will blow a gale before morning.

You think you would like to see the skull? I've no objection.
There's no reason why you shouldn't have a look at it, and you
never saw a more perfect one in your life, except that there are
two front teeth missing in the lower jaw.

Oh yes — I had not told you about the jaw yet. Trehearn
found it in the garden last spring when he was digging a pit for a
new asparagus bed. You know we make asparagus beds six or
eight feet deep here. Yes, yes — I had forgotten to tell you that.
He was digging straight down, just as he digs a grave; if you want
a good asparagus bed made, I advise you to get a sexton to make
it for you. Those fellows have a wonderful knack at that sort of
digging.

Trehearn had got down about three feet when he cut into a
mass of white lime in the side of the trench. He had noticed that
the earth was a little looser there, though he says it had not
been disturbed for a number of years. I suppose he thought that
even old lime might not be good for asparagus, so he broke it
out and threw it up. It was pretty hard, he says, in biggish
lumps, and out of sheer force of habit he cracked the lumps
with his spade as they lay outside the pit beside him; the
jawbone of a skull dropped out of one of the pieces. He thinks
he must have knocked out the two front teeth in breaking up
the lime, but he did not see them anywhere. He's a very

experienced man in such things, as you may imagine, and he said at once that the jaw had probably belonged to a young woman, and that the teeth had been complete when she died. He brought it to me, and asked me if I wanted to keep it; if I did not, he said he would drop it into the next grave he made in the churchyard, as he supposed it was a Christian jaw, and ought to have decent burial, wherever the rest of the body might be. I told him that doctors often put bones into quicklime to whiten them nicely, and that I suppose Dr. Pratt had once had a little lime pit in the garden for that purpose, and had forgotten the jaw. Trehearn looked at me quietly.

'Maybe it fitted that skull that used to be in the cupboard upstairs, sir,' he said. 'Maybe Dr. Pratt had put the skull into the lime to clean it, or something, and when he took it out he left the lower jaw behind. There's some human hair sticking in the lime, sir.'

I saw there was, and that was what Trehearn said. If he did not suspect something, why in the world should he have suggested that the jaw might fit the skull? Besides, it did. That's proof that he knows more than he cares to tell. Do you suppose he looked before she was buried? Or perhaps — when he buried Luke in the same grave —

Well, well, it's of no use to go over that, is it? I said I would keep the jaw with the skull, and I took it upstairs and fitted it into its place. There's not the slightest doubt about the two belonging together, and together they are.

Trehearn knows several things. We were talking about plastering the kitchen a while ago, and he happened to remember that it had not been done since the very week when Mrs. Pratt died. He did not say that the mason must have left some lime on the place, but he thought it, and that it was the very same lime he had found in the asparagus pit. He knows a lot. Trehearn is one of your silent beggars who can put two and two together. That grave is very near the back of his cottage, too, and he's one of the quickest men with a spade I ever saw. If he wanted to know the truth, he could, and no one else would ever be the wiser unless he chose to tell. In a quiet village like ours, people don't go and spend the night in the churchyard to see whether the sexton potters about by himself between ten o'clock and daylight.

What is awful to think of, is Luke's deliberation, if he did it; his cool certainty that no one would find him out; above all, his nerve, for that must have been extraordinary. I sometimes think it's bad enough to live in the place where it was done, if it really was done. I always put in the condition, you see, for the sake of his memory, and a little bit for my own sake, too.

I'll go upstairs and fetch the box in a minute. Let me light my pipe; there's no hurry! We had supper early, and it's only half past nine o'clock. I never let a friend go to bed before twelve, or with less than three glasses — you may have as many more as you like, but you shan't have less, for the sake of old times.

It's breezing up again, do you hear? That was only a lull just now, and we are going to have a bad night.

A thing happened that made me start a little when I found that the jaw fitted exactly. I'm not very easily startled in that way myself, but I have seen people make a quick movement, drawing their breath sharply, when they had thought they were alone and suddenly turned and saw someone very near them. Nobody can call that fear. You wouldn't, would you? No. Well, just when I had set the jaw in its place under the skull, the teeth closed sharply on my finger. It felt exactly as if it were biting me hard, and I confess that I jumped before I realized that I had been pressing the jaw and the skull together with my other hand. I assure you I was not at all nervous. It was broad daylight, too, and a fine day, and the sun was streaming into the best bedroom. It would have been absurd to be nervous, and it was only a quick mistaken impression, but it really made me feel queer. Somehow it made me think of the funny verdict of the coroner's jury on Luke's death, 'by the hand or teeth of some person or animal unknown'. Ever since that I've wished I had seen those marks on his throat, though the lower jaw was missing then.

I have often seen a man do insane things with his hands that he does not realize at all. I once saw a man hanging on by an old awning stop with one hand, leaning backwards, outboard, with all his weight on it, and he was just cutting the stop with the knife in his other hand when I got my arms round him. We were in mid-ocean, going twenty knots. He had not the smallest idea what he was doing; neither had I when I managed to pinch my finger between the teeth of that thing. I can feel it now. It was exactly as if it were alive and were trying to bite me. It would if it could, for I know it hates me, poor thing! Do you suppose that what rattles about inside is really a bit of lead? Well, I'll get the box down presently, and if whatever it is happens to drop out into your hands that's your affair. If it's only a clod of earth or a pebble, the whole matter would be off my mind, and I don't believe I should ever think of the skull again; but somehow I cannot bring myself to shake out the bit of hard stuff myself. The mere idea that it may be lead makes me confoundedly uncomfortable, yet I've got the conviction that I shall know before long. I shall certainly know. I'm sure Trehearn knows, but he's such a silent beggar.

I'll go upstairs now and get it. What? You had better go with me? Ha, ha! do you think I'm afraid of a bandbox and a noise? Nonsense!

Bother the candle, it won't light! As if the ridiculous thing understood what it's wanted for! Look at that — the third match. They light fast enough for my pipe. There, do you see? It's a fresh box, just out of the tin safe where I keep the supply on account of the dampness. Oh, you think the wick of the candle may be damp, do you? All right, I'll light the beastly thing in the fire. That won't go out, at all events. Yes, it sputters a bit, but it will keep lighted now. It burns just like any other candle, doesn't it? The fact is, candles are not very good about here. I don't know where they come from, but they have a way of burning low occasionally, with a greenish flame that spits tiny sparks, and I'm often annoyed by their going out of themselves. It cannot be helped, for it will be long before we have electricity in our village. It really is rather a poor light, isn't it?

You think I had better leave you the candle and take the lamp, do you? I don't like to carry lamps about, that's the truth. I never dropped one in my life, but I have always thought I might, and it's so confoundedly dangerous if you do. Besides, I am pretty well used to these rotten candles by this time.

You may as well finish that glass while I'm getting it, for I don't mean to let you off with less than three before you go to bed. You won't have to go upstairs, either, for I've put you in the old study next to the surgery — that's where I live myself. The fact is, I never ask a friend to sleep upstairs now. The last man who did was Crackenthrope, and he said he was kept awake all night. You remember old Crack, don't you? He stuck to the Service, and they've just made him an admiral. Yes, I'm off now — unless the candle goes out. I couldn't help asking if you remembered Crackenthorpe. If any one had told us that the skinny little idiot he used to be was to turn out the most successful of the lot of us, we should have laughed at the idea, shouldn't we? You and I did not do badly, it's true — but I'm really going now. I don't mean to let you think that I've been putting it off by talking! As if there were anything to be afraid of! If I were scared, I should tell you so quite frankly, and get you to go upstairs with me.

Here's the box. I brought it down very carefully, so as not to disturb it, poor thing. You see, if it were shaken, the jaw might get separated from it again, and I'm sure it wouldn't like that. Yes, the candle went out as I was coming downstairs, but that was the draught from the leaky window on the landing. Did you hear anything? Yes, there was another scream. Am I pale, do you say? That's nothing. My heart is a little queer sometimes, and I went upstairs too fast. In fact, that's one reason why I really prefer to live altogether on the ground floor.

Wherever the shriek came from it was not from the skull, for I had the box in my hand when I heard the noise, and here it is now; so we have proved definitely that the screams are produced by something else. I've no doubt I shall find out some day what makes them. Some crevice in the wall, of course, or a crack in a chimney, or a chink in the frame of a window. That's the way all ghost stories end in real life. Do you know, I'm jolly glad I thought of going up and bringing it down for you to see, for that last shriek settles the question. To think that I should have been so weak as to fancy that the poor skull could really cry out like a living thing!

Now I'll open the box, and we'll take it out and look at it under the bright light. It's rather awful to think that the poor lady used to sit there, in your chair, evening after evening, in just the same light, isn't it? But then — I've made up my mind that it's all rubbish from beginning to end, and that it's just an old skull that Luke had when he was a student; and perhaps he put it into the lime merely to whiten it, and could not find the jaw.

I made a seal on the string, you see, after I had put the jaw in its place, and I wrote on the cover. There's the old white label on it still, from the milliner's, addressed to Mrs. Pratt when the hat was sent to her, and as there was room I wrote on the edge: 'A skull, once the property of the late Luke Pratt, M.D.' I don't quite know why I wrote that, unless it was with the idea of explaining how the thing happened to be in my possession. I cannot help wondering sometimes what sort of hat it was that came in the bandbox. What colour was it, do you think? Was it a gay spring hat with a bobbing feather and pretty ribands? Strange that the very same box should hold the head that wore the finery — perhaps. No — we made up our minds that it just came from the hospital in London where Luke did his time. It's far better to look at it in that light, isn't it? There's no more connection between that skull and poor Mrs. Pratt than there was between my story about the lead and —

Good Lord! Take the lamp — don't let it go out, if you can help it — I'll have the window fastened again in a second — I say, what a gale! There, it's out! I told you so! Never mind, there's the firelight — I've got the window shut — the bolt was only half down. Was the box blown off the table? Where the deuce is it? There! That won't open again, for I've put up the bar. Good dodge, an old-fashioned bar — there's nothing like it. Now, you find the bandbox while I light the lamp. Confound those wretched matches! Yes, a pipe spill is better — it must light in the fire — I hadn't thought of it — thank you — there we are again. Now, where's the box? Yes, put it back on the table, and we'll open it.

That's the first time I have ever known the wind to burst that window open; but it was partly carelessness on my part when I last shut it. Yes, of course I heard the scream. It seemed to go all round the house before it broke in at the window. That proves that it's always been the wind and nothing else, doesn't it? When it was not the wind, it was my imagination. I've always been a very imaginative man: I must have been, though I did not know it. As we grow older we understand ourselves better, don't you know?

I'll have a drop of the Hulstkamp neat, by way of an

exception, since you are filling up your glass. That damp gust chilled me, and with my rheumatic tendency I'm very much afraid of a chill, for the cold sometimes seems to stick in my joints all winter when it once gets in.

By George, that's good stuff! I'll just light a fresh pipe, now that everything is snug again, and then we'll open the box. I'm so glad we heard that last scream together, with the skull here on the table between us, for a thing cannot possibly be in two places at the same time, and the noise most certainly came from outside, as any noise the wind makes must. You thought you heard it scream through the room after the window was next open? Oh yes, so did I, but that was natural enough when everything was open. Of course we heard the wind. What could one expect?

Look here, please. I want you to see that the seal is intact before we open the box together. Will you take my glass? No, you have your own. All right. The seal is sound, you see, and you can read the words of the motto easily. 'Sweet and low' — that's it — because the poem goes on 'Wind of the Western sea', and says, 'blow him again to me', and all that. Here is the seal on my watch-chain, where it's hung for more than forty years. My poor little wife gave it to me when I was courting, and I never had any other. It was just like her to think of those words — she was always fond of Tennyson.

It's of no use to cut the string, for it's fastened to the box, so I'll just break the wax and untie the knot, and afterwards we'll seal it up again. You see, I like to feel that the thing is safe in its place, and that nobody can take it out. Not that I should suspect Trehearn of meddling with it, but I always feel that he knows a lot more than he tells.

You see, I've managed it without breaking the string, though when I fastened it I never expected to open the bandbox again. The lid comes off easily enough. There! Now look!

What? Nothing in it? Empty? It's gone; man, the skull is gone!

No, there's nothing the matter with me. I'm only trying to collect my thoughts. It's so strange. I'm positively certain that it was inside when I put on the seal last spring. I can't have imagined that: it's utterly impossible. If I ever took a stiff glass with a friend now and then, I would admit that I might have made some idiotic mistake when I had taken too much. But I don't, and I never did. A pint of ale at supper and half a go of rum at bedtime was the most I ever took in my good days. I believe it's always we sober fellows who get rheumatism and gout! Yet there was my seal, and there is the empty bandbox. That's plain enough.

I say, I don't half like this. It's not right. There's something wrong about it, in my opinion. You needn't talk to me about supernatural manifestations, for I don't believe in them, not a little bit! Somebody must have tampered with the seal and stolen the skull. Sometimes, when I go out to work in the garden in summer, I leave my watch and chain on the table. Trehearn must have taken the seal then, and used it, for he would be quite sure that I should not come in for at least an hour.

If it was not Trehearn — oh, don't talk to me about the possibility that the thing has got out by itself! If it has, it must be somewhere about the house, in some out-of-the-way corner, waiting. We may come upon it anywhere, waiting for us, don't you know? — just waiting in the dark. Then it will scream at me; it will shriek at me in the dark, for it hates me, I tell you!

The bandbox is quite empty. We are not dreaming, either of us. There, I turn it upside down.

What's that? Something fell out as I turned it over. It's on the floor, it's near your feet, I know it is, and we must find it! Help me to find it, man. Have you got it? For God's sake, give it to me quickly!

Lead! I knew it when I heard it fall; I knew it couldn't be anything else by the little thud it made on the hearthrug. So it was lead after all, and Luke did it.

I feel a little bit shaken up — not exactly nervous, you know, but badly shaken up, that's the fact. Anybody would, I should think. After all, you cannot say that it's fear of the thing, for I went up and brought it down — at least, I believed I was bringing it down, and that's the same thing, and by George, rather than give in to such silly nonsense, I'll take the box upstairs again and put it back in its place. It's not that. It's the certainty that the poor little woman came to her end in that way, by my fault, because I told the story. That's what is so dreadful. Somehow, I had always hoped that I should never be quite sure of it, but there is no doubting it now. Look at that!

Look at it! That little lump of lead with no particular shape. Think of what it did, man! Doesn't it make you shiver? He gave her something to make her sleep, of course, but there must have been one moment of awful agony. Think of having boiling lead poured into your brain. Think of it. She was dead before she could scream, but only think of — oh! — there it is again — it's just outside — I know it's just outside — I can't keep it out of my head! — oh! — oh!

You thought I had fainted? No, I wish I had, for it would have stopped sooner. It's all very well to say that it's only a noise, and that a noise never hurt anybody — you're as white as shroud yourself. There's only one thing to be done, if we hope to close an eye tonight. We must find it and put it back into its bandbox and shut it up in the cupboard, where it likes to be. I don't know how it got out, but it wants to get in again. That's why it screams so awfully tonight — it was never as bad as this — never since I first . . .

Bury it? Yes, if we can find it, we'll bury it, if it takes us all night. We'll bury it six feet deep and ram down the earth over it, so that it shall never get out again, and if it screams we shall hardly hear it so deep down. Quick, we'll get the lantern and look for it. It cannot be far away; I'm sure it's just outside — it was coming in when I shut the window, I know it.

Yes, you're quite right. I'm losing my senses, and I must get hold of myself. Don't speak to me for a minute or two; I'll sit quite still and keep my eyes shut and repeat something I know. That's the best way.

'Add together the altitude, the latitude, and the polar distance, divide by two and subtract the altitude from the half-sum; then add the logarithm of the secant of the latitude, the cosecant of the polar distance, the cosine of the half-sum and the sine of the half-sum minus the altitude' — there! Don't say that I'm out of my senses, for my memory is all right, isn't it?

Of course, you may say that it's mechanical, and that we never forget the things we learned when we were boys and have used almost every day for a lifetime. But that's the very point.

When a man is going crazy, it's the mechanical part of his mind that gets out of order and won't work right; he remembers things that never happen, or he sees things that aren't real, or he hears noises when there is perfect silence. That's not what is the matter with either of us, is it?

Come, we'll get the lantern and go round the house. It's not raining — only blowing like old boots, as we used to say. The lantern is in the cupboard under the stairs in the hall, and I always keep it trimmed in case of a wreck.

No use to look for the thing? I don't see how you can say that. It was nonsense to talk of burying it, of course, for it doesn't want to be buried; it wants to go back into its bandbox and be taken upstairs, poor thing! Trehearn took it out, I know, and made the seal over again. Perhaps he took it to the churchyard, and he may have meant well. I daresay he thought that it would not scream any more if it were quietly laid in consecrated ground, near where it belongs. But it has come home. Yes, that's it. He's not half a bad fellow, Trehearn, and rather religiously inclined, I think. Does not that sound natural, and reasonable, and well meant? He supposed it screamed because it was not decently buried — with the rest. But he was wrong. How should he know that it screams at me because it hates me, and because it's my fault that there was that little lump of lead in it?

No use to look for it, anyhow? Nonsense! I tell you it wants to be found — hark! What's that knocking? Do you hear it? Knock — knock — knock — three times, then a pause, and then again. It has a hollow sound, hasn't it?

It has come home. I've heard that knock before, It wants to come in and be taken upstairs, in its box. It's at the front door.

Will you come with me? We'll take it in. Yes, I own that I don't like to go alone and open the door. The thing will roll in and stop against my foot, just as it did before, and the light will go out. I'm a good deal shaken by finding that bit of lead — too much strong tobacco, perhaps. Besides, I'm quite willing to own that I'm a bit nervous tonight, if I never was before in my life.

That's right, come along! I'll take the box with me, so as not to come back. Do you hear the knocking? It's not like any other knocking I ever heard. If you will hold this door open, I can find the lantern under the stairs by the light from this room without bringing the lamp into the hall — it would only go out.

The thing knows we are coming — hark! It's impatient to get in. Don't shut the door till the lantern is ready, whatever you do. There will be the usual trouble with the matches, I suppose — no, the first one, by Jove! I tell you it wants to get in, so there's no trouble. All right with that door now; shut it, please. Now come and hold the lantern, for it's blowing so hard outside that I shall have to use both hands. That's it, hold the light low. Do you hear the knocking still? Here goes — I'll open just enough, with my foot against the bottom of the door — now!

Catch it! it's only the wind that blows it across the floor, that's all — there's half a hurricane outside, I tell you! Have you got it? The bandbox is on the table. One minute, and I'll have the bar up. There!

Why did you throw it into the box so roughly? It doesn't like that, you know.

What do you say? Bitten your hand? Nonsense, man! You did just what I did. You pressed the jaws together with your other hand and pinched yourself. Let me see. You don't mean to say you have drawn blood? You must have squeezed hard, by Jove, for the skin is certainly torn. I'll give you some carbolic solution for it before we go to bed, for they say a scratch from a skull's tooth may go bad and give trouble.

Come inside again and let me see it by the lamp. I'll bring the bandbox — never mind the lantern, it may just as well burn in the hall, for I shall need it presently when I go up the stairs. Yes, shut the door if you will; it makes it more cheerful and bright. Is your finger still bleeding? I'll get you the carbolic in an instant; just let me see the thing.

Ugh! There's a drop of blood on the upper jaw. It's on the eye-tooth. Ghastly, isn't it? When I saw it running along the floor of the hall, the strength almost went out of my hands, and I felt my knees bending; then I understood that it was the gale, driving it over the smooth boards. You don't blame me? No, I should think not! We were boys together, and we've seen a thing or two, and we may just as well own to each other that we were both in a beastly funk when it slid across the floor at you. No wonder you pinched your finger picking it up, after that, if I did the same thing out of sheer nervousness in broad daylight, with the sun streaming in on me.

Strange that the jaw should stick to it so closely, isn't it? I suppose it's the dampness, for it shuts like a vice — I have wiped off the drop of blood, for it was not nice to look at. I'm not going to try to open the jaws, don't be afraid! I shall not play any tricks with the poor thing, but I'll just seal the box again, and we'll take it upstairs and put it away where it wants to be. The wax is on the writing-table by the window. Thank you. It will be long before I leave my seal lying about again, for Trehearn to use, I can tell you. Explain? I don't explain natural phenomena, but if you choose to think that Trehearn had hidden it somewhere in the bushes, and that the gale blew it to the house against the door, and made it knock, as if it wanted to be let in, you're not thinking the impossible, and I'm quite ready to agree with you.

Do you see that? You can swear that you've actually seen me seal it this time, in case anything of the kind should occur again. The wax fastens the strings to the lid, which cannot possibly be lifted, even enough to get in one finger. You're quite satisfied, aren't you? Yes. Besides, I shall lock the cupboard and keep the key in my pocket hereafter.

Now we can take the lantern and go upstairs. Do you know, I'm very much inclined to agree with your theory that the wind blew it against the house. I'll go ahead, for I know the stairs; just hold the lantern near my feet as we go up. How the wind howls and whistles! Did you feel the sand on the floor under your shoes as we crossed the hall?

Yes — this is the door of the best bedroom. Hold up the lantern, please. This side, by the head of the bed. I left the cupboard open when I got the box. Isn't it queer how the faint odour of women's dresses will hang about an old closet for years? This is the shelf. You've seen me set the box there, and now you see me turn the key and put it into my pocket. So that's done!

Goodnight. Are you sure you're quite comfortable? It's not much of a room, but I daresay you would as soon sleep here as upstairs tonight. If you want anything, sing out; there's only a lath and plaster partition between us. There's not so much wind on this side by half. There's the Hollands, on the table, if you'll have one more nightcap. No? Well, do as you please. Goodnight again, and don't dream about that thing if you can.

The following paragraph appeared in the *Penraddon News*, 23rd November, 1906:

MYSTERIOUS DEATH OF A RETIRED SEA CAPTAIN

The village of Tredcombe is much disturbed by the strange death of Captain Charles Braddock, and all sorts of impossible stories are circulating with regard to the circumstances, which certainly seem difficult of explanation. The retired captain, who had successively commanded in his time the largest and fastest liners belonging to one of the principal transatlantic steamship companies, was found dead in his bed on Tuesday morning in his own cottage, a quarter of a mile from the village. An examination was made at once by the local practitioner, which revealed the horrible fact that the deceased had been bitten in the throat by a human assailant, with such amazing force as to crush the windpipe and cause death. The marks of the teeth of both jaws were so plainly visible on the skin that they could be counted, but the perpetrator of the deed had evidently lost the two lower middle incisors. It is hoped that this peculiarity may help to identify the murderer, who can only be a dangerous escaped maniac. The deceased, though over sixty-five years of age, is said to have been a hale man of considerable physical strength, and it is remarkable that no signs of any struggle were visible in the room, nor could it be ascertained how the murderer had entered the house. Warning has been sent to all the insane asylums in the United Kingdom, but as yet no information has been received regarding the escape of any dangerous patient.

'The coroner's jury returned the somewhat singular verdict that Captain Braddock came to his death "by the hands or teeth of some person unknown". The local surgeon is said to have expressed privately the opinion that the maniac is a woman, a view he deduces from the small size of the jaws, as shown by the marks of the teeth.

The whole affair is shrouded in mystery. Captain Braddock was a widower, and lived alone. He leaves no children.'

[*Note.*—Students of ghost lore and haunted houses will find the foundation of the foregoing story in the legends about a skull which is still preserved in the farmhouse called Bettiscombe Manor, situated, I believe, on the Dorsetshire coast.]

XV

The Tale of Philo

Sir H. Rider Haggard

*Anyone who has been captivated by the unknown terrors that
accompanied the mystic rites of the Ancient Egyptians, and,
judging by the devotees of* The Mummy, *these are legion, cannot
fail to share my delight at being able to include of this perfect little
tale by Sir H. Rider Haggard. That these strange gods and their
chilling minions are not completely forgotten, that they are still
secretly worshipped and that their powers have endured far longer
than any other recorded religion, all adds to the depth of the
mystery and dread. The tale is set in an era when Egypt has been
invaded: Noot the high priest of Isis and the new priest Kallikrates
have sailed away down the Nile. Ayesha, high priestess of Isis,
guided by the sea captain Philo, is endeavouring to find them.*

Once more it was the night of full moon. As we had done for
many days, we were sailing before that steady wind along the
coast of Libya, having his upon our right hand, and upon our
left at a distance a line of rocky reef upon which breakers feel
continually.

It was a very splendid moon that turned the sea to silver and
lit up the palm-grown shore almost as brightly as does the sun. I
sat upon the deck near to my cabin and by me stood Philo
watching that shore.

'For what do you seek, Philo? Are you in fear of sunken
rocks?'

'Nay, child of Isis, yet it is true that I seek a certain rock of
which by my reckoning we should now be in sight. Ah!'

Then suddenly he ran forward and shouted an order. Men
leaped up and sprang to the ropes while the rowers began to get
out the sweeps. As they did this the *Hapi* came round so that
her bow pointed to the shore and the great sail sank to the deck.
Then the long oars drove us shorewards.

Philo returned.

'Look, lady,' he said. 'Now that the moon has risen higher you can see well,' and he pointed to a headland in front of us.

Following his outstretched hand with my eyes I perceived a great rock many cubits in height and, carven on the crest of it, a head far larger than that of the huge Sphinx of Egypt. Or perchance it was not carved; perchance Nature had fashioned it thus. At least there it stood and will stand, a terrible and hideous thing, having the likeness of an Ethiopian's head gazing eternally across the sea.

'What is it?' I asked.

'Lady, it is the guardian of the gate of the land whither we go. Legend tells that it is shaped to the likeness of the first king of that land who lived thousands upon thousands of years before the pyramids were built; also that his bones lie in it, or at least, that it is haunted by his spirit. For this reason none dare to touch and much less to climb yonder monstrous rock.'

Then he left me to see to the matters of the ship, because, as he said in going, the entrance to the place was narrow and dangerous. But I sat on alone upon the deck watching this strange new sight.

Within an hour, rowing carefully, we entered the mouth of a river, having the rock shaped like a negro's head upon our right. Then it was that I saw something which put me in mind of Philo's tale about an ancient king. For there, unless I dreamed, upon the very point of the skull of the effigy, of a sudden I perceived a tall form clad in armour which shone silvery bright in the moon's rays. It leaned upon a great spear and when we were opposite to it, it straightened itself and bent forward as though to stare at our ship beneath. Next, thrice it lifted the spear in salutation; thrice it bowed, as I thought in obeisance to me, and having done so, threw its arms wide and was gone.

Afterwards I asked Philo if he also had seen this shape.

'Nay,' he answered in a doubtful voice as though the matter were one of which he did not wish to talk, adding.

'It is not the custom of mariners to study that head in moonlight, because the story goes that if they do and chance to see some such ghost as that you tell of, it casts a spear towards them, who then are doomed to die within the year. Yet at you, child of Isis, he cast no spear, only bowed and gave the salute of kings, or so you tell me. Therefore doubtless neither you nor any of us, your companions, are marked for death.'

I smiled and said that I whose soul was in touch with heaven, feared not the wraith of any ancient king, nor did we speak more of this matter. Yet in the after ages it came into my mind that there was truth in the story and that this long-dead chieftain appeared thus to give greeting to her who was destined to rule his land through many generations; also that perchance he was not dead at all, but, having drunk of a certain cup of life of which I was to learn, lived eternally there upon the rock.

I laid me down and slept and when I woke in the bright morning, it was to find that we had passed from that river into a canal dug by man, which, though deep, was too narrow for the sweeps to work. Therefore the *Hapi* must be pushed along with poles and towed by ropes dragged at by the mariners from a path that ran upon the bank.

For three days we travelled thus making but slow progress, since the toil of dragging so large a ship was great, and at night we tied up to the bank, as boats do upon the Nile. All this while we saw no habitation though of ruins there were many. Indeed, that country was very desolate and full of great swamps that were tenanted by wild beasts, the haunt of owls and bitterns, where lions roared and serpents crept, great serpents such as I have never seen.

At length at noon on the fourth day we came to a lake where the canal ended, which lake once had been a harbour, for we saw stone quays to which were tied some boats that seemed to be little used. Here Philo said that we must disembark and travel on by land. So we left the *Hapi*, sadly enough for my part, because those were happy, quiet days that I had spent on board of her, veritable oases in the storm-swept desert of my life.

Scarcely had we set foot upon the land when appeared, I knew not whence, a company of men, handsome, hook-nosed, sombre men, such as I had seen among the crew upon the *Hapi*. These men, though so fierce of countenance, were not barbarians for they wore linen garments that gave to them the aspects of priests. Moreover, their leaders could speak Arabic in its most ancient form which, having studied it as it chanced, I knew. With this army, who bore bows and spears, came a multitude of folk of a baser sort that carried litters, or burdens, also a guard of great fellows who, Philo told me, were my escort. Now my patience failed so that I turned to Philo saying angrily,

'Hitherto, friend, I have trusted myself to you, because it seemed decreed that I should do so. Tell me, I pray you, for what reason I journey over countless leagues of sea into a land untrod, and whither I go in the fellowship of these barbarians? Because you brought me a certain writing in an acceptable hour, I gave myself into your keeping, nor did I so much as ask light from the goddess or seek to solve the mystery of its spells. Yet, now, as the Prophetess of Isis, I demand the truth of you, her humbler servant.'

'Lady divine,' answered Philo, bowing himself before me, 'what I have withheld is by command, the command of a very great one, of none less than Noot, the aged and holy. You go to an old land that is yet new, to find Noot, your master and mine.'

'In the flesh or in the spirit?' I asked.

'In the flesh, prophetess, if he lives, as these men say, and see, I accompany you, I whom you have found faithful in the past. If I fail you, let my life pay forfeit, and for the rest, ask it of the holy Noot.'

'It is enough,' I said. 'Lead on.'

We entered the litters; we laded the bearers with the treasures of Isis and with my own peculiar wealth, and having placed the ship *Hapi* under guard, marched into the unknown, like to some great caravan of merchants. For days we marched, following a broad road that was broken down in places, over plains and through vast swamps, at night sleeping in caves, or covered by tents which we had brought with us.

This was a strange journey which I made surrounded by that host of hook-nosed, silent, ghost-like men, who, as I noted, loved the night better than they did the day. Almost I might have thought that they had been sent from Hades to conduct us to those gates from which for mortals there is no return. My fellowship of the priests and priestesses grew afraid and clustered round me at night, praying to be led back to familiar lands and faces.

I answered them that what I dared, they must dare also, and that the goddess was as near to us here as she had been in Egypt, nor could death be closer to us than it was in Egypt. Yea, I bade them have faith, since without faith we could not be at peace one hour, who, lacking it, must be overwhelmed with terrors, even within the walls of citadels.

They listened, bowing their heads and saying that whatever else they might doubt, they trusted themselves to me.

So we went on, passing through a country where more of these half-savage men, that I learned were called *Amahagger*, surrounded by their cattle, dwelt in villages or by colonies in caves. At last there arose before us a mighty mountain whose towering cliffs had the appearance of a wall so vast that the eye could not compass it. By a gorge we penetrated that mountain and found within it an enormous, fertile plain, and on the plain a city larger than Memphis or than Thebes, but a city half in ruins.

Passing over a great bridge spanning a wide moat, once filled with water, that now here and there was dry, we entered the walls of that city and by a street broader than any I had ever seen, bordered by many noble, broken houses, though some of these seemed still to be inhabited, came to a glorious temple like to those of Egypt, only greater, and with taller columns. Across its grass-grown courts that were set one within another, we were carried to an inner sanctuary. Here we descended from the litters and were led to sculptured chambers that seemed to have been made ready to receive us, where we cleansed ourselves of the dust of travel, and ate. Then came Philo who conducted me to a little lamp-lit hall, for now the night had fallen, where was a chair of state such as high-priests used, in which at his bidding I sat myself.

I think that being weary with travel, I must have slept in that chair, since I dreamed or seemed to dream, that I received worship such as is given to a queen, or even to a goddess. Heralds hailed me, sweet voices sang to me, spirits appeared in troops to talk to me, the spirits of those who thousands of years before had departed from the earth. They told me strange stories of the past and of the future; tales of a fallen people, of a worship and a glory that had gone by and been swallowed in the gulfs of time. Then gathering in a multitude they seemed to hail me, crying,

'Welcome, appointed queen! Build thou up that which has fallen. Discover thou that which is lost. Thine is the strength, thine the opportunity, yet beware of the temptations, beware of the flesh, lest the flesh should overcome the spirit and by its fall add ruin unto ruin, the ruin of the soul to the ruin of the body.'

I awoke from my vision and saw Philo standing before me.

'Harken, Philo,' I said. 'I can bear no more of these mysteries. The time has come when you must speak, or face my wrath. Why have I been brought to this strange and distant land where it seems that I must dwell in a place of ruins?'

'Because the holy Noot so commanded, O child of wisdom,' he answered. 'Was it not set down in the writing I gave you at the Isle of Reeds upon the Nile?'

'Where then is the holy Noot?' I asked. 'I see him not. Is he dead?'

'I do not think that he is dead, lady. Yet to the world he is dead. He has become a hermit, one who dwells in a cave in a perilous place not very far from this city. Tomorrow I will bring you to him, if that be your will. Thus only can you see him who now for years has never left that cave, or so I think, unless it be to fetch the food which is prepared for him.'

'A strange tale, Philo, though that Noot should become a hermit does not amaze me, for such was ever his desire. Now tell me how he came here, and you with him?'

'Lady, you will remember that in the bygone years when Nectanebes, he who was Pharaoh, fled up Nile, the holy Noot embarked upon my ship, the *Hapi*, to sail to the northern cities, that there he might treat with the Persians for the ransom of those temples of Egypt that remained unravished.'

'I remember, Philo. What chanced to you upon that journey?'

'This, lady: that we were very nearly slain, every one of us, for whom the Persians had set a trap, thinking to snare Noot and his company, and torture him till he revealed where the treasures of the temples of Isis were buried. Nevertheless, because I am a good sailor and because that warrior priest, Kallikrates, was brave, we escaped into the canal which is called the *Road of Rameses*, and so at last out to sea, for to return up Nile was impossible. Then Noot commanded that I should sail on southerly upon a course he seemed to know well enough; or perhaps the goddess taught it to him; I cannot say. At least I obeyed, so that in the end we reached that harbour which is guarded by a rock carved to the likeness of an Ethiopian's head, and thence travelled to this place, still guided by the wisdom of Noot who knew the road.'

'And Kallikrates? What chanced to Kallikrates — who, it seems, was with you?' I asked in an indifferent voice, though my heart burned to hear his answer.

'Lady, so far as it is known to me, this is the story of Kallikrates and the Princess Amenartas.'

'*The Princess Amenartas!* By all the gods, what is your meaning, Philo? She went up Nile with Nectanebes her father, he who was Pharaoh.'

'Nay, lady, she went *down* Nile with Kallikrates, or perhaps with Noot, or perhaps with herself alone. I do not know with whom she hid, since I never saw her, nor learned that she was aboard my ship until we were two days' journey out to sea, with the coasts of Egypt far behind us.'

'Is it so?' I asked coldly, though I was filled with bitter anger. 'And what did the holy Noot when he found that this woman was aboard his vessel?'

'Nothing, lady, except look on her somewhat doubtfully and lead her to the cabin — that which was yours.'

'And the priest, Kallikrates? Did he strive to be rid of her?'

'Nay, lady, indeed that would have been impossible, unless he had cast her overboard. He, too, did nothing except talk with her — that is, so far as I saw.'

'Then, Philo, where is she now, and where is Kallikrates? I do not see him in this place?'

'Lady, I cannot tell you, but I think it probable that they are dead and in the fellowship of Osiris. When we had been some weeks at sea we were driven by storm to an island off the coast under the lee of which we took shelter, a very fertile and beautiful island, peopled by kindly folk. After we had sailed again from that island it was discovered that the priest Kallikrates and the royal Princess Amenartas were missing from the ship, nor because of the strong wind that blew us forward, was it possible for us to return to seek for them. I enquired of the matter and the sailors told me that they had been fishing together and that a shark which took their bait, pulled them both into the sea; in which case doubtless they were drowned.'

'And did you believe that story, Philo?'

'Nay, lady. I understood at once that it was one which the sailors had been bribed to tell. Myself I think that they went to the island in one of the boats of the people who dwell there; perhaps because they could no longer bear the cold eyes of Noot fixed upon them, or perhaps to gather fruit, for which those who had been long upon the sea often conceive a great desire. But,' he added simply, 'I do not know why they should have done this, seeing that the island-dwellers brought us aplenty of fruits in their boats.'

'Doubtless they preferred to pluck them fresh with their own hands, Philo.'

'Perhaps, lady; or perhaps they wished to stay awhile upon that island. At least I noted that the Princess took her garments and her jewels with her, which she could scarcely have done if the shark had dragged her into the sea.'

'Are you so sure, Philo, that she did not leave some of those jewels behind — in *your* keeping, Philo? It is very strange to me that the Princess Amenartas could have come aboard your ship and have left your ship and you know nothing.'

Now Philo looked up innocently and said.

'Surely it is lawful for a captain to receive faring money from his passengers, and that I admit I did. But I do not understand why the child of wisdom is so wroth because a Greek and a great lady were by chance left together upon an island where, for aught I know, one or other of them may have had friends.'

'Am I not the guardian of the honour of the goddess?' I answered. 'And do you not know that under our law Kallikrates was sworn to her alone?'

'If so, prophetess, doubtless that captain, or that priest, remembers his oaths and deals with this princess as though she were his sister or his mother. At the least, the goddess can guard her own honour, so why should you fret your soul concerning it, prophetess? Lastly, it is probable that by now both of them are dead and have made all things clear to Isis in the heavenly halls.'

Thus he prattled on, adding lie to lie as only a Greek can do. I listened until I could bear no more. Then I said but one word. It was 'Begone!'

He went humbly, yet, as I thought, smiling.

Oh! now I understood. Noot had made a plot to remove Kallikrates far from me, so that I might never look upon him again. Philo knew of this plot, and through him Amenartas knew it also. Unknown to Noot, she bribed Philo to hide her upon his ship till they were far from land, though whether the plan was known to Kallikrates I could not say, nor did it greatly matter. Then the rest followed. Amenartas appeared upon the ship and cast her net about Kallikrates who had sworn to have done with her, and the end can be guessed. Noot was wroth with them, so wroth that when the chance came, they fled away, purposing to stay upon that island until they could find a ship to take them back to Egypt, or elsewhere. Thus, I was sure, ran the story, and, as it proved afterwards, I was right.

Well, they were gone and as I hoped, dead, since only death could cover up such a sin, and for my part I was glad that I had done with Kallikrates and his light-of-love. And yet there, seated on the couch of state, I wept — because of the outrage done to Isis whom I served. Or was it for myself that I wept? I cannot say, I only know that my tears were bitter. Also I was very lonely in this strange and desolate place. Why had I been brought here, I wondered. Because Noot had commanded it, sending for me from afar, and what he commanded, that I must obey. Where, then, was Noot, who Philo swore, still lived? Why had he not appeared to greet me? I covered my eyes with my hands and threw out my soul, to Noot, saying,

'Come to me, Noot. Come to me, my beloved master.'

Lo! a voice, a well-remembered voice answered.

'Daughter, I am here.'

I let fall my hands. I gazed with my tear-stained eyes, and behold! before me, white-robed, gold-filleted, snowy-beared; grown very ancient and ethereal, stood the prophet and high-priest, my master. For a moment I thought that it was his spirit which I saw. Then he moved and I heard his white robes rustle, and knew that there stood Noot himself whom I had travelled far to find.

I rose; I ran to him; I seized his thin hand and kissed it, while he, murmuring, 'My daughter, at last, at last!' leaned forward and with his lips touched me on the crown.

'Far away your summons reached me in an hour of peril,' I said. 'Behold! I obeyed, I came. In faith I came, asking no questions, and I am here in safety, for I think the goddess herself was with me on that journey. Tell me all, O Noot. What is this place? How were you brought to it and why have you called me to you?'

'Harken, daughter,' he said, seating himself beside me on the throne-like couch. 'This city is named Kôr. Once she was queen of the world, as after her Babylon, Tyre, Thebes, and Athens are, or have been queens. From Kôr thousands of years ago in the black, lost ages Egypt was peopled, as were other lands. In those dim days, by another title, her citizens worshipped Isis, queen of heaven, only they named her *Truth* whom in Egypt you know as Maat. Then apostasy arose and many of this great people, abandoning the pure and gentle worship of Isis wrapped in the veil of truth, set up another god under the name of Rezu, a fierce sun-demon, to whom they made human sacrifices, as the Sidonians did to Moloch. Yea, they sacrificed men, women, and children by thousands, and even learned to eat their flesh, first as a sacred rite, and afterwards to satisfy their appetites. Heaven saw and grew wrath. Heaven smote the people with a mighty pestilence, so that they perished and perished till few were left. Thus Kôr fell by the sword of God as, for like cause, fell Sidon.'

'Of all this afterwards,' I answered impatiently. 'Tell me first, how came you here? Long years ago you sailed down Nile to treat with the Persians for the ransom of the temples of Isis, a mission in which it seems you failed, my father.'

'Aye, Ayesha, I failed. It was but a trap, since those false-hearted fire-worshippers thought to take me captive and hold my life in gage against all the treasures of Isis. By the cunning and seamanship of Philo and the courage of a priest named Kallikrates, whom you may still remember after all these years — ' here he glanced at me sharply, 'I escaped when a gang of them disguised as envoys, strove to snare me. But the road up Nile being barred, we were forced to fly south, down Pharaoh's great ditch, till at length, after many wanderings and adventures, we came to this land, as it was fated that I should do. You will remember daughter that I told you I believed that we were parting for a long while, although I believed also that we should meet again in the flesh.'

'I remember well,' I answered, 'also that I swore to come to you at the appointed hour.'

'I came to this land,' went on Noot, 'but Kallikrates, the

Greek captain who was a priest of Isis, never reached it. He was lost on the way.

'With another, my father. I have heard that story from Philo.'

'With another who caused him to break his vows. Be sure daughter, that I knew nothing of her plot or that she was hidden aboard the ship, though perchance Philo knew. The goddess hid it from me, doubtless for her own purposes.'

'Are this pair dead, or do they still live, my father?'

'I cannot say; that soon or late for such sacrilege vengeance will fall upon the head of one, if not of both of them. Peace be to them. May they be forgiven! At least, as I think they loved each other much and, since love is very strong, all should have pity on them who have ever loved where they ought not,' and again his questioning eyes played upon my face.

XVI

Confidences

'Sea-Wrack'

And so the final story is reached, and I think it is a fitting finish to such a collection as this one. I have aimed to give readers a rich mixture of sea and terror and hope I have succeeded. Confidences, like the majority of the stories in this collection, can be read at two levels, as a straightforward ghost story of the sea, or, alternatively, as a reflection on the strange affinity man had always had for that inert collection of steel plates known as a ship. The story illustrates both aspects perfectly.

In a lonely, deserted corner of the yard I came across her — that old ship of mine. There she lay, pathetically motionless; and already she seemed to be shrouded in that mantle of patient resignation which surrounds like an aura of doom the vessel that has run her predestined course.

And because I had loved her — though years past — I sat heavily down on a decrepit bollard on the jettyside and let my eye wander over the rusted plates and the stark barrenness of her dismantled frame.

High above me, in the near-dusk, as if dark with suppressed pain, the untenanted hawse-pipes — for the bower anchors and cables were gone — peered down at me with a quiet air of recognition. No need for me to walk along the jetty and try to decipher the battered lettering on the sheer of the stern. Just as a man will pick out his own kin from a multitude, so did I know that this was indeed my old destroyer.

The evening breeze freshened so that the lap of the water rose in a brisk chatter. The sun sank low in the west, but still I sat on. And now I saw that my old ship moved a little uneasily at her berth. Under my right foot, as it rested on the wire 'spring', the eye of which was made fast round the bollard, I could feel a tremor — sentient and strangely moving, like a message bidding me stay, if only for a brief while. And there, in

the loneliness of that deserted shipyard, I felt the companionship of my old boat, as I have felt it so many years before.

But now it came, that feeling, with a poignancy that opened
wide the floodgates of memory. And with memory there came
words of my own that I had written, leaping to my mind, so
that I muttered under my breath:

'It seems as if ships speak at night. Little rattles, squeaks, and
groans emphasize the stillness on board. . . .'

'As if ships speak at night. . . .'

'Oh, come!' a Voice seemed to break into my train of
thought, 'come and see me — your old ship — before it is too
late. There is so much to talk about, and so little time. . . .'

'So little time and so much to talk about. . . .'

I rose to my feet and shivered.

It was dusk.

'So little time. . . .' The eternal cry of mankind, century
after century, aeon after aeon.

And suddenly there, in that graveyard of ships — ships that
had once been proud and strong and gallant, ay, and
gay — there came to me an instinctive feeling that I should go.
The appeal must not remain unanswered. It was as if an old and
trusted friend lay in the dark valley and whispered, stretching
out a hand.

So, looking round me, I turned up the collar of my coat and
stumbled through the debris towards a plant that stretched
from the jetty to the upper deck. And as I walked the call grew
more insistent. Rats scuttled before me as I stepped delicately
over the narrow brow. Below, in the black chasm, dirty water,
iridescent with the sheen the oil, gurgled and lapped as if
choking in torture, while fenders grunted protestingly at the
pressure exerted by the old hull.

The ship stood high: the old trim waterline four feet above
the surface, for boilers and engines — those splendid turbines
that never once had failed me — had gone already.

There were no guard-rails, so I stepped out, with a sigh of
relief, on to a barren, devastated deck. I looked about with
horror; searching in vain for this and that: for the torpedo-
tubes and the glow from the galley-fire: for the 'pom-pom',
that venomous small piece of artillery that had played havoc
with unskilful fingers and thumbs: and the midship gun-

platform, that half-way refuge from the bridge aft to the wardroom when driving seas had swept the upper deck. All, all were gone.

But as I stood, and while memory drove bitter contrast home, the steel of the deck under my feet moved safely, reassuringly, with the sturdy strength that I had always relied upon. That at least was still there.

Seventeen years!

With a profound shock, I realized what a long passage of time had separated us. How many hundreds of thousands of feet had since passed and repassed along that now echoing upper deck? Blithe feet, shod with the fine carelessness of youth; and dragging, wounded feet, ay, and there in my own time — instinctively I glanced at the deck abreast the after funnel — still bodies, torn and blackened, whose eyes had stared through the White Ensign with the stern, direct gaze of death at the muted stars under whose pale light their souls had fled. And the sure, steady feet of my old Captain, that characteristic tread of his sounded suddenly in my ears, so that I peered aft, searching the shadows while my heart drummed. For a flashing moment the voices of my old messmates came to me distinctly, cheerfully, from the past, as the revealing beam of a lighthouse illumines a sector of sea and shore. I heard the rapid patter of the wardroom steward's rush aft with welcome meals from the galley. I caught again the Sub's busy stride — a bundle of charts thrust under his arm. . . .

In a maze, I paused suddenly to listen, while imperceptibly, impalpably, but strong as the permeating essence of a powerful scent, there came to me in a single, all-embracing wave of reunion, the very spirit of my old ship.

For a second I strove instinctively to control it. I looked around at the fading landmarks, noting how night was coming into her own, and my gaze was restless, anxious — for I was suddenly afraid.

'Don't be a fool!' a prosaic, matter-of-fact voice was saying. 'You have gone aboard to have a look round your old destroyer; no need to let idiotic ideas get hold of you. . . .'

But the cold, narrow forces of logic and reason beat in vain at the outer ramparts of the subconscious; for under my feet the steel deck moved uneasily, as the old ship gently heaved, and a long-drawn-out sigh of disappointment seemed to emanate from the shadows; issuing from the very hawsers and fenders, and even from the tattered canvas 'dodgers' that hung like a witch's rags from the bridge-rails.

'So little time . . . ' the Voice breathed, 'and so much to say.'

Hesitatingly, I turned for'ard towards the charthouse, and as I looked up at the bare, stark lines of the skeleton-like bridge, the memories of many a wild night came surging back out of the past. Like tiny, rapid exposures of a microscopic camera, pictures, blindingly vivid, flashed across the screen of memory, so that I lived again in a moment whole months of experience. Once more the biting easterly gale drove in my face. I saw the metallic-looking moon; the high, crested combers, and the yellow, yeasty wave-tops. Instinctively, as I had done so often seventeen years before, I clutched at the nearest refuge — the funnel-casing rail — and felt the high, shuddering climb, and the sickening plunge. 'Bump, bump, bump,' as the sharp, sturdy bows ploughed a resistless way through the heart of a giant wave. My breach caught as I watched the green sea break in thunder on the echoing fo'c'sle and saw the creaming torrent overwhelm the fo'c'sle gun. And the voice from the shadows, growling, grumbling, was the voice of my old Captain.

'Bumping, Sub, she's bumping like fury. Twenty-five knots into a full gale. Blast the battle-boats; never think of us poor coves escorting 'em. . . .'

The wind howled and the topmast rattled. The moon had gone. My head in a whirl, I gripped afresh the rail under my hand.

'Look out, Sub, hold tight!' The voice was rising. 'Hold her up Quartermaster, hold her up, man, for heaven's sake — last leg of the zig-zag — twenty-five knots right into it. Hell! we'll be lucky if we have a bridge in an hour's time.' Then, in a changed voice: 'Hullo! what's that? Quick, man, port twenty! Bear him a hand, signalman! Our next ahead's damaged; the *Sarpedon*'s caught one: she's hauling out of the line. Blast those battle-boats! Look at her bridge, Sub — it's gone; topmast gone, wireless gone, charthouse stove in!' The burly figure in the oilskins and sou'wester shook an impotent fist in the direction of the starboard quarter, where the vast black shapes wallowed their majestic way through the storm. 'Bridge gone;

there's Jenkins — good skipper, Sub — crawling his way through the wreckage. I can see him; he's alone, crawling, crawling his way through the wreckage. I can see him; he's alone, crawling, crawling through the wreckage; poor devil, he's hurt. He's got to the wheel; he's found one spoke left. His left arm looks bust; but he's getting her nose back to it. No sign of the quartermaster. Officer of the watch's gone, too. And we can't stop, Sub — orders; can't do anything; no boat would live in this sea. Oh, *blast* those battle-boats. . . .'

The leaping seas were flattening out; the fury was calming. Gradually, still gripping the funnel casing rail, I re-focused my eyes, looking round in amazement at the stark ship on whose deck I stood.

'I was reminding you,' the Voice said. 'That and much more we have shared. Come.'

I mounted the ladder to the fo'c'sle and stood a moment looking aft. It was from this spot that I had been hurled aft one night — caught by a huge wave just after leaving the bridge. In spite of myself, I shivered. It had been a near thing. Two hundred feet I had gone in a flash that had yet seemed endless, and without once touching the upper deck. The funnels, the torpedo-tubes, the after-gun-platform: all these I had encountered with varying degrees of violence, until. . . .

'I did my best,' the Voice said, earnestly. 'I think I saved you that night. I made a supreme effort to raise my upper deck before the wave carried you over the stern. Hundreds of tons of water I threw off my back — and just did it, for my magazine-hatch caught you. It was painful' — instinctively I rubbed my knee, which had held seventeen stitches — 'but you did not go over the side. . . .'

I nodded, well satisfied; then, as I looked aft, slowly a constriction came to my throat. From this spot I had given my young, confident orders, many times, for the hoisting of the whaler. It seemed suddenly a long time ago. I heard again the tramping feet, and saw once more the two long lines of men surging aft on the boat's falls, their rhythmic passage imbuing the responsive hull under their feet with a lilting quiver that continued for a moment, like an echo, after the long drawn out order, 'High enough!'

'Was that really me?' I muttered, catching for an instant a

glimpse of a young figure on whose cuff there proudly gleamed one golden stripe and curl.

'Yes,' the Voice replied; 'for we are all atoms in Time, passing on our ways purposefully down the ringing avenues of Light, knowing not this nor that, but catching every once in a while a glimmer of the music that is pure Truth.'

Slowly, I let fall my hands from those stanchions I had gripped so often seventeen years before. Stumbling, I directed my steps those few well-worn yards to the open charthouse door. An odour drifted out to me — of cheese and mouldering biscuit and stale billycan; for humanity, following its vocation of ship-breaking, had sheltered oft in there from rain and storm: had taken its dinner-hour there. Dimly, the cobweb-encrusted portholes showed pale and grey in the for'ard bulkhead, like unlighted moons.

For a moment I hesitated; then went through that well-remembered doorway. And in some strange way memory showed me, simultaneously with my passage, a young sub-lieutenant, his face eager and laughingly beckoning me on; while alongside me, an older edition of the sub-lieutenant walked with me and on his sleeve were two golden stripes. His face was grave, for he carried the authority of a First Lieutenant of Destroyers. Startled, I peered over my shoulder, for yet another figure loomed close behind me. It was that of the acting Captain; older still, the face more lined, the eyes weary-looking, but burning with a steady light.

So, as I passed through that doorway, there seemed to be accompanying me the shades of my former selves: three separate yet linked individualities; the young sub-lieutenant, the graver, more responsible, First Lieutenant, and finally the rather weary, yet dogged, acting Captain.

I found myself leaning on the skeleton-frame of my old chart-table — in vain I felt for the polished slab of mahogany — and the vivid mental images grew out of the pale light of the portholes with an insistency that was overwhelming.

'Let them come,' the Voice said; 'it is good, sometimes, to remember the past; for out of the past grows the present, merging into the future, and the wise man knows that that way wisdom comes.'

'You are a woman,' I said suddenly to that Voice, the spirit of my old ship; 'and a beautiful one,' I added with conviction.

The spirit seemed to me to smile: a slow, tender smile.

'We are all women,' the Voice said. 'Once I was beautiful and you loved me. Do you remember when you first saw me? When you first came aboard? When I lay on the banks of the Clyde and emerged, a gorgeous grey lady, from the squalor of the slips?'

'Yes, I remember,' I answered slowly; 'you were the most beautiful ship I had ever seen, with the lovely, flowing lines and the slender, steely strength of perfect proportion.'

The Voice sighed. 'We always know when we are loved, and to those we give all.'

'But tell me!' I cried, with a rising excitement — for here at last I might, I thought, penetrate that secret which had always intrigued me — 'tell me why you are all different? Almost as if you were human, and possessed the frailties and splendours, the fickleness and steadfastness of womankind.'

'Because,' said the Voice, proudly, 'we are fashioned by men, nay, more — by artists very frequently. For six months, five hundred men worked day and night to make of me a thing of strength and beauty: and every blow of a riveting-hammer added something more than steely endurance to my slender frame; for a man cannot fashion truly without giving something of himself. Every day and night, for six months, five hundred of the finest workmen in the world imbued me with something of their steadfastness and devotion, while the finest designing brains watched carefully over my growing pains. So that inherent in me is the sum total of their endeavours. They gave me more than strength and beauty — they endowed me with a soul.'

'Ah!' I said, slowly, 'so that is why ships are so different one from the other.'

'To those who love us — we give all,' the Voice repeated, proudly; 'for them we fight till the last. In the roar of the gale you will hear our battle-cry, as our backs bend and our ribs recoil to the pounding of the giant waves. We fight with the fury of feline cunning for those we love and honour as masters: so that our sisters ashore will remember us in their prayers when we bear their men home in safety through the storm. And sometimes we take the bit in our teeth — ' The Voice hesitated;

then: 'I will tell you one of my secrets — '

Something was happening to my vision. The cobwebby portholes faded. I looked out over a choppy sea from the bridge, standing alongside my old Captain, who searched the surrounding waters anxiously through his glasses. Suddenly, my heart leapt, for the Captain had jumped in a wild leap to the voice-pipe. 'Hard-a-starboard, Quartermaster! Half astern, port: full speed ahead, starboard engines! Quick, man, jump to it!' Then a moment later:

'Blazes, man, you've got the wrong helm on! "Starboard," I said, not "port"! Sub, jump below and see what's the matter with that damned fool of a quartermaster: there's a torpedo coming straight for us — only five hundred yards away.'

The vision faded. I was looking again through the dirty portholes in the charthouse; and my brow was wet with sweat.

'Yes,' I muttered, huskily, 'I remember. A few seconds later we thanked our lucky stars for that apparent lapse of the quartermaster's, for the torpedo sank before it reached us — and, if we *had* been carrying starboard helm, we should have run straight into a couple of mines floating low in the water — '

'I did that,' said the Voice, gravely. 'I knew it was the only hope. Usually' — the Voice was low and strangely womanly — 'I was quicker when danger was near.'

'Yes, I know,' I said, 'I noticed that often; it was almost as if you understood — especially that night in the Pentland Firth.'

'And now,' the Voice breathed, and I think, faltered for the first time, 'you must go. It is getting late and you are cold.'

'Ah, dear and gallant lady,' I whispered, 'it is sad to leave you yet once again. To me, you are still that lovely ship of seventeen years ago. I see that creaming, flashing bow-wave: and the lilt of your swift stride like deer grazing the grass-tops in full flight. And the jaunty toss of your head, and the trim, raking beauty of your hull; the gleam of torpedo-tube and burnished steel: the intimate tinkle of telegraph-bell: and the hoist of gay bunting fluttering colourful from the slender straightness of the main. And you were mine. But now — '

'Life is all flux and change,' the Voice replied; 'we come, we pass, and we go, but life flows on: it is the work that matters . . . to do that well. I, myself, pass on, but I pass in pride and my steely strength endures, melted, transmuted so that sisters yet unborn may benefit; thus the work that was done on the Clyde, those seventeen years ago, is not wasted. Nothing is lost in the Cosmic Law.'

Dazed, I stretched my cramped limbs, staring, there, through those cobwebby portholes, and the Voice whispered: 'Take it; it will remind you of all those happy days we had together when we were young.'

My mind in a whirl, I found myself stumbling off the upper deck with something clutched firmly in my left hand. The gentlest zephyr of wind suddenly brushed my cheek and forehead, fragrant as pine, yet strong with the tang of the south-east trade.

'Farewell!' the Voice breathed softly; 'I cannot guard you ashore as I guarded you when we were shipmates long ago. Step carefully, for it is dark and the way is difficult.'

There was a curious mistiness in my vision, but gentle hands seemed to guide me over the rotten gang-plank, and I stood at last on the jetty, then stumbled blindly away. An intolerable sense of loss assailed me, so that I staggered carelessly into débris and obstacles that bestrewed my path.

Halting, I looked back, but could see nothing in that pit of darkness. I raised my hand as if in salute.

'Farewell, gallant lady,' I muttered, 'farewell.'

And so, stumbling often, barking shins and feet on hard, unyielding obstacles, and after sundry adventures, I arrived finally at a ramshackle building near the gates, which was the superintendent's hut and office. A dull light gleamed under the torn curtain which shrouded the window. I knocked and entered.

An old bent man, with metal spectacles hanging precariously from a long, melancholy nose, rose shakily from a chair to greet me. I asked him if I could keep a memento from my old ship, and after a moment repeated my request.

He looked at me in a peculiar way, his gnome-like body throwing a curious, distorted shadow on wall and ceiling, dim like the light of the hurricane-lamp that illuminated the room.

'Where was this ship?' he asked me in return, and in his voice, husky, nervous, there seemed to sound a tremor of fear.

I told him, and his ancient's face paled.

'What've ye got in your hand?' he asked, tremulously; 'this memento ye told me about?'

Then, for the first time, I opened my left hand and laid on the table the article I had been clutching.

We stared at each other over the narrow table, with a growing apprehension. 'What is it?' he muttered.

'It's a lead weight, I said with a catch of the breath. 'I used to use it in my old ship for keeping corners of the chart down on the chart-table. See, it's covered with green baize so that it won't slip when the ship's rolling and pitching — and,' I added suddenly, as I examined it more closely with a rising excitement, 'it's one I lost when the charthouse got washed out one night in the Pentland Firth. Look! there are my initials, and the number. I numbered them all — I can't quite think why — there were six of 'em; this is number five.'

The old watchman-superintendent regarded me with a blank, watery gaze, curiously shut, as if he had closed the door of his senile mind on some alarming apprehension. His face had gone a dull grey colour, out of which there stood out in frightful contrast his huge red beak of a nose, decorated by a criss-cross pattern of veins, like the drooping proboscis of some mournful night-bird.

'What was your ship?' he inquired, as if the words were slowly squeezed out of him.

I told him, and at my answer he staggered to his chair and sat down, raising and dropping his hands in a gesture of despair.

'I wouldn't go to that corner of the yard after nightfall if I was you, sir,' he quavered. Then, looking anxiously at me, he said slowly: 'There's not been a ship there these eighteen months. Your'n were the last: she were broke up just a year and a half ago.' He shambled out of his chair, and put a reassuring claw on my arm, as I swayed.

'Don't take it hard, sir,' he said, tremulously. 'I wouldn't go to that corner of the yard after nightfall, misself, for all the gold in the Indies.'

'*Not a ship* . . . ' I muttered, aghast.

'No, sir, not a — ship,' came the quivering but earnest reply, and I weighed the peculiar emphasis on the last word, while we stood staring at each other, pale of face, there, under the flickering lamplight.